Johann Georg Korb, Count MacDonnell

Diary of an Austrian secretary of Legation

At the Court of Czar Peter the Great - Vol. II

Johann Georg Korb, Count MacDonnell

Diary of an Austrian secretary of Legation
At the Court of Czar Peter the Great - Vol. II

ISBN/EAN: 9783743408449

Manufactured in Europe, USA, Canada, Australia, Japa

Cover: Foto ©Raphael Reischuk / pixelio.de

Manufactured and distributed by brebook publishing software (www.brebook.com)

Johann Georg Korb, Count MacDonnell

Diary of an Austrian secretary of Legation

DIARY

OF

AN AUSTRIAN SECRETARY OF LEGATION

AT THE

COURT OF CZAR PETER THE GREAT.

TRANSLATED FROM THE ORIGINAL LATIN

AND EDITED BY

THE COUNT MAC DONNELL,

K. S. J. J., &c., &c., &c.

IN TWO VOLS.—VOL. II.

LONDON:

BRADBURY & EVANS, 11, BOUVERIE STREET.

1863.

The Diary of

AN AMBASSADOR AT THE COURT OF MOSCOW.

—⋅⋅+)€+⋅⋅—

MAY 1.—We tafted to-day, for the firft time, the fifh dried in the air, which the Samoïeds eat inftead of bread.

2.—No letters are allowed to leave Azow or Veroneje for Mofcow; hence there is a dark rumour that fifty of the Azow rebels were put to death at Veroneje.

3.—The Czar claims the monopoly of the fale of brandy.* Some of the lower orders—

---

* It is ftill a ftate monopoly in Ruffia Proper: not fo in Ruffian Poland, where the landed proprietors were never de-prived of the monopoly of baking, and of that of diftillation and fale (*propinatio*) of intoxicating drinks for the vaffals of their re-fpective feignories. Indeed, the fabrication and fale of ftrong liquors, farmed out ufually to Jews, forms often no fmall propor-tion of the income of a Polifh nobleman's ill-managed eftate. The ufurious Jews, to whom noble and ferf alike are igno-minioufly tributary, immorally entice the peafants to drunken-

thoſe called Jemſkoi—were offering it for ſale in
their private houſes, contrary to the exprefs inhi-
bition of the Czar. So the Treaſurer, Peter
Ivanowicz Proforowſki, wanting to chaſtiſe them,
had fifty ſoldiers at his orders that he had aſked
of General Gordon. Along with theſe he ſent a
ſcribe, armed with a warrant to ſeize as contra-
band and bring to the Czar's ſtores all the brandy
they could find in ſuch places. But when they
attempted to put the warrant in execution, a mob
of Jemſkoi aſſembled ; and, repelling force by
force, killed three ſoldiers by running them
through, and wounded ſeveral. The Jemſkoi,
moreover, threatened fiercer vengeance if ſuch
another ſeizure ſhould be attempted. The daring
of this conduct is ſuch, that it keeps the autho-
rities of the city in great anxiety whether it is
better to employ force or diſſemble.

5.—When one of the footmen belonging to
the Daniſh Envoy was going to Sboſeck, a
Ruſſian ſhouted an opprobrious name at him.

---

neſs, and cheat them, of courſe. Theſe privileges of ſeignorial
monopoly, and this miſerable ſervitude to the uſurious Jews,
both grew up, in times out of mind, under the old national
government of Poland.—TRANSLATOR.

The footman at once fprang from his horfe to ftrike the fellow for the infult: for the word was a contumelious one that they addrefs to the Germans. But the Ruffian ran away, and called up the Guard, faying that the German was on the point of murdering him, and that he was a robber. The foldiers roufed by this ftory ran up, arrefted the footman, and brought him as a robber to the Pricaffa; where, his innocence being manifeft, he was, on payment of one griffna, allowed to return home.

· Everything is in confufion in Mufcovy. The Czar, at leaving, commended the fafe keeping and prefecture of the city to Knes Tzerkafki. To Gordon he faid: " To thee, meanwhile, I commit everything: everything is entrufted to your hands and to your loyalty." But fome fcribe arrogates to himfelf the fupreme military direction which belonged to Knes Romadonowfki, pretending that it devolved upon him at the departure of the latter, and confequently that cognifance of everything is of his competency.

6.—Count Bergamini, who had come to Mufcovy at great coft to pay his court to the Czar, was actually on his way to Veroneje, when hearing that the Czar was no longer there, he came back at once, and to-day obtained his paffport to return to Poland.

7, 8, 9, 10, 11.—To our very great delight, the moft clement Imperial letters of recall came by the poft. About one o'clock at night a great ftorm arofe—thunder, lightning, rain, and wind raged with incredible violence throughout the night.

12.—The Calmuck Ambaffador of the Tartars was honoured with a Czar's entertainment— flender enough and in fuit with the manners of the receiver.

At laft, leave is given to the four Francifcan fathers to go through Perfia to China. The Czar had indeed given orders that thefe fathers fhould be provided with a fhip and all the provifions they might want as far as the Cafpian Sea, in the fame way as the Archbifhop of Ancyra was previoufly furnifhed. But Galizin, the Viceroy of Caffan and Aftracan, whofe bufinefs this was, as foon as the Czar had left for Azow would give them nothing of the kind. Thus it became incumbent on the Lord Envoy Extraordinary to make the outlay, and with ſignal Chriſtian charity he procured for them as well a ſhip as a ſupply of proviſions,—wine, beer, brandy, meat, bread, flour,—with a capital ſtore of which they began their journey.

13, 14.—Notice came by a ſure meſſenger that Dumnoi Emilian Ignatowicz Ukrainzow, whom the Czar has appointed Envoy Extra-ordinary, was about going by the Black Sea to Conſtantinople, and that His Majeſty the Czar would accompany him as far as the Cimmerian Boſphorus, or the Straits of Kaffa. With refer-ence to this miſſion, on which the Dumnoi is ſent to ratify the peace which Procop Woſnizin had haughtily and imprudently neglected, a cer-tain perſon made the following witty remark : "It ſeems to me juſt like as if a fool had broken a pane of glaſs, and a man of ſenſe were obliged to make it whole again."

/ Dumnoi Andrew Artemonowicz, whoſe father was thrown by the rebel Strelitz out of a window of the Caſtle of the Kremlin, received upon lances and murdered, was named Ambaſſador in ordi-nary to their High Mightineſſes the States of Holland, and has the Czar's commands to remain there with his wife and children for three years. Eight fons of Boyars go along with him, to acquire a knowledge during that time of feamanfhip and naval matters.

15.—A hundred and fifty veffels, laden with barley and oats, have come here by the river Wolga. Three hundred are following them with cargoes of wheat.

When the Czar was leaving Veroneje for Azow, and was already on board, that Alexander, who is fo confpicuous at court through the Czar's graces, was whifpering fomething in his ear, which put the Czar in a fudden paffion, and he inflicted fome boxes on his importunate monitor, fo that he lay ftretched at full length, quite like a dying man at the feet of irate Majefty.

The mutiny of the garrifon of Azow gained ftrength with its duration. The mutineers demand an oath from him whom they fhould revere as the arbiter of life and death. But what have treafonable fubjects, after trampling on the authority of their prince, ever left whole, untouched, and undared? It is a folace to thofe whofe unholy difobedience has thus loft them,

to leave nothing untried, that daring can fug-
geft, which may avail them to conjure the ruin
which they have called down upon themfelves.
Although the Czar faw, with a great fenfe of
grief, his dignity compromifed by treafon, neverthelefs, he did not rejeĉt the condition put to
him, nor the oath which was exaĉted as its
guarantee; left, by obftinately upholding His
Majefty, he fhould open the way to peril of
worfe evils. He defcended to make a paĉt with
his fubjeĉts, and, repeating the words after them,
bound himfelf by his royal truth and dignity,
that all the Strelitz in the city of Azow fhould
go unpunifhed. It remains to be feen whether
he will adhere to this pledge given under compulfion. For what is extorted wrongfully from
princes they often requite by another wrong, nor
do they confider themfelves in juftice bound to
their own injury.

16, 17.—Several days of continual rain have
rendered the ftreets in the German Slowoda im-
paffable: carts are lying about everywhere fo
deep in the mud that the horfes were unable to
draw them out.

18.—General de Gordon, and the Colonel,

his fon ; Colonel Acchenton, Colonel de Grage ;
the two miffionaries — Doctor Carbonari and
Mr. Guafconi—met at the Lord Envoy-Extra-
ordinary's, to confult about keeping up the
Church and the Catholic community. The
care of the money matters of the Church is
committed to General de Gordon and Mr.
Guafconi.

19.—They celebrated to-day with the greateft
pomp, the feftival of Saint Nicholas, patron of
Mufcovy, which is the grand *Brafnick* of the
Ruffians. It is quite fhameful—they think it,
in fact, unworthy of them—not to reel with wine
or brandy on this day, for the greater the folemnity of the feftival the more correct they confider
it to give themfelves up to drunkennefs and
other gratifications. This night, as the Envoy
of Denmark came back from Veroneje, when
he arrived at the gate, a difpute arofe about
money which the foldiers infifted upon—what
is called *das Sper-Geld*—for he refufed to pay
for the foldiers that the Czar had given him as
an efcort.

20.—The Envoy of Denmark told among
other ftories the following. That two German

colonels who were accufed by a Mufcovite of treafon, imprifoned and fubjected to the worft tortures of the rack, could not be made to confefs the crime which the informer had laid to their charge. Meanwhile the Ruffian had repented of his falfe accufation, and with the fame effrontery as he before had accufed thefe innocent men, he made known to the Czar that the Germans had been wrongfully tortured, and that it was only his envy that made him accufe innocent men of fuch a heinous offence. This atrocious man's malice put the Czar in fuch a heat of indignation, that he ftruck off his hateful head, as he richly deferved.

The foldiers of the regiment of Bebrafchentfko are divided among the fhips. They fay that the veffel to which none but the Czar and his principal Boyars put a hand, is unique, and the handfomeft of his Majefty's fleet.

21, 22.—On account of the lofs of his palace, which was burnt down in the late fire, Leo Kirilowicz Narefkin got leave of abfence from the Czar, and came back to Mofcow from Veroneje.

23.—The fecretary was fent very early in the

morning to the Boyar, juſt named, with the following meſſage, to ſay that the Lord Envoy
Extraordinary congratulated the Boyar on his
happy return from Veroneje, and would be extremely glad to have another interview with him
in his capacity as Prime Miniſter of the Muſcovites ; that he truſted the letters he had written
to him had reached him ſafely, but as he had as
yet no anſwer to them, and ſubſequent commands
had arrived meantime from the Moſt Auguſt the
Emperor, he deſired an occaſion of conferring
with him in reference to them, and conſequently
begged that the Boyar would have the kindneſs
to appoint a convenient time to call upon him.
To theſe points the Boyar replied ; that he returned thanks for theſe polite attentions, and with
his reciprocal ſalutations to the Lord Envoy,
that he had received the letters which notified the
marriage of the King of the Romans, and that
he would take care to appoint a convenient time
for conference.   He alſo inquired why the Lord
Envoy would not come to Veroneje, ſaying that
the Czar's orders to ſummon him thither had
been ſent to Moſcow, and further that the Czar
had waited ſix days for his arrival.   But this

appeared paradoxical ; for where were the letters?
—where had the orders come ?—what courier
brought the letters?—why had there been no
queftion on the fubjeƈt ? For the Lord Envoy
had heard nothing of all thefe things. But
another explanation was given that wore a greater
femblance of truth,—that thefe orders had been
fent enclofed to Dumnoi Ukrainzow to intimate them properly, and as the letters did not
reach Mofcow until Dumnoi was on the road
to Veroneje, they had been fent thither after
him by another link of the chain of accidents.
The circumftances of the time made it advif-
able to accept, in a ftraightforward credulous
way the excufe alleged, without queftioning its
truth.

24.—The Brandenburgh refident, Timothy
de Zadora Kefielfki, had gone for the purpofe of
fpeaking to Boyar Leo Kirilowicz Narefkin.
After a whole hour's patience, the Boyar at laft
came into the antechamber, where he knew he
was waited for. When he looked at the Refident, as if he wondered at his being there, he
rudely queftioned him with this haughty addrefs :
" What doft thou want ? " To which the Refi-

dent anſwered : " Thou knoweſt that I have not come to beg a cruſt of bread from thee : if thou doſt not conſider the attention of my viſit an honour to thee, I ſhall diſpenſe myſelf in future of that trouble." The unexpected tartneſs of the anſwer ſtruck the Boyar ſo home, that in a harſh and contemptuous tone he was beginning to taunt the Reſident, ſaying ; "What durſt thou ſay to me, thou petty little Chamberlain ? " Upon which the Reſident, with no leſs warmth, inſtantly retorted: "I hold myſelf highly honoured in being a Chamberlain of my moſt Serene Prince. If the rank I hold be beneath thy ambition, he that ſent me could confer a higher upon me, but it would be difficult for him to confer any which the impotency of your ſtilted mind would not deſpiſe as far beneath you."

26.—Sixteen hundred roubles in ready money, and ſixteen hundred more in ſable furs, were delivered to Dumnoi Ukrainzow, for the ex-penſes of his journey to Conſtantinople. At length the council of Boyars begin to entertain more practical ideas about the ratification of peace. The Czar has determined to call upon the brotherly friendſhip of the Moſt Auguſt

Emperor, in order to obtain fair conditions through his falutary offices.

27, 28, 29.—The miner Urban has at length, after his long and fqualid imprifonment, been reftored to liberty once more; and though an exprefs mandate of the Czar for his liberation, which was granted as a favour at the Lord Envoy's folicitation, commanded that he fhould be fet free without ranfom, neverthelefs he had to pay a bribe of fifteen roubles to the Diak and fcribes for his liberty. Nothing is fafe in Mufcovy from thefe harpies.

30, 31.—A hundred and fifty Strelitz brought here from the camp at Azow.

Y

JUNE 1.—The Brandenburgh Refident entertained the Imperial Lord Envoy and the Dumnoi of the Siberian *Pricaffa*, Wignius. The fame day the Danifh Envoy received at dinner Andrew Artemonowicz, the Ambaffador Defignate to the States of Holland.

2.—Half the Lord Envoy's fervants went with the Miffionary, Mr. John Berula, to the monaftery called Jerufalem, fix German miles diftant from Mofcow.

3.—Mr. John Caſſagrande, the Miſſionary of the Venetian Shipbuilders, who was ſent from this to Veroneje, a year ago, along with Baron de Burcherſdorff, who was then ſetting out for Azow, has died there, and his body, which was ſent back to Moſcow by command of the Czar himſelf, arrived on the very day of the month on which he left this city in order to fulfil the duties and functions of his holy miſſion, which he preſided over ſo as to earn everybody's good word, and give univerſal edification.

4, 5.—The body of the deceaſed Miſſionary was interred in the garden of the Imperial Miſ-ſionaries, near the Gordon tomb. The Lord Envoy Extraordinary and all his ſuite, beſides a great many other Catholics, were pleaſed to attend the funeral.

6.—Michael-Louis de Buchan, Captain in Beiſt's regiment of horſe, was ſent to His Majeſty the Czar, from the King of Poland, and being about to ſtart immediately for Azow with letters of great importance, dined at our table.

Doubtful reports came by letters that the Czar's Ambaſſador Prokop, who lately departed

with the higheft honours from the Imperial
Court, is either dead on the road, or lying
dangeroufly ill at Königfberg : peftilent fruit of
an ill weed.*

To-day being the feaft of Pentecoft, branches
and foliage of trees were bleffed by the Ruffian
priefts [*a Ruthenorum myftis*]; and this is the
only day on which they pray for God's aid
kneeling ; on every other feftival they fay their
ufual prayers ftanding erect. They account for
it by faying that the Apoftles and all the dif-
ciples of our Redeemer proftrated themfelves
upon the earth at the time of the coming of the
Holy Ghoft—and thence they took a handle to
blefs all the fruits of the earth.

8, 9.—The Lord Envoy Extraordinary drove
out to the Monaftery dedicated to the Moft
Holy Refurrection, diftant fix German miles
from Mofcow. The Bazilian monks took the
moft laudable pains to receive the Lord Envoy
honourably. They ferved up with moft lavifh
politenefs a vaft quantity of frefh fifh out of their
own fifhponds, beer, brandy, and difhes dreffed

---

* " Malæ herbæ peffimus fructus."—ORIG.

in the Ruſſian faſhion. The Czar's miniſters had recommended the monks to ſhow all this civility of polite preparation.

10.—We were led by a monk through the monaſtery, which is encloſed with huge walls. The refectories for the whole community were ſhown to us, as were the cells of the monks; the latter are ſeparated by a very thin partition. The church is a large and very noble pile, ſumptuouſly built by the Patriarch Nichon, and, carried out exactly on the model of that on Mount Calvary in Jeruſalem, repreſents every circumſtance of Chriſt's paſſion, in different chapels. While we were examining the church at our leiſure, Wignius arrived with the Branden-burgh Reſident, in company with whom we had our dinner here; at which a Ruſſified Pole, who ſpoke good Latin, and two other monks high in office, were preſent; after which we ſet off to an eſtate of his (Wignius's), that lay ſome miles further on. His houſe, conſtructed of brick, is built with various conveniences. The ſtream that glides paſt it, and the wide open fields around it, afforded a charming view. We firſt amuſed ourſelves delightfully boating, and en-

ticing the unwary fifh into the cunning net, a
diverfion all the more pleafant, when we knew
we fhould have them to fupper, for which it was
delightful to catch them. Our hoft omitted
none of thofe attentions that might denote fincere
affection and truth.

11.—After fowling and dinner duly performed,
and friendly greetings had been mutually ex-
changed, the Brandenburgh Refident defired to
return to Mofcow, along with the Imperial Lord
Envoy. At a village called Angeliko, on an
eftate belonging to the monaftery, we paffed
that night.

12.—After accomplifhing four miles, we
reached Mofcow, and the Ambaffadorial Palace,
at about ten in the day. In a grove, an hour
diftant from the city—where the Germans are in
the habit of going to amufe themfelves—there
grew fo hot a quarrel between Captains Erchel
and Printz, that fwords were drawn, and wounds
given on both fides.

13.—The feaft of St. Anthony of Padua
folemnly celebrated.

14.—With unaccuftomed civility Diak Boris
Michalowicz, that was fometime refident at

Warſaw, was ſent by Leo Kirilowicz Nareſkin to the Lord Envoy to inquire after the ſtate of his health.

15.—Again came Boris Michalowicz to the Lord Envoy with preciſely the ſame civil errand as yeſterday. Two Ruſſians with a complete ſpecification of the whole ſea fleet, deſerted to the Tartars from Banzina. Though it appeared that no blame for this deſertion could be imputed to the Vice-Commandant (whom they ſtyle Sotik),* nevertheleſs by order of the Czar he was *hanged*, for not being ſharp enough in preventing the criminals in their deſign. But what Argus could have eyes enough for the malicious wiles of traitors?

16.—Again came Boris Michalowicz, by command of Nareſkin, announcing that the time for the conference ſolicited, would ſhortly be appointed. The Grand Embaſſy of the Swedes halted near the borders of Moſcovy; hence orders are deſpatched to the Woivodes of the frontier cities to impreſs 450 *potwoda*.

17.—Conference had by the Lord Envoy with Nareſkin touching the notification of the

---

* Sotnik.

marriage of the Moſt Serene King of the Romans.

18, 19.—General de Gordon received all the Engliſh and Scotch merchants at dinner.

20.—Two houſes in the German Slowoda, and ſome hundreds of dwellings in the city, were confumed by a moſt difaſtrous fire.

21, 22, 23, 24.—No time was allowed to the Venetian ſhipwrights to purify their conſciences by ſacramental confeſſion, they are kept working as hard as they can by the Czar, toiling without reſt at ſhipbuilding. Their prieſt, as I have already mentioned, died lately ; but that they might not be deſtitute of the confolation of this annual devotion, the Imperial Miſſionary at Mofcow, a man of great and moſt devoted zeal, yielded with the greateſt readineſs to their entreaties. When he was about ſtarting for Veroneje, the miniſtry granted him four *potwoda* at the mediation of the Lord Envoy.

25.—The Lord Envoy honoured the eſpoufals of Captain Rickmann with his prefence.

26.—Major* de Straus celebrated his marriage with a coufin of the Daniſh Envoy.

* Supremis-Vigiliarum-præfeſtus, literally in German, *Oberſl-*

27.—A boy caught in a theft committed ſuicide, out of fear of the penalty that awaited him.

28.—The Lord Envoy viſited Prince* Szeremetow. It was noiſed abroad that Prokop had arrived, but extremely ill; ſo one of the chief ſcribes was deſpatched with an account to the Czar at Azow.

29, 30.—Mr. Schrader, paſtor of the Sectaries of the Confeſſion of Augſburg, breathed his laſt between eleven and twelve at night.

JULY 1, 2.—It remained for the Lord Envoy, according to the Imperial injunction and letters, to announce to His Majeſty the Czar, the marriage contracted under ſuch happy auſpices ſome time ſince between the Moſt Serene the

wachtmeiſter, the title given to an Auſtrian major to the preſent day.—TRANSL.

* Szeremetow's rank was ſtrictly that of Boyar, not Prince. The frequency of the uſe of the title Prince in this Diary to perſons not belonging to the families ſtrictly entitled to that rank, leads me to ſuppoſe that it was thus abuſively given in Muſcovite ſociety to ſome of the great magnates of the Boyar claſs. Even now it is frequently uſurped by petty Tartar and Calmuck and Georgian chieftains' families, ſettling or living in Ruſſia.—(See Dolgoruki, *Notices des principales familles*, &c.)— TRANSL.

King of the Romans and Hungary, Jofeph I., and the Moft Serene Princefs Wilhelmina-Amelia, Duchefs of Brunfwick and Luneburg.* May God grant, that thofe whom by his infcrutable bounty, for the weal of Chriftendom, the fruitful increafe of the Moft Auguft Houfe of Auftria, the ineffable confolation of fubject nations, and · the moft ardent prayers of good citizens, auguft love hath joined, may after the confummation of the newly begun century, be brought fcathelefs to old age, to live in the conftant and moft anxioufly defired fucceffion of moft ferene off-fpring, among the pofterity of ages hereafter to come, with immortal fame for ever and aye.

The Czar's Majefty was abfent—his avidity to acquire glory, which is his inmoft defire, and the

---

* This princefs was coufin-german to King George I., being daughter and co-heirefs (with her fifter, who married the Duke of Modena) of John Frederick, a Catholic, *third* fon of George, Duke of Hanover: the *fourth* fon, Erneft Auguftus, Bifhop of Ofnaburg, and fubfequently, by creation of the Emperor Leopold, Elector of Hanover, was father of George I. Her mother was daughter of Edward, Prince Palatine of the Rhine, brother of the Electrefs Sophia of Hanover, whofe fon George fucceeded to the throne of England, as the neareft Proteftant, to the exclufion of the nearer Catholic heirs ; the eldeft defcendant of whom in our days is Francis V., Duke of Modena, as reprefentative of the Princefs Henrietta of England, fifter of Charles II. and of James II.—TRANSL.

pleaſure he takes in new ſhips, having ſummoned him with laudable impulſe, nearly three hundred miles away to the Palus Meotides,* not far from the Straits of the Cimmerian Boſphorus.† Still the function demanded a ſolemnity which the Prime Miniſter, Leo Kirilowicz Nareſkin, pre-pared with becoming zeal. There was a ſix-horſe coach of the Czar's for the Lord Envoy, and horſes from the Czar's ſtables adorned with the cuſtomary glittering trappings. When the Lord Envoy reached the court-yard of the houſe where the Boyar had appointed to receive the letters of notification, he was met by two Diaks, who con-ducted him through many ante-chambers to the apartment deſtined for this ſolemn ceremony, in the veſtibule of which the Boyar ſtood awaiting him. The officials of the Lord Envoy, for the greater dignity of the act, had taken their places ſtanding along with a great crowd of the Czar's ſcribes in that room. But when the Boyar prayed of the Lord Envoy to be ſeated and the confer-ence began, all were ordered out except Diak Boſnikow, the ſecretary, and the interpreter.

---

* The Sea of Azow.—TRANSL.
† The Straits of Jenikale.—TRANSL.

Mutual proteftations enfued, in which affurances were interchanged that the fincere and fraternal love of the Moft Clement Lords Principals fhould be always cultivated and kept up. The ceremony and polite offices being gone through, the Lord Envoy was led back by two Diaks to his coach, and by a *priftaw* to the Ambaffadorial Palace ; and on driving paft the Czar's caftle, the foldiers on guard faluted with the cuftomary prefenting of arms and waving of colours.

3, 4.—St. John's day celebrated with the feftive ftrains of the muficians in choir and ftreet.

5, 6.—A Ruffian merchant claimed a debt of four roubles from a certain German for goods bought. When the German denied that he owed fo much, the Ruffian with much vociferation, feveral times moft atrocioufly calling on all the powers celeftial and infernal to witnefs, endeavoured to prove his claim. So the German appointed the Ruffian arbiter on his proffered oath; who thereupon entering the neareft church, falfely made the requifite oath. In a fhort time after he himfelf confeffed that the German did not owe him four roubles, but only two ;

that the other two were due to him by another, alfo a German, and that he could claim
them in turn.   This is refpect for an oath !
this is piety towards God ! the taking of whofe
name in vain is no fcruple of confcience to this
people.

7.—The Lord Envoy received letters written
from the camp at Azow by the Lord Boyar,
Feodor Alexiowicz Golowin, at the command of
the Czar's Majefty, to the effect that His Majefty
had given it in command to his minifter refiding
here to difmifs the Lord Envoy with fuch degree
of honours in the fulleft manner in every refpect,
as had never hitherto fallen to the lot of any
minifter of the fame rank.

8.—The Eve of the Holy Apoftles, Peter and
Paul, was celebrated by the Mufcovites with
great feftivities.   The Czarewicz had appointed
public prayers for the fafety of His Moft Serene
Father the Czar.

9.—The Mufcovites perform the annual
feftival of the Holy Apoftles, Peter and Paul,
and of the Czar, who was named Peter in
baptifm.

The Czar's caftle of Ismailow, laid out moft

agreeably for a fummer refidence, is furrounded
by a grove of trees, not thickly planted, but
growing to a prodigious height, and affording
an admirable refuge beneath the cool fhade of
their lofty and fpreading branches from the burning heat of fummer. It pleafed the Lord Envoy
to go and fee the delightful neighbourhood of
this wood, to contemplate and enjoy the famous
charms of the place. Muficians followed to aid
the gentle whifperings of the woods and winds
with fweeter harmonies. The Czarine, the
Czarewicz, and the unmarried princeffes, énticed
by the gentle feafon of the year, were then ftaying at that caftle, and they were fond of rambling
through the denfe thickets to the pleafant glades
of the foreft, and killing time in the fweet dif-
ports and forgetfulnefs of bufy repofe. It fo
happened that they were thus engaged at the
moment when the fweet fymphony of clarions
and reed inftruments gufhed in gentleft meafure
upon their ears, and made them ceafe awhile
from their occupation. The muficians grew
ambitious upon finding themfelves obferved, and
were giving fatisfaction to the obfervers, and
with moft graceful emulation they ftrove one

with another who fhould bear off the palm in witching with his fweet fkill, thefe ears Moft Serene to longeft forgetfulnefs. They remained a quarter of an hour, and praifed exceedingly the fkill of all the muficians.

10.—A Lithuanian Catholic boy, feduced by the Mufcovites, fled from our kitchen to a certain Ruffian prince, to embrace the Ruffian religion, in the hope of getting a wife, as they had pro- mifed him upon that condition. Knes Repnin,* Colonel of the Dragoons,† and his fervants, ftung by fome gad-fly to frenzy, broke violently in upon the city guard, and as he was on the point of fnatching away the colours, the enfign received him upon his pike in the moft creditable manner. Several others were wounded in the ftrife on both fides.

11.—In the evening a fire broke out not far from Narefkin's houfe, and reduced to afhes a

---

* Prince Anikita Repnin, who was a conftant friend of Peter the Great. He rofe to be a field-marfhal. The family is extinct in the male line.—TRANSL.

† The Latin expreffion is, *dimacharum præfectus.* I fuppofe the author muft mean dragoons, for *dimachae*, or διμαχαι, were foldiers that fought both on foot and on horfeback, as dragoons originally did.—TRANSL.

hundred and thirty houfes between poor and handfome.

12.—Knes Boris Alexiowicz Galizin has come back from the frontiers of Cafen and Aftracan to Mofcow.

13.—The boy that lately ran away was fent back by the Prime Minifter to the Lord Envoy. During the Czar's abfence the Prime Minifter was empowered to give the Czar's re-credentials in the name and by the authority of His Majefty. Of the reft of their cuftomary ceremonial hardly anything was omitted by them. An apartment was appointed in the Czar's caftle for the performance of this ceremonial. There was a *priftaw*, the Czar's Vice-Mafter of the Horfe, with an interpreter, a fix-horfe coach of the Czar's; horfes gorgeoufly decked, as ufual, with trappings of gold and filver, and a fquadron of dragoons fwelled the cortège. Guards were everywhere drawn up in long array, and waved their colours, and prefented arms. The body-guards filled the court of the caftle, as far as the veftibule of the firft apartment, Lieutenant-Colonel de Colom, Meffieurs de Bach and Erchel as Captains, performing their refpective

funations. A fon of the Boyar, along with
Diak Bofnikow, received the Lord Envoy at the
threfhold, and conduated him to his father.
When the re-credential letters were delivered, it
was explained what the one wifhed to be announced to the Emperor, and what the other
wifhed to be announced to the Czar, and placing
a laft wreath, the Lord Envoy commended himfelf, and all his fuite, the Imperial Miffionaries,
and the whole Catholic community to the benig-
nity of the Czar. The Czar's good grace being
thereupon promifed to all by the Boyar, Diak
Bofnikow thus began :—" The Czar's Majefty
deigns all his grace to the Lord Envoy, and has
commanded that he fhall not only receive out of
his liberality the ufual letters, but alfo a *priftaw*,
an efcort of foldiers, and *potwoda*, as far as the
confines of Mufcovy and Lithuania, and whatever elfe he defires to his full fatisfaction. This
being over, the Lord Envoy handed the Czar's
re-credentials to the Secretary, and was led, with
the moft exquifite politenefs, by the Prime
Minifter and his fon, as far as the court, where
the foldiers ftood drawn up in array, and feated
himfelf with the *priftaw* in the Czar's coach,

before which the Secretary rode upon a gorgeous
fteed, bearing the Czar's re-credentials, wrapped
in red filk, brocaded with gold, held in fuch a
way as that everybody could fee them. Befides the Czarewicz, the Dowager Czarine,
and other princeffes of the Czar's court, were
looking curioufly out of their windows, at our
entry into, and our exit from, the Kremlin
caftle.

14.—Came Diak Jacob Nikonow, having
heard of the complaints of fome of our people,
who had been uncivilly affronted lately by the
watch, and after previoufly examining the accufed
dragoons, condemned them all eight, notwithftanding the fplendour of their birth—for they
were noble—to the penalty of the *battok.* By
order of the Czar the fentence was executed in
the Court of the Ambaffadorial Palace, the
number of blows with which they were to be
chaftifed was left to the arbitrement of thofe
to whom their evil ftars had led them to give
very ill-treatment.

A Czar's banquet, not inferior in opulence
and fplendour to that given to us before, was
carried to the Lord Envoy with the ufual folemn

ftate and proceffion of two hundred men. After a fip of brandy, which was brought round in a cup made of a precious ftone, the firft toaft was to the health of the Moft Auguft Emperor; the fecond, that of the Moft Serene Czar; the third, of the Moft Serene King of the Romans; the fourth, the Czarewicz; the fifth, the Lord Envoy. The mutual wordy compliments of the *priftaw* and of the Lord Envoy, confifted in proteftations of fincere friendfhip.

15.—Thofe who had any part of care or trouble in yefterday's Imperial banquet, conference, and folemn difmiffal, ftood awaiting with moft greedy hopes, the largefs of the Lord Envoy, and received gifts in proportion to their feveral functions.

16, 17, 18.—The Ruffians celebrated the feftival of the Bleffed Virgin of Cafan. The Mufcovites believe that the image which they venerate under that name had always been fufpended in the clouds, and was feen by the entire Ruffian army that beleaguered Cafan, during the whole time of the fiege; but that after the city was ftormed, the image fell from the fky to the ground, and was with the utmoft reverence lifted

up by the Ruſſians, and has ever ſince been held
in worſhip.

About evening came the head ſcribe of the
Ambaſſadorial Chancery, attended by many others
from the ſame office, and diſtributed the Czar's
preſents, conſiſting of ſable furs, to the Lord
Envoy and the whole of his ſuite.

19, 20.—Yeſterday and to-day leave-taking
began ; farewell being bidden to all that were
familiar and intimate friends. Full-ſize portraits
of their Imperial Majeſties, the Emperor and
Empreſs, of the Moſt Serene King of the
Romans, and of the Moſt Serene Archduke
Charles, were ſent as a preſent to the Prime
Miniſter, Leo Kirilowicz Nareſkin.

21, 22.—Having performed the laſt civility
of farewell viſits in the German Slowoda, we all
prepared for to-morrow's departure. The Lord
Envoy has been ſeveral times invited by the
Prime Miniſter to a ſeat of his called Filli, ſome
werſts diſtant from Moſcow.

At four miles diſtant from Moſcow the Grand
Swediſh Embaſſy lay, awaiting the order for
entering the city. For their ſuitable lodging
there was aſſigned a houſe formerly inhabited

by popes, and commonly called *das Pfaffen-Haus.*

RETURN OF THE IMPERIAL LEGATION
FROM MUSCOVY TO VIENNA.

JULY 23.—Although no ſuch practice or cuſtom be in force in any European Court, as accompanying the departure of the Miniſters of foreign Princes with a public ſolemnity and extraordinary exhibition of pomp; ſo that for ages it had come to be conſidered a uſeleſs ex- penſe of public honours to wait on their departure with ſtate or ſplendour; neverthelefs the Court of Ruſſia departed in our time by a contrary uſage from this general ſentiment, honouring Mr. de Printz, Envoy Extraordinary of the Elector of Brandenburgh (as an eſpecial friendly diſtinction, in order to exhibit more abundantly the fraternal bonds lately confirmed between the two princes), with the fame ſtate ceremonial at his departure as that with which they received him on his arrival, and had thought fit to accom- pany his entry into their walls. The like was

intimated to the Lord Envoy alfo, after the ceremonial of giving him his re-credentials. He
indeed fet himfelf againft this novel and unufual
method of demonftrative friendfhip; but it was
labour in vain. After his multifarious objec-
tions, the commands of His Majefty the Czar
were brought back, directing that the Lord
Envoy fhould be difmiffed with fuch honours as
had never fallen to the lot of any minifter before
him. So after duly providing by folemn proteft,
that the Mufcovites fhould not pretend to make
thefe unufual ceremonies a precedent at the Emperor's Court, he left it to their own free will to
diftinguifh his departure with whatever honours
they might choofe. Now, it was in no particular different from the handfome ceremonial
which they had appointed for our entry. There
were fquadrons of the new cavalry; detachments
of the light troops, a moft gorgeous coach of the
Czar's, and horfes glittering with new trappings
of gold and filver and gems, awaited the Lord
Envoy's officials. Along with the Lord Envoy,
their fate in the coach a *priftaw* in ordinary, as
well as the interpreter, and they were to conduct
him as far as the place where fifteen months ago

the ceremonial of reception had been folemnly gone through.

Through the leading ftreets of the city, every-where befet by a countlefs throng of men, we reached the banks of the river of Mofcow. The croffing was not quite exempt from danger, for the bridge was only in the middle of the ftream, and did not reach the bank at either fide ; fo that the afcent and defcent were of no little difficulty. But the dangers of fuch ill-made bridges feems little or nothing to the Mufcovites, though they fwallow up no few people that are deceived by the unexpected declivity. Jemfka Slowoda (the coachmen's fuburb) occupies the further bank. The *priftaw's* attendance was limited to the bounds of this fuburb. Here the coach ftopped, the *priftaw* bade farewell, and capped the adopted ceremonial with the laft compliments. The noble eftate of the Prime Minifter and Boyar, Lord Leo Kirilowicz Narefkin, called Filli, is only feven werfts diftant from Mofcow. He had fome days previoufly invited the Lord Envoy, at his departure, to a dinner, which he got up there in moft fplendid ftyle. Scarcely was the ceremo-nial at an end, when one of the officials of that

Boyar, who was fent by his mafter to fhow the way to the eftate, prefented himfelf, politely begging that the Lord Envoy would deign to follow him. Thus with the whole train and baggage, which was carried by ninety *potwoda*, he left the high road efcorted by the reprefentatives of foreign minifters and feveral officers of the Czar's army. So great were the compliments of the guefts upon entering the place, which was for the moft part thronged with the principal Germans, that you might have thought they were contending for a prize. There was a great and general ftudioufnefs of friendfhip ; fovereign was the emulation of many to exprefs with greater force the integrity of their feelings, till at length the fummons to the coftly banquet that was ferved brought back the guefts to themfelves. Except the Prime Minifter and his kinfman, and our ufual interpreter, Mr. Schwerenberg, no Ruffian gueft was there. The Germans, in numbers, were invited inftead of them. The following was the order of the feats after the Lord Envoy : the Envoy of Denmark, General de Gordon, the Brandenburgh Refident, Adam Weyd; the Imperial Colonel of Artillery de

Grage, Colonel James Gordon ; Colonel Acchenton ;* the Imperial Miſſionary, John Berula ;
the Czar's doctor, Carbonari ; Guaſconi, a Catholic merchant ; Wolff, Brand, and Lips, non-
Catholic merchants ; mixed among whom there
alſo ſat eight of the Lord Envoy's officials. The
banquet was not inferior to Royal ſumptuouſneſs,
nor was it cooked in the Ruſſian faſhion, but well
dreſſed to the German taſte. The rare profuſion
of viands, the coſtlineſs of the gold and ſilver
plate, the variety and exquiſiteneſs of the bever-
ages, beſpoke plainly the near blood-relation of
the Czar.† After dinner there was an archery
match : nobody was excuſed becauſe of the exerciſe being ſtrange to him, or for his want of ſkill
in a matter to which he was unaccuſtomed. A
ſheet of paper ſtuck in the ground was the butt.
The Prime Miniſter perforated it ſeveral times,
amidſt general applauſe. As the rain drove us
from this moſt pleaſant exerciſe, we retired again
to the apartments of the Boyar. Nareſkin,
taking the Lord Envoy by the hand, led him to

* Acchintown, or Auchindown, an ancient caſtle and ſeat of
the Gordons in Scotland.
† Nareſkin's ſiſter was the Czarine, mother of Peter I.

his wife's chamber to falute and be faluted. There is no higher mark of honour among the Ruffians. He is honoured in the higheft degree whom the hufband invites to embrace his wife, and to receive the extreme compliment of a fip of brandy from her hand. Nor fhould I pafs unmentioned the liberality which the Boyar exhibited in his gift of a coftly peliffe of fables to the Lord Envoy. Yet this munificence was not altogether devoid of fome thought of his own advantage. For the Boyar labouredly fought an occafion of moving difcourfe, and calling to remembrance the honours of the day, when the Moft Auguft Emperor's clemency diftinguifhed Bafil Kirilowicz Galizin, who held the firft place of authority in Mufcovy fourteen years ago, fending him a coach by Mr. Kurz. Eager, no doubt, that the Emperor fhould exhibit equal condefcenfion to him who ambitioufly occupies the fame place and office at prefent. Whither tended the atrocious threats againft Diak Bafil Bofnikow, that there was no fcarcity of cudgels to chaftife his impertinence towards him? Certainly this meant to mollify the Lord Envoy, who was querulous about this Diak's rude manners, and to make fair

fail for the objeƈt of his ambition by the Lord
Envoy's favourable report. But he loſt his oil
and his labour, when, after General Gordon
having already occupied the ſeat of honour, he
invited the Imperial Envoy to get into his coach,
that he might conduƈt him to another eſtate of his
two werſts further on. Yet the man was rather
to be pardoned for his ſimplicity than reprehended
for craftineſs ; and ſo he was horror-ſtricken when
the Lord Envoy ſaid: " You poſtpone the Imperial Envoy to General Gordon ! " While he
was ſeeking to remedy this, the Imperial Envoy
got into his own carriage, and ſo drove off with
the reſt to that eſtate. Receiving his gueſts there
with much politeneſs, the proprietor pointed out
his conveniences for the chaſe on an adjacent hill
that was ſtudded with little thickets, and ſloped
with a gentle declivity into a valley ; and he
ſought to win back the offended ſpirit of the Lord
Envoy by the offer of two ſporting dogs, which
he warranted capital. After tarrying for a brief
ſpace here, thanks were given and farewell bidden
not only to the Boyar, but to all the gueſts preſent and above-named. Colonel Gordon's main
taſk was to excuſe his father of the offence

received in his perfon from the Boyar. Colonel
de Grage and the Czar's doctor, Carbonari, followed our tents three werfts further.—Beneath
the open fky, under canvas, we paffed the night.
But as a fcarcity of water was apparent, the Lord
Envoy not unjuftly inveighed againft the Czar's
priftaw, for it was incumbent on him to have
provided againft fuch circumftances. Although
there was no inn near, ftill we were not afflicted
with any fcarcity of eatables or drinkables. Nor
did we ever experience fuch barren days as thofe
eight continuous days that Wickart details in his
" Mufcovite Itinerary," fol. 126. People may
take the blame to themfelves who do not make
provifion of what is neceffary from place to place.
Perhaps in that inftance it was nothing but parfi-
mony, under the cloak of economy, that had
introduced fafting.

24.—After folemn leave-taking on both fides,
thofe returned to Mofcow, who, as I have already
faid, accompanied us to the field and to our
tents; and we too fpeedily ftarted on an oppofite route, and came at dinner hour to Pir-
gufcowa, a village belonging to Knes Ivan
Bafilowicz. After dinner, paffing the village of

Veſonka, which belongs to Prince Boris Alexiowicz, we went on ſome miles further through
rough and broken ways, and over many little
bridges between, to our night's reſting place in
the woods.   Oats were bought in that village ;
for they are not to be had in every place.   This
prince has built at his own coſt a handſome
church, at the further ſide of the ſtream that
flows through the place, which is no mean ornament.   This prince had ſent forward one of his
officials to furniſh all that the Lord Envoy or
his whole ſuite might need ; but he did not
meet us becauſe we did not ſtop there.

25.—By Kuckliza Lararega to Scoloma Brach-
entſka, where we dined.   This place belongs to
the Stolnok (that is, noble) Ianow.   Here a
ſurgeon that we brought with us, a great boaſter
of his ſkill, ſhowed himſelf in a diſpute with
one of the ſerfs, more anxious about oil for the
wheels than about that of roſes.   On our evening drive through the foreſts ſeveral white hares
were ſeen—the Lord Envoy ſent a ball through
one, a diſh for to-morrow's dinner.   Not far
from Moſaiſko, in a glaſſy glade of the foreſt,
ſupper was prepared, and we ſlept.

26.—We arrived early at the city of Mofaiſko.* Saint Nicholas is revered as patron there. Formerly the Muſcovite Czars were in the habit of coming to this neighbourhood, laying aſide the cares of ſtate, and recreating themſelves with the chaſe, eſpecially of white hares, of which there are great quantities hereabouts. But the preſent Autocrat of Ruſſia, never, or hardly ever, indulges in the chaſe, by the various kinds of which his predeceſſors uſed to divide the ſeaſons of the year. This fortreſs and wooden town are diſtant eighteen German miles from Moſcow ; and here proviſion was made of a change of *potwoda*—the ſame in number as at Moſcow. After fifteen *werſts* we paſſed the night in the foreſt.

27.—Dinner in the foreſt alſo, cloſe to the village of Oſtroſchock ; but our afternoon journey was very diſagreeable from the ſwamps, dykes, and little bridges. All the carriages would ſtick ſo as hardly to be got along, ſo that we had to remain on the road till midnight,

---

* In the neighbourhood of Mofaiſk, which is a pretty little town of 2,500 ſouls, was fought in 1812, the great battle of the Borodino.—TRANSL.

for the lightly burdened had been fent on in advance to look out for a convenient place for our night halt; and heedlefs of the difficulty of the road, which they did not feel, they had gone on too far. Two horfes that fome of our company would have follow us loofe were loft in the darknefs of the night; one that was fent off to inquire about them only brought back indications of their having been ftolen. At laft we had fupper in a foreft on the banks of a ftream.

28.—Paffing through Biala Kabaka, where capital beer was found, we dined near the village of Waffeiniz Czariwa, which Wickart calls Sumiefchne Tzariwa, others pronounce Segmeftia Tzariovoa. The founder of this place was Ivan Bafilowicz,* whofe reign began in 1533, and who, after a tyranny of fifty-one

---

* Ivan IV., ftyled the Cruel, or, as the Ruffians fometimes prefer to call him, the Terrible, who was a fuitor in 1579 for the hand of Queen Elizabeth of England. He eftablifhed in 1568 the fovereign's body guard, called the Strelitz, which for repeated feditions and treafonable confpiracies, under Peter the Great, was abolifhed with the fanguinary vengeance detailed in this Diary; and which has no parallel fo ftriking as the maffacre in 1826 of the Janiffaries, with whom the Strelitz had fo many other points of refemblance, as has been frequently remarked.—TRANSL.

years, perifhed miferably in the year 1584. The village now belongs to the Boyar Bucchin, by gift of the Czar. The laft Czar built a new church here. There are feven bells there that chime like an organ ; they rang out in honour of the Lord Envoy when he was pafling through. Fifteen *werfts* further on we fupped in the foreft.

29.—We arrived by an exceffively rough road to Viafma, a wooden town and caftle of confiderable fize. The then Woivode was one of the Bucchins ;* he would admit none of our people into the city ; infifting upon a mandate of Czar Michael Feodorowicz, that has grown quite obfolete in the modern ftate of things, or quite abolifhed. Here was the fecond change of *potwoda*, and the firft of the foldiers to whom, becaufe they belonged to Gordon's regiment, the Lord Envoy gave fome imperials. The river Hugra wafhes this city, after crofling which we paffed the bridge called the Mile-and-half Bridge. Indeed, almoft the whole way from Vefonka to the fortrefs of Smolenfko is difficult,

* Bucchin, probably Pouchkin.—TRANSL.

on account of the countlefs and exceedingly long
bridges. We fupped in the foreft.

30.—We arrived at Semblowa at dinner hour.
The Ruffians were celebrating the feaft of Saint
Elias. They alleged as the reafon for this feftival, that for three years and fix months con-
tinuoufly no rain had fallen in that part of Mufcovy, and that God at length granted it to their
prayers on that day. In the evening arrived
at Tfchowodofelo, which Wickart calls Scho-
bodognia. How inhuman and untractable the
Mufcovites fhow themfelves at times, the following occurrence will teach. We had a carriage
broken; a peafant was called to mend it, and
taking it as an omen of the worft, he jumped
into the water, threatening with his drawn knife
to defend himfelf againft anybody that would
attempt to take him out.

31.—The Lord Envoy's birthday fell out
to-day. Having fuitably performed our congratulations—after paffing the Bafilean Monaftery, called Bogdin—we refrefhed ourfelves with
dinner outfide the village of Madilowa, on the
Boryfthenes. Three noble brothers are lords of
this village. They refufed to repair the bridge

over the Boryfthenes at their own coft until the
Lord Envoy threatened to denounce them to
the Czar's Majefty, and hinted the penalty of
hanging, or knout-flogging, that would be the
infallible confequence. The ferocity of the
brothers vanifhed at hearing of fuch horrid
punifhments, and becoming vaftly mild they
proffered milk, and did all that was in their
power to repair the bridge. We fupped outfide the city of Drogobufa, which lies on the
bank of the Boryfthenes. The deep river
Hugra rifes not far from this town in a foreft,
and flows into the Occa between Kalouga and
Vorotinfk. This river formerly divided Lithuania from Ruffia. One of the return *potwoda*
(for here we had the third change of *potwoda*)
ftole a fack of oats and harnefs from another,
but, being caught in the .fact, received as the
penalty of his difhonefty an abundant thwacking
of *battoks.*

✝ August 1.—The *priftaw* leaving the ufual
road brought us by a fhort cut. After paffing
the monaftery of Wefukol, fituated upon a
high hill, we prepared dinner in a foreft, and

fupped clofe by the river Wob, which it took
us till midnight to crofs. The Lord Envoy
received a prefent of fifh from a noble ftaroft of
a neighbouring village.

2.—We halted for dinner in a vaft open
plain at the village of Moeft; our journey in
the evening was incommoded by a thunder-
ftorm, and we fpread our tents on a beauteous
flat on a lofty hill in the foreft.

3.—We were ferioufly admonifhed by an
indifpofition of the Lord Envoy to ftrike our
tents later than ufual. As we travelled on,
medicines had to be prepared, and the malady
was on the increafe; when, at dinner-time, we
arrived at Smolenfko. This city, the metropolis
of the Duchy of Smolenfko, feated upon the
bank of the Boryfthenes, poffeffes a citadel built
of oaken timbers, in the midft of which there is
a church, dedicated to the Holy Virgin, built
upon a rock. The city itfelf lies in a valley
cinctured on every fide with hills and vaft forefts.
The Lord Envoy was received in the moft
honourable way outfide the gate by a frefh
priftaw and two companies of foldiers, who
accompanied his coach to his lodging, for which

a houfe fuitable to his rank was affigned. After everybody had inftalled himfelf in his room, the fecretary was fent to the Woivode Peter Samuelowicz Soltikow to announce our arrival, and perform the other ceremonies of falutation. He, in return, fent a moft polite meffage of wifhes for our health, and faid that he would call to-day on the Lord Envoy, if he did not believe it might incommode him, as he had heard he was rather indifpofed.

4.—But to omit nothing which could be expected from the politeft of men, he deputed his own fon, eight years old, to make particular inquiries about the Lord Envoy's ftate of health. The Lord Envoy, however, having fomewhat recovered his ftrength, went off to return the very great civility of this gentleman, with no lefs promptitude to the Woivode, along with his fon, to give and receive in turn tokens of true mutual friendfhip.

5.—Here was the fourth change of *potwoda.* Cuftomarily another *priftaw*, too, is appointed; but as the Lord Envoy, in anfwer to the Woivode's inquiry, whether he would prefer the fame *priftaw*, or a frefh one, faid that he would prefer the offices of the former, as he knew him already ;—he was not changed. His name was Alexi Michita Lichoni. Everything being arranged we quitted Smolenſko, and paſſed that night in a meadow.

6.—We arrived in the plain before the village of Dolſtihi at dinner hour. One of the officials was ſent forward from this place with letters for the Governor of Kadzin, to beg he would have the goodneſs to aid that official in collecting carters. We ſlept that night cloſe to Tohuſoff.

7.—We arrived at the Muſcovite village, called by ſome Richena, and by others Gregorwſki. Outſide this village, near Kadzin, a nameleſs rivulet marks the frontier between Lithuania and Muſcovy. When lately, in the year 1614, negotiations for peace were going on between theſe two moſt puiſſant nations, a houſe was built over this rivulet, in which the ambaſſador of either country ſat within his own territory. Here the *priſtaw* and the *potwoda* bade farewell, and in their ſtead we found carters, to whom we were to pay two imperials for every horſe to bring our baggage to Mohilow. There were twenty of them in all; fixteen from Richena and four from Kadzin. The Lord Envoy went by invitation to the governor of this frontier town, having fent him a handfome prefent previoufly. As we were pitching our tents in the fields outfide of Kadzin, the governor fent us fifh.

8.—The bridges, and the frequency of fteep hills gave much trouble and labour with the carts, which were heavily laden. We arrived outfide the city of Hori about noon; afterwards, paffing Gratfchma* and Krug Bern (they call their inns Krug), we fupped in Kirojetfcha. But ceafelefs rain forced us to abandon our tents, and betake ourfelves to the fmoky dens of the ruftics.

9.—At Schivanni we refted in the foreft about noon. Here the Governor of Sclovia, Mr. John Modlock, a native of Dantzick, returning from his eftate to Sclovia, vifited the Lord Envoy, who flept that night beyond Stanowicz, in the fields.

10.—At a mile from Mohilow we had to

---

* A corruption of *Karfzmat*, pronounced Karshmat, the local name for the vile Polifh ale-houfes, the only inns out of the great towns, and dens of matchlefs filth.—TRANSL.

crofs the Boryfthenes, the paffing of which occupied three hours. Count Bergamini, Captain of Irregular horfe (*equitum defultoriorum magifter*), who had come into Mufcovy in our time, but to no purpofe, and who had come back to his foldiers without feeing the Czar, was the firft to falute the Lord Envoy. A major and a company of foldiers, by command of General de Beift, received the Lord Envoy with proper refpect on the farther bank of the river, and efcorted him all the way to Mohilow.

General de Beift, after our arrival had been duly notified to him, fent his greetings through his regimental auditor, announcing that he would call in perfon. But his vifit was politely declined, and the meeting put off on both fides till the morrow. Meanwhile, a corporal and eight men were fent for our guard.

11.—Next day we infpected the new Jefuits' church at Mohilow, and another belonging to the Carmelites. The Bernardines,* too, have a monaftery, and the Bafileans an immenfe

---

* A branch of the Francifcan order is called fo in Poland, as I am informed.—TRANSL.

abbey. Of one of the Bernardines who took occafion to beg an alms of us, the following ftory was told : That this monk was formerly not a Catholic, that he had long made up his mind to embrace our orthodox faith, which gave the evangelicals who were ftaying there occafion to traduce the good man's intentions, that finally impatient of being teafed any longer he at laft anfwered fomebody : "I will not become a Catholic, but a Bernardine;" as if that order were not comprehended in the Catholic religion. The Lord Envoy dined with General de Beift, and gave him two Aftracan fheep, rare animals in thefe regions. Eighteen horfes were got together, for each of which we paid five imperials for taking us as far as the city of Minfk.

12.—We dined in the town of Knafchiz, where the Dominicans venerate an image of the Mother of God, copied after the miraculous image of Tfceftochov.* In the evening we

---

* Czenftcchow, or Czçftochow, or Czenftochau, in Ruffian Poland, clofe to the frontiers of Pruffian Silefia. A renowned place of pilgrimage, where there is an image of the Mother of God, which was crowned as Queen of Poland, in the 17th century, by King John Caffimir.—TRANSL.

halted at Halawzi, a village of which General Sluſki is lord.

13.—Travelling through Ceerin, we arrived at Paulowicz at dinner time. This place belongs to Oginſki. Some of his domeſtics that were ſetting out along with us to Warſaw, with a great number of dogs, aſſeverated that they had taken fifty bears in that diſtrict. In the evening it was raining, when we entered Illa.

14.—Paſſing through the town of Bober, ſo called from the river Bober that flows paſt it, we refreſhed ourſelves with dinner in Krupke. The cold to-day was ſo great, that ſome of our folk were not aſhamed to put on furs.* Paſſed through Naſhot, and ſupped in Loſchniz.

15.—We made our mid-day halt at Boriſ-ſowa, where there is a long bridge: the river Berezina, by the inhabitants called Breiſen, cutting up the land repeatedly with its windings and turns. The townsfolk were celebrating the dedication of the church. Hence, the Secretary,

---

* The Poles have an old jeſting proverb, to the effect that one ſhould wear fur until St. John's day (24th June), and not put them off after it : which is tantamount to ſaying that in their climate furs muſt be worn the whole year round. The Ruſſians, indeed, wear them often travelling, even in ſummer.—TRANSL.

going to fpeak to the Procurator of the College
of Minfk, who was then there, found feveral
noble guefts of both fexes at the parifh prieft's.
The fame river waters the village of Berwiz,
which we paffed, and we halted that night in
the town of Sodin, which others call Boguflaw.

16.—Dinner in Schmolowiz; thence by a
road, in fome places bad, and in others eafy,
we arrived in Gratfchma Horodziffeze, where
we prepared fupper.

17.—We arrived at the city of Minfk, in
which the Jefuits, the Dominicans, the Fran-
cifcans, the Bernardines, have their colleges and
monafteries. The river Suiflowiz interfects the
city, and flows into the fea at Riga. So defo-
lated by war, and feveral conflagrations, in this
place, that though formerly rich in merchandife,
it has now but few fhops to fhow.

18.—Here we tarried while the carriages,
which on our journey into the country we were
obliged, on account of the badnefs of the roads,
to leave behind us, with the fathers of the fociety,
were repaired and loaded again. The Superior
of the Jefuits and his *focius* dined with us by
invitation. Our hoftefs, whofe father was bur-

gomafter (*confulatum tenebat*), was honoured in the fame way.

19.—Setting on the afternoon, we got as far as Viafen, paffing through Molfchgabiz.

20.—Through the city of Goudanow to Palagniawiz, and after dinner went to Gratfchma Safiulle.

21.—At Schokobora we croffed the river Niemen, an arm of which had flooded more than a mile of the road, and converted the flimy foil into a fwamp. One of the coachmen plumped unexpectedly into a hole, upfetting the carriage; and it could not be got out for a long time,—fo that the water got into the trunks and their precious contents. Afterwards we went on to Mira, which belongs to Radziwil.

22.—On account of our mifhap in the water yefterday, we remained here.

23.—We fet out after dinner, and arrived at the Gratfchma,* or hoftelry, called Wolna.

24.—We comforted ourfelves with dinner in the city of Stolowiz, a place poffeffing a Loreto chapel as well as its parifh church. The church

---

* *Recte* Karzmatt, the Polifh name for the rude filthy *caravanferais* of that country.—TRANSL.

is ferved by a Provoft and two Vicars. There
is a yearly fair here after St. Bartholomew's
day. Paffing through Neumofch, we got on
to Poloncka, where there is a Dominican Monaftery, and ftopped for the night.

25.—Paffing Gratfchma Takimlowiz, we arrived at the city of Slonim : here there are
both Dominicans and Jefuits. After dinner, as
we were going off, we were oppofed by a fwarm
of bees that had fwarmed out on the high road,
and had lately killed a horfe and ftung many
people in the face and hands. They were kept
at bay with fire, and everybody ran paft the place
as faft as he poffibly could. At nightfall we
arrived at Gratfchma Schmelnize. A river
called the Ruida flows paft this inn.

26.—We arrived early at Rofana, and heard
mafs at the Uniat Ruthenians. A fon of General
Sapieha was then refiding at this place, and he
not only fent us a guard of eight foldiers, but
alfo handfomely entertained the Lord Envoy
at dinner. In this city Jew carters were collected, with whom we bargained for fix imperials for each horfe to bring our baggage to
Warfaw.

27.—After dinner we ftarted for Lifkowa, where we remained for the night.

28.—Dinner in the inn at Stoteniki, and fupper in the village of Jalowka.

29.—Dinner clofe by the river Nareff, in a town of the fame name. Supped in Klenick.

30.—After getting over a mile of road, we came to Drefdianka, where the depth of the water,—the bridge being broken down,—denied us paffage ; in confequence of which we had to take the road by Lochniza, and fo we dined in the royal city of Bilfeck. Bzanifki is ftaroft for General Sapieha. Befides a monaftery of Uniat Bafilians there, the Carmelites, too, have a foundation of forty thoufand Polifh florins : the Polifh florin is worth fix pfennings.* A peafant wanted to force one of the Grooms of the Chamber, who went forward with the Jew carters, to pay the tolls, though it was no bufinefs whatever of his ; and the fellow's audacity went fo far as to try with oftentatious violence to drag about a horfe and to draw a piftol from the

* The Polifh florin, ftill current in Ruffian Poland, amounts alfo to fixpence Englifh ; and is about the fourth of the value of the German florin.—TRANSL.

holfter. But when he perceived that the Ambaffador and the reft of the train were coming up, he tried to fave himfelf by running away. The blackfmith followed him, and unhorfed him with his lance, and brought the peafant's horfe with him into the city, as a *pièce de conviction*, the fellow himfelf having got away. The fellow belonged to a canon, who with the greateft politenefs begged pardon for the exceeding infolence committed by his ferf. When the peafant was fent to the Lord Envoy for chaftifement, he pardoned him the outrage, moved by the kindnefs of the canon, who interceded for him. At night we came to the city of Bodki,—others write Bodfki : a little, winding river of the fame name runs paft this place.

31.—Half a mile beyond Bodki we entered the boundaries of Mafovia. The inhabitants are a dangerous race, gaping thievifhly at what belongs to other folk, and notorious for night marauders and robberies.* Dinner in the inn at Mironowfki. Towards evening we arrived at the Buck (*Bóg*), a river of immenfe width,

---

* "Natio periculofa, alienis furtive inhians, nocturnifque graffatoribus, et latrociniis nota."—ORIG.

the city of Granada being on the right bank, and on the left that of Kremeniz, where we paffed that night, after getting fafely acrofs the river.

September 1.—At Semkowa for dinner; Wenkenow, where we bought oats; and, after fording the river Liba, arrived at the town of that name.

2.—On the road we met the train of General Carlowiz, who was going to Mofcow again. He was taking miners with him. Dined in the town of Dobre. Paffing through Staniflowa we fupped in the inn at Michalowa.

3.—At ten o'clock to-day we reached Praga, on the Viftula. The width of the river rendered the paffage difficult; it took three hours to get acrofs. Warfaw, the capital of the Kings of Poland, ftands upon the oppofite bank. All the Polifh magnates and the ambaffadors of crowned heads live in palaces in the fuburbs. We put up at an inn in the ftreet they call Cracow Street. General Carlowiz called on the Lord Envoy.

4.—The moft eminent Cardinal Radziowfki,

and the moft illuftrious lord, Monfignor Avia, the Nuncio Apoftolic, were notified of our arrival through the fecretary. It was, moreover, intimated to the former that the Lord Envoy was the bearer of letters of the King of Perfia for his Majefty the King, and that in the King's abfence he would deliver them to his Eminence, as Primate of this kingdom.* The Lord Envoy honoured the Apoftolic Nuncio with the firft vifit; and he returned it with no lefs promptitude in the afternoon. The Lord Envoy was alfo vifited by Baron de Blumberg, who was formerly affociated with Mr. Zierowfki, Imperial ambaffador to the Court of Mofcow. Father Conrad, a Carmelite, about to go back to Perfia, whence he returned a few years ago, alfo had the politenefs to call.

5.—The Lord Envoy vifited Baron de Blumberg and General Carlowiz. He was called

---

* The Primate of Poland, Archbifhop of Gnefen and Pofen, was the higheft dignitary of the old Polifh kingdom. He enjoyed the privilege of wearing fcarlet like a Cardinal; and was, *virtute officii*, Regent of the kingdom, with the title of Inter-Rex, during vacancies of the throne; and, during the period of inter-Regency, laid claim to the ftyle of Moft Serene, which, however, the kings of France denied even to the crowned kings of Poland.—TRANSL.

away to the moft eminent Cardinal Radziowfky
to give him the Perfian letters. We ftrolled
to amufe ourfelves to the Lubomirfki garden,
the bath of which is much praifed for its beauty
and art. The hermitage there is fo artiftically
conftructed that I muft not pafs it over in
filence.

6.—The Lord Envoy went to dine at the
Apoftolic Nuncio's. Letters written from Mufcovy fince we left arrived, telling of a great
conflagration that broke out in the city the
fame day as the grand Swedifh Embaffy was
brought in in folemn ftate. The Palace of
the Ambaffadors, that of General Schachin,
Prince Galizin's, with feveral more befides,
and fifteen thoufand houfes, were burnt to
the ground; and the letters told how amidft
the general difmay the Danifh Envoy had
fled to Mr. Adam Weyd's, how the Swedes
were brought to the late General Lefort's
wooden palace beyond the Taufa, how eight
incendiaries had been caught, and that two of
them, popes, confefs that the Strelitz were the
originators of the fire, and would never be at
reft until all Mofcow lay in afhes. Louis de

Buchan, who was recently fent to the Czar, came back to-day from Mufcovy.

7.—The fecretary was fent to the Apoftolic Nuncio to tell him the news that came yefter-day of the great fire in Mofcow. The late King's* body embalmed lay ftill provifionally at the Capuchins; we went to fee it, and alfo the rooms which he had built in the monaftery of thofe fathers, in order to retire there from time to time from public cares for a brief fpace. The Mufcovite refident delivered to the Lord Envoy letters from the Czar to the Emperor. They announced that a miflion had been fent to Conftantinople, and requefted of the Emperor to interpofe his friendly and fraternal offices in the negotiations for peace that were to be refumed.

8.—Not far from the church dedicated to the Holy Crofs there is a chapel called the Mufcovite Chapel, becaufe it was built by two Czars that were made prifoners in days of yore, and buried there. About evening the Nuncio Apoftolic baptifed a fon of Prince Seuterizki.†

---

* John III., the chivalrous Sobiefki.—TRANSL.

† Probably the name here difguifed by the old fecretary's odd orthography fhould be *Czartorifki.*—TRANSL.

A quarrel arofe from fome trifling caufe on the bank of the Viftula, and the Poles, mobbed together in countlefs numbers, maffacred three Saxon foldiers in a pitiable way with ftones and fticks.

9.—A Jew baptifed at the Church of Holy Crofs; the fponfors were Cardinal Radziowfki and the wife of the Grand Chancellor of Lithuania. The neophyte received the name of Michael. The Nuncio Apoftolic fet out on a vifitation of the religious houfes in Lithuania.

10.—The Mufcovite refident vifited the Lord Envoy.

11.—We procured horfes, for which we are to pay eightpence per mile each. The head carter's name is Rolant, who being elated beyond what he ought, was the caufe of our leaving later than we intended. We halted for the night in Bulow.

12.—We ftopped in Uffudar precifely at noon, and in the evening in the city of Amfcenow.

13.—Dined in the village of Pabfki, and paffed through the town of Rawa to Kaminfka, where we fupped.

14. — Dined in Lafchifka, bought oats in Velbor, fupped in Petrikow. In Velbor fome of the fervants fell into a difpute with a Pole; but the Pole, being ftruck in the face, ran away and gave up the conteft.

15. — Dined in Caminfka, fupped in Radumfki.

16. — Dinner in Zaporowa, fupper in the city of Jfcheftokow.* The monaftery here is enclofed with a very ftrong wall, and is always garrifoned with Polifh troops. Monks of the order of St. Paul inhabit it. Their provincial, a man advanced in years, received the Lord Envoy with extreme politenefs, and, introducing him to the richly-provided pharmacy of the monaftery, prefented him with Hungarian wine.

17.—Out of particular devotion to the Mother of God we performed our devotions here; for there is a miraculous image of the Moft Bleffed Virgin venerated here, which ftill retains fcars and marks upon the face which were made by a peafant with a whip, and is renowned for numbers

---

* Czenftochow, near the frontier of Pruffian Silefia, a place of pilgrimage ftill greatly frequented.—TRANSL.

of miracles. It was given by Ladiſlaus, Duke of
Oppeln. Afterwards we inſpected the treaſury
of the church, which is exceedingly rich in relics.
There is a veil (*velum*) of St. Philip Neri; a
miraculous croſs that belonged to St. Charles
Borromeo, which is very efficacious in caſes of
obſeſſion. In our preſence an obſeded woman
bellowed horribly during maſs. Starting again
after dinner we ſupped in Caminiza.

18.—We ſtopped for dinner in Turenberg,
and for ſupper in Tarnoberg.

19.—There are two Jeſuit miſſionaries here;
and alſo the firſt imperial poſting ſtation, of which
the Lord Envoy availed himſelf to go on before us to Vienna. We followed in his track
after dining, and reached Klawiz late that
evening.

20.—In Rauda there is a monaſtery of Ciſ-
tercians. We dined there, and ſupped in the
town of Ratibor, which is watered by the Oder,
and half a mile before which there is an unuſu-
ally long bridge built over a ſwamp.

21.—At dinner hour we arrived in Troppau,
which belongs to Prince Liechtenſtein ; and halted
in the evening at Dereſchdorff.

22.—Paffing through the town of Hoft, we dined in Berna, and fupped in Olmutz.

23.—On account of an eclipfe we did not fet out until it had ceafed to darken the heavens. So, as we only left in the afternoon, we halted at Teifchniza.

24.—Paffed through the town of Wifhau, and had dinner prepared in the village of Raufniz, a place belonging to His Excellency the Count von Kauniz. When dinner was over we prepared to fet out; but a dangerous riot that arofe between our train and the Jews that lived in that village detained us beyond an hour; a ftone thrown by a Jew knocked out the right eye of one of the grooms of the chamber. Several on both fides were injured.

25.—That evening the fecretary fet off to give a full account of the riot above-mentioned to the Lord Envoy Extraordinary; and took the poft at Nickolburg in order to gain time. But the reft of the fuite had dinner in that town, and fupped in Kezelfdorff.

26.—Dined in Wolckerfdorff; fupped in Stamerfdorff.

27.—From thence we arrived fafely in Vienna.

A COMPENDIOUS DESCRIPTION

PERILOUS REVOLT OF THE STRELITZ IN MUSCOVY.

REVOLT OF THE STRELITZ.

——+♦❈♦+·——

By a common fport of fortune it very often
happens that when a friend would extinguifh the
houfes of his neighbours which the flames are
devouring, his own is involved in the fame peril.
And fo it is not without reafon that we deplore
a calamity that may befal ourfelves as often as
Ucalegon hard-by is on fire.

Everybody knows that when the Poles were
about to proceed to the vote for the election of a
monarch to the throne of their widowed Republic,
their ftruggles were divided between two candidates. Thefe wild gufts burfting beyond the
narrow limits of the Diet, among this fiery
people, burning as they are with fubtle and active
intrigue, menaced a tempeft fraught with univer-
fal danger. The Czar of Mufcovy, roufed by
the proximity of the peril, ordered a ftrong body
of troops under the command of General Knes

Michael Gregorowicz Romadonowſki, to lie in
obſervation upon the frontiers of Lithuania, ſo
as to be able, ſhould public diſorders ariſe out of
the ſtrife of private individuals, to ſettle them
promptly and repreſs with ſtrong ſuccours the
diſturbers of the public peace, and force them
the more efficaciouſly into the reverence due to
their lawfully elected king.

But how wonderful are the viciſſitudes of fortune and of human affairs ! The flood burſt in
wild rage upon him, who raſhly thought to brave
the unruly inundation that menaced the quiet
of a neighbouring nation. Four regiments of
Strelitz, which lay upon the frontier of Lithuania, had nefariouſly plotted to change the ſove-
reignty. The regiment of Theodoſia abandoned
Viaſma, the Athanaſian regiment quitted Picla,
the Ivano-Tzernovio-Wlodomirian left Oſtheba,
and the Ticchonian quitted Dorogobuſa, in which
places they were in garriſon. They drove away
the loyal officers that happened to be among
them, diſtributed military rank among themſelves,—the readieſt for crime being held the
fitteſt for command. At once they menaced
death to all in their next neighbourhood, if they

would not freely join their party or fhould refift their defign.

Many reports fpread through Mofcow about the danger that was fo near at hand, but what real truth was in them nobody knew : until at length the meetings of the Boyars, their confultations repeated day after day, their affembling by night, and their affiduous conferences might have proved to any body how grave a bufinefs it was, and what imminent need there was to prefs on their conclufions to maturity. The Czar, before his departure, had chofen the Boyar and Woivode Alexis Simonowicz Schahin,* generaliffimo of his land forces. No other than the man whom the Czar's majefty had already entrufted with the command-in-chief of the army could be charged with the execution of the meafures required. But the orders were not fufficiently decifive, everybody wifhed to take counfel of events; fhould they hold out perfeveringly and refufe to confefs their fault and crave pardon, it would be then time enough to take fevere meafures againft this flagitious mutiny. Schachin agreed to

* Schein.

accept the power they, the Boyars, would entruſt to him, but upon condition that the decree approved unanimouſly ſhould be alſo confirmed by all their ſeals and ſignatures. Although what he required was fair, there was not one among them all that did not refuſe to put his hand to the reſolution. It was hard to ſay whether this was through fear or envy: but the danger was too near to admit of delay, and the dread was left the ſeditious cohorts of the Strelitz ſhould penetrate into Moſcow. Nor was it without reaſon that they were in terror of the mixing of the rebels and the maſſes. It appeared more adviſable to march out againſt them than to await an invaſion ſo fraught with the verieſt peril.

The regiments of the guards got notice to hold themſelves in readineſs to march at an hour's notice, and that thoſe who ſhould decline to aɕt againſt the ſacrilegious violators of the Majeſty of the Crown would be held guilty of miſpriſion of their crime,—that no ties of blood or kindred held binding when the ſalvation of the ſovereign and the ſtate were at ſtake,—nay, that a ſon might ſlay his father if he roſe to ruin his fatherland. General Gordon ſtrenuouſly executed this Spartan meafure, and exhorted the troops entrufted to him to perform their noble tafk, telling them how there could be no more glorious meed than to have faved the fovereign and the ftate. Nor was the circumftance of this expedition againft the mutineers being under-taken on the very feftival of Pentecoft, devoid of happy omen that the fpirit of truth and juf-tice would confound the councils of the wicked,— as the event clearly fhowed. For there was dif-cord between the three principal chiefs of the rebellion, which delayed their march for three days, and fo gave the loyal army time to en-counter the traitor Strelitz at the monaftery dedicated to the moft Holy Refurrection which fome call Jerufalem. For the ftupendous nature of their crime, brought dread, delay, and divided counfels: the concord that is fworn for crime is feldom indeed lafting. Had the rebels reached that monaftery but one hour fooner, fafe within its ftrong defences, they might perhaps have worn out the loyal troops with fuch long and fruitlefs labour that they might have loft heart, and Victory, hoftile to Loyalty, might have fet her garland upon the brow of Treafon. But

Fortune denied to their turbulent counfels the
object that they fought. A flender ftream not
far diftant waters the rich land hereabouts. On
its hither banks the Czar's troops, and on the
oppofite the rebel columns had begun to appear.
The latter were trying the ford and if they had
been really determined to pafs, the Czar's force
could hardly have hindered them. Fatigued with
a long march, and ftill without fufficient force,
Gordon, fetting wifdom in the place of ftrength,
ftrolled alone to the bank to talk with the Strelitz. He found them deliberating about crof-
ing, and diffuaded them from their undertaking
with words like thefe : " What did they mean
to do ? Whither were they going ? If they were
thinking of Mofcow, the night was too clofe at
hand to admit of their reaching it,—there was
not room for them all on the hither bank, they
would do much better to remain at the other fide
of the river and give the night to thinking
fenfibly of what they ought to do on the morrow.
The feditious multitude could not refift fuch
friendly advice ; they were too much fatigued in
body to have ftomach for a fight where they did
not expect one.

Meantime, Gordon having well examined all the advantages of the ground, occupied an advantageous height with his troops. Schachin confenting, he diftributed the pofts, and fortified himfelf, leaving nothing undone that could contribute to his own defence and fecurity or to the detriment and damage of the enemy. With equal loyalty and refolution the imperial colonel of artillery, De Grage, bravely performed his part. He made a lodgement upon the height, placed his great guns in advantageous pofition, and diftributed all in fuch excellent order, that almoft the whole fuccefs that attended the affair was due to the artillery. At the firft dawn of day, by command of General Schachin, General Gordon went again to parley with the Strelitz, and after blaming fomewhat the difobedience of the regiments, he difcourfed largely of the Czar's clemency, telling them, that it was not by fedition and mobbing together that the defires of foldiers fhould be made known to the Czar. Why, contrary to their ufual dutiful behaviour, contrary to the fanction of difcipline, had they deferted the places that had been entrufted to their loyal keeping? Why fhould they have

driven away their officers, and have broken out
in defigns of violence?   Let them rather pro-
pofe their requefts peaceably, and, mindful of
the loyalty they owed, return to their appointed
ftations, that fhould he fee them yield to their
duty, fhould he hear them beg for it, he would
get them both fatisfaction for their requefts,
and pardon, when they confeffed it, for their
fhameful conduct.   But Gordon's fpeech did
not move the now hardened ftubbornefs of the
falfe traitors;   and they only faucily anfwered
that they would not go back to their appointed
quarters until they had been allowed to kifs
their darling wives at Mofcow, and had received
the arrears of their pay.

Gordon related to Schachin the perfectly determined wickednefs of the Strelitz.   But as the
latter was unwilling to defpair altogether of the
repentance of the criminals, Gordon did not decline to try a third time to mollify the fierce paffions of the rebels with offers of payment of their
arrears, and pardon for the crime they were bent
upon.   Not only was advice utterly fruitlefs, but
they were in fuch a ftate of exafperation, that
the negotiator was near to have paid dearly for

his pains. Already they loudly upbraided and
rebuked this man of grave authority, their former
general; they warned him to be off forthwith,
and not to wafte his words to no purpofe, unlefs
he wanted a bullet to chaftife his marvellous
audacity; that they recognifed no mafter, and
would liften to orders from nobody : that they
would not go back to their quarters; that they
muft be admitted into Mofcow; that if they were
forbidden, they would open the road with force
and cold fteel. Their unexpected fiercenefs ftung
Gordon, and he deliberated with Schachin and the
other military officers prefent what was to be
done. There was no difficulty in deciding the
courfe that fhould be adopted againft men that
were predetermined to try the ftrength of their
arms. Everything was made ready, confequently,
for the onfet and the fight, as the ftubborn unani-
mity of the traitors forced on that laft refort.
Nor were the Strelitz lefs bufy; they drew up
their array, pointed their artillery, dreffed their
ranks, and, as if the ftrife in which they were
about to mingle was a ftruggle with a foreign
foe, they preceded it with the cuftomary prayers
and invocation of God. Even malice does not

dare to fhow its head in the face of the world
without difguifing itfelf in the colours of virtue
and righteoufnefs.

Countlefs figns of the crofs being made on
both fides, the attack began on both fides from a
diftance. The firft reports of cannon and fmall
arms proceeded from the lines of General Schachin, by whofe command none of the pieces were
loaded with ball; for he entertained a fecret hope
that the reality of refiftance might terrify them
into a fubmiffive return to obedience. But the
firft volley paffing without wound or flaughter,
only added courage to guilt. Vaftly emboldened,
they refponded by a difcharge, by which fome
were laid lifelefs, and feveral were bloodily
wounded. When death and wounds had given
a fufficient leffon that ftronger remedies muft
be applied, Colonel de Grage was no longer
required to diffemble his ftout will, and allowed
to difcharge his great guns, fraught with deadly
lead and iron. Colonel de Grage had been
anxioufly waiting for this command, and loft
no time in firing with fuch precifion into their
rebel ranks that their furious paffions were
checked, and the ftrife of refiftance and fkir-

mishing of the mutineers was changed into a piteous slaughter.

When they saw that some were stretched life-less, courage and fiercenefs at once deserted the terror-stricken Strelitz, who broke in diforder. Thofe that retained any prefence of mind, endea-voured by the fire of their own artillery to check and filence that of the Czar; but all in vain; for Colonel de Grage had anticipated that defign, and directing the fire of his pieces upon the artil-lery of the feditious mob, whenever they would go to their guns, vomited fuch a perfect hurri-cane upon them, that many fell, numbers fled away, and none remained daring enough to return to fire them. Still Colonel Grage did not ceafe to thunder from the heights into the ranks of the flying. The Strelitz faw fafety nowhere; arms could not protect them; nothing was more ap-palling to them than the ceafelefs flafh and roar of the artillery fhowering its deadly bolts upon them from the German right. And the fame men who, but an hour before, had fpat upon prof-ferred pardon, offered in confequence to fur-render—fo fhort is the interval that feparates victors from vanquifhed. Suppliant, they fell

proftrate, and begged that the artillery might
ceafe its cruel ravages, offering to do promptly
whatever they were ordered. The fuppliants
were directed to lay down their arms, to quit
their ranks, and obey in everything that would
be enjoined to them. Though they at once
threw down their arms, and proceeded to the
places to which they were ordered ; neverthelefs,
for a little while, the fire of the artillery was kept
up, left with the ceffation of the caufe of their
terror, their rafh daring fhould return, and the
mutinous ftrife be renewed. But when they
were truly and thoroughly frightened, they were
treated with contemptuous impunity. Thoufands of men allowed themfelves to be fettered,
who, if they had but rather inftead have tried
their real ftrength, would, beyond the leaft doubt,
have become the victors of thofe that vanquifhed
them. But it is God that fcatters the counfels
of the malignant, that they may not profper in
their undertaking.

When the ferocious arrogance with which they
were fwollen had been made to fubfide com-
pletely, in the manner we have juft narrated, and
all the accomplices of the mutiny had been caft

into chains, General Schachin inftituted an inquiry, by way of torture, touching the caufes, the
objects, the inftigators, the chiefs, and the accomplices of this perilous and impious machina-
tion. For there was a very ferious fufpicion
that more exalted people were at the head of it.
Every one of them freely confeffed himfelf de-
ferving of death; but to detail the particulars of
the nefarious plot, to lay bare the objects of it,
to betray their accomplices, was what no perfon
could perfuade any of them to do. The rack
was confequently got in readinefs by the executioner, as the only means left to elicit the truth.
The torture that was applied was of unexampled
inhumanity. Scourged moft favagely with the
cat, if that had not the effect of breaking their
ftubborn filence, fire was applied to their backs,
all gory and ftreaming, in order that, by flowly
roafting the fkin and tender flefh, the fharp pangs
might penetrate through the very marrow of
their bones, to the utmoft power of painful fen-
fation. Thefe tortures were applied alternately,
over and over again. Horrid tragedies to witnefs
and to hear. In the open field above thirty of
thefe more than funeral pyres blazed at the fame

time, and thereat were thefe moſt wretched creatures under examination roaſted amidſt their horrible howlings.   At another ſide refounded the
mercilefs ſtrokes of the cat, while this moſt ſavage
butchery of men was being done in this very pleafant neighbourhood.

After numbers had been proved by the torture,
at laſt the obſtinacy of a few was found to yield ;
and one of them detailed the following particulars
of this moſt perverſe plot.   He ſaid that he was
not unaware how great their fault was, that all
had deſerved to lofe their lives, and that perhaps
none would be found that would ſhirk death.
That had fortune attended their undertaking they
would have decreed the fame penalty againſt the
Boyars, as, now they were vanquiſhed, they
expeᶜted themſelves ; for that they had the intention to ſet on fire, fack and ruin the whole
German ſuburb, and when all the Germans,
without exception, had been got rid of by maſ-
facre, to enter Mofcow by force, to murder all
that would make refiſtance, taking the reſt with
them to aid in their nefarious deeds ; that they
meant to inflict death upon fome of the Boyars,
exile upon others, and to drag them all down

from their offices and dignities, in order the more
eafily to conciliate to themfelves the fympathies of
the maffes. That fome popes were to carry an
image of the Bleffed Virgin, and another of
Saint Nicholas, before them, in order that it
might appear they had been driven to take up
arms by the neceffity of defending the faith, and
not out of malice. That when they had got
poffeffion of authority they meant to fcatter
papers among the public, to affure the people
that the Czar's majefty, who had gone abroad, in
confequence of the pernicious advice of the Germans, had died beyond feas. But that left the
barque of the State fhould be buffeted at hazard
by the billows to perifh a wreck upon the firft
rock, that Princefs Sophia Alexiowna was to be
raifed to the throne until the Czarewicz fhould
have attained his majority and the ftrength of
manhood. That Bafil Galizin was to have been
recalled from exile, to aid Sophia with prudent
advice.

Now, as any one of the points of this confeffion was of itfelf weighty enough to merit
death, General Schachin had the fentence that
was drawn up againft them, promulgated and

executed. Numbers were condemned to be
hanged and gibbeted; many laid their heads
upon the fatal block and died by the axe; many
were referved to certain vengeance, and laid in
cuftody in places in the environs. It was contrary to General Gordon's and Prince Ma-
fatfki's advice that the General proceeded to
execute the rebels; as in this manner the chiefs
of the revolt may, without fufficient examination,
have been removed, by premature death, from
further inqueft. Hence, he drew upon himfelf,
not undefervedly, the fury of a more wary
avenger, when, amidft the gaieties of a royal
banquet he would have died the death, had not
the ftout arm of General Lefort drawn back
and refrained the hand that was defcending to
the ftroke. But, at the time in queftion,
Schachin was of a different opinion, believing
that timely feverity would have the falutary confequence of reftoring to the minds of numbers
reverence for the monarch and fear of punifhment. And for this reafon—to ftrike terror into
the reft by an example of public vengeance—he
on one day broke feventy, and another ninety,
upon the crofs they fo richly deferved.

How fharp was the pain, how great the indignation to which the Czar's Majefty was mightily
moved, when he knew of the rebellion of the Strelitz, betrayed openly a mind panting for vengeance.
He was ftill tarrying at Vienna, quite full of
the defire of fetting out for Italy ; but, fervid
as was this curiofity of rambling abroad, it was,
neverthelefs, fpeedily extinguifhed on the an-
nouncement of the troubles that had broken out
in the bowels of his realm. Going immediately
to Lefort (the only perfon almoft that he con-
defcended to treat with intimate familiarity), he
thus indignantly broke out : "Tell me, Francis,
fon of James, how I can reach Mofcow, by the
fhorteft way, in a brief fpace, fo that I may
wreak vengeance on this great perfidy of my
people, with punifhments worthy of their flagitious crime. Not one of them fhall efcape with
impunity. Around my royal city, of which,
with their impious efforts, they meditated the
deftruction, I will have gibbets and gallows fet
upon the walls and ramparts, and each and every
of them will I put to a direful death." Nor
did he long delay the plan for his juftly excited
wrath ; he took the quick poft, as his ambaffador

fuggefted, and in four weeks time, he had got
over about three hundred miles* without accident, and arrived on the 4th of September,—a
monarch for the well-difpofed, but an avenger
for the wicked. His firft anxiety, after his
arrival, was about the rebellion. In what it
confifted? What the infurgents meant? Who
had dared to inftigate fuch a crime? And as
nobody could anfwer accurately upon all points,
and fome pleaded their own ignorance, others
the obftinacy of the Strelitz, he began to have
fufpicions of everybody's loyalty, and began to
cogitate about a frefh inveftigation. The rebels
that were kept in cuftody, in various places in
the environs, were all brought in by four regiments of the guards, to a frefh inveftigation and
frefh tortures. Prifon, tribunal, and rack, for
thofe that were brought in, was in Bebrafchentfko.
No day, holy or profane, were the inquifitors
idle; every day was deemed fit and lawful for
torturing. As many as there were accufed there
were knouts, and every inquifitor was a butcher.†

* German miles, each equal to about five Englifh.—Transl.
† "Quot rei tot knuttæ, quot quæfitores tot carnifices."—
Orig.

Prince Feodor Jurowicz Romadonowſki ſhowed himſelf by ſo much more fitted for his inquiry, as he ſurpaſſed the reſt in cruelty. The very Grand Duke himſelf, in conſequence of the diſtruſt he had conceived of his ſubjeᶜts, performed the office of inquiſitor. He put the interrogatories, he examined the criminals, he urged thoſe that were not confeſſing, he ordered ſuch Strelitz as were more pertinacioufly filent, to be ſubjeᶜted to more cruel tortures; thoſe that had already confeſſed about many things were queſtioned about more; thoſe who were bereft of ſtrength and reaſon, and almoſt of their ſenſes, by exceſs of torment, were handed over to the ſkill of the doᶜtors, who were compelled to reſtore them to ſtrength, in order that they might be broken down by freſh excruciations. The whole month of October was ſpent in butchering the backs of the culprits with knout and with flames: no day were thoſe that were left alive exempt from ſcourging or ſcorching, or elſe they were broken upon the wheel, or driven to the gibbet, or ſlain with the axe—the penalties which were inflicted upon them as ſoon as their confeſſions had ſufficiently revealed the heads of the rebellion.

Major* Karpakow was faid to be as far beyond the other rebels in treafon as he was in official rank. So after being knouted, fire was applied to roaft his back to fuch a degree that he loft both fpeech and confcioufnefs; and then, as it was feared that death might remove him prematurely, he was commended to the fkill of the Czar's phyfician, Dr. Carbonari, that he might apply fuch remedies as would have the effect of reftoring his expiring ftrength, and as foon as he was in fome degree reftored, he was fubjected to the queftion anew, and fainted away under the fharpeft tortures.

Batfka Girin, the infurgent ringleader, after undergoing four times the moft exquifite tortures, confeffing nothing, was condemned to be hanged. But on the very day appointed for his execution, there was led out of prifon, with the rebel Strelitz, to the queftion, a certain youth of twenty years of age, on being confronted with whom, he, of

* Vice-Colonellus locumtenens. —ORIG.

his own accord, broke his ftubborn filence, and
revealed the counfels of the traitors, with all the
circumftances. Now that youth of twenty had
fallen in by chance with thefe rebels near the
borders of Smolenfko, and being forced to wait
on the principal inftigators of the mutiny, they
took no notice of his liftening, nor was his prefence forbidden even when they ufed to deliberate
about the fuccefs of their nefarious enterprife.
When he was dragged along with the rebels
before the tribunal, he, in order to prove his
innocence the more eafily, caft himfelf at the
judge's feet, and with the moft ardent fighs im-
plored not to be fubjected to the torture—that
he would confefs all that he knew with the moft
exact truth. Batfka Girin, who was condemned
to the halter, was not hanged before having made
his judicial confeffion ; for he was one of the
prime rebels, and an excellent witnefs of what he
very truly detailed.

Borifka Brofkurad was executed in the camp,
by command of General Schachin.

Takufka, who had been chofen firft Major of
the White Regiment, and two other inferior
officers, among whom, as they were approaching

Mofcow, a difpute arofe which occafioned fome days' delay, were the caufe of their own deftruction, and faved the lives of all well-difpofed people.

Deacon Ivan Gabrielowicz had, fome years previoufly, courted the Princefs Marpha to yield to his paffion. The rebels would have this fellow married to Marpha, to be protector of the Strelitz or high chancellor; but in confequence of the finifter turn of their criminal undertaking, his funeral and obfequies, inftead of his nuptials, marked the event.

Certain popes that were connected with the Strelitz became fharers in their treafon. For they put up prayers to God to favour the efforts of treafon, and it was they who carried the images of the Bleffed Virgin and Saint Nicholas among armed men, and who had promifed to draw the people to the fide of the revolt, under the pretence of the marked juftice of the caufe, and of true piety. Hence one of them was hanged by the Czar's buffoon, near the high church dedicated to the moft Holy Trinity; another, being firft beheaded with the axe, was fet upon the wheel near the fame place. Dumnoi Diak

Jichon Mofciwicz (whom the Czar calls his patriarch), was forced to be the butcher of the latter.

SOPHIA.

Wherever ambition has entered into poffeffion there is no room for juftice. For ambition has always reafons to allege in its own behalf, and is unmoved at the gulf that lies between empire and fubjection. Princefs Sophia has the reputation of having intrigued, for the laft fourteen years, againft her brother's life, and has already been the caufe of feveral feditious movements. She, by her open fchemes and factioufnefs, drove him, who is at once her fovereign and her brother, to confult for his own fafety ; efpecially as the late perils bore ample witnefs that, as long as fhe was at liberty, there would be nothing ftable in Mufcovy. Shut up on this account in the monaftery of Nuns, watched daily in the ftricteft manner, by a guard of the Czar's troops, neverthelefs the wiles of this moft ambitious princefs could not be quite guarded againft by all thofe watchful eyes. She promifed to put herfelf at the head of a new confpiracy of the

Strelitz, and communicated her advice to them—fuggefting the manner and the frauds by which the Strelitz might bring their dark and malignant defigns into effect. She was interrogated by the Czar himfelf, touching thefe attempts, and it is ftill uncertain what fhe anfwered. But this much is certain—that in this act the Czar's Majefty wept for his own lot and Sophia's. Some will have it the Czar was on the point of fentencing her to death, and ufed this argument : " Mary of Scotland was led forth from prifon to the block, by command of her fifter Elizabeth, Queen of England—a warning to me to exercife my power over Sophia." Still once more the brother pardoned a fifter's crime, and, inftead of penalty, enjoined that fhe fhould be banifhed to a greater diftance, in fome monaftery.

It was rather the luft of fating her paffions than the defire of transferring dominion, that had entangled Princefs Marpha in the fame rebellious machinations. She wanted to indulge more at eafe in her illicit connection with Deacon Ivan Gabrielowicz,* whom fhe had maintained at her

* Souvarow was his furname. This cleric was the grandfather of the famous Souvárow, and was attached to one of the

own coft, for fome years, for that purpofe. With her head fhaved, fhe has been thruft into a monaftery and does penance for the paft.

Fiera and Schukowa, the former Sophia's, the latter Marpha's confidential chamber-woman, were dragged from the Czar's Caftle to Bebraf-chentfko—the place of inquifition—and were both fubjeɗed to the torture. When Fiera, ftripped naked to the loins, was being fcourged with what they call the *knout*, the Czar obferved that fhe was pregnant; and on being afked whether fhe knew the faɗ, fhe did not deny it, and, moreover, indicated a certain chorifter as the caufe of her burden. By this fhe liberated herfelf from further fcourging, but not from the penalty of death. For, afterwards, fhe and Schukowa, who had undergone a long fcourging, and had confeffed her fhare in the operations of the traitorous Princefs, both expiated their

churches in the Kremlin. His fon Bafil entered the army as a common foldier, rofe by his merit to be an officer, and, confe-quently, noble, afcended ftep by ftep to the rank of full General, and is faid to have been a well-informed foldier and an upright man. The fon of General Bafil, the renowned Field-Marfhal Souvarow, created Prince of Italy (Knes Italinfki) in 1799, was born in 1729.—Transl.

crimes with their lives. Nothing is yet certain about the manner of their execution : fome will have it that they were buried up to the neck alive ; others, that they were thrown into the river Ianga that flows juft there.

THE CORRESPONDENCE OF SOPHIA WITH
THE REBELS.

No garrifon is fafe where malice and treafon have once adopted the idea of upfetting the fortrefs. Malice is never a moment idle ; examines minutely every fmalleft nook in which fhe may fafely hide the emiflaries of her nefarious defigns. It was certainly with no other defign that fo large a guard of foldiers kept watch and ward, day after day, without the gates of the monaftery of Nuns, than to obferve, with all poffible minutenefs, this dangeroufly ambitious Princefs, fo that fhe might be unable to plot anything againft the fafety of the ftate and the fovereign. Yet all thefe Argus eyes were not able to hinder her from contriving to raife a truly great and moft perilous flame of civil war by means of an abject wretched little mendicant that ufed to frequent the very guard. This was a little old woman that begged her daily bread. Sophia took her affections by storm with profufe liberality and, with promife of higher rewards, feduced her to forbidden deeds.

When the old hag, full of fuch grand hopes, promifed to execute to the minuteft detail all her lady's bidding, Sophia taught her what to guard againft and what to do, and told her that fhe would pretend to give her a loaf as her ufual alms, that fhe would bring it to the Strelitz and fhould wait to fee whether they would entruft her with any anfwer. There were letters enclofed in the loaf, in which fhe affured the rebels that fhe would make ftrong efforts in aid of their laudable undertakings; let them only come to the mona-ftery, flay all the guards that would refift; that things had come to fuch a pafs, that there was no happy aufpices for them without fhedding blood. The rebels in like manner tranfmitted their anfwers to Sophia in a loaf. The thing was done feveral times and the foldiers had no fufpicion of it—fo ingenious is malice in plotting mifchief. After all fhe deceived herfelf; and that loaf of which they meant to make the bread of death to

fo many innocent people, led to their own richly-
deferved ruin, and was moft fatal to themfelves,
as will be plainly underftood from the following
fentence.

THE SENTENCE PASSED UPON THE REBELS ON 10TH OCTOBER, 1698.

" Thieves, plunderers, traitors, tramplers on the
Crofs (crucis tranfgreffores), and rebels of
the regiment of Theodofius Kolpokow,
of the regiment of Athanazius Tzabanow,
of the regiment of Ivan Zornoi, of the
regiment of Tichon Hundertmark, javelin-
cafting Strelitz: The Grand Dominator,
King and Grand Duke Peter Alexiowicz,
Autocrat of Great, Little and White Ruffia,
commands there be told unto them :—

"On the 27th of October laft year, (*i.e.*
1698*) according to the letters of him the Grand
Dominator and of the Roferati, (the mandate
chancery†) there were ordered from Storopzo,

---

* *Sic*, but properly 1697.—TRANSL.

† Litteras Roferati (*cancellariæ mandatoriæ.*)—*See* ORIGINAL.

with the army of the Senator and General Prince Michael Gregorowicz Romadonowſki, with his aſſociates, his Colonels and Lieutenant-Colonels, to be at his, the Grand Dominator's, command in the cities and place appointed.

Theodoſius's regiment at Viaſma.
Athanaſius's regiment at Piella.
Ivan's regiment at Oſtheba-Wlodomirowa.
Tichon's regiment at Dorogobuſki.

And they, contrary to his, the Grand Dominator's mandate, went not into theſe appointed towns, with the ſaid colonels and lieutenant-colonels; but ordered them and their lieutenant-colonels and captains forth of their regiments aforeſaid; and in lieu of the ſame did elect into the ſaid offices rebels, their brother javelin throwers; and with the cannons of the regiments did march in arms from Storopzo upon Moſcow ; and when below the monaſtery of the Reſurrection the ſaid javelin throwers met Alexius Simonowicz Schachin, with his aſſociates, and a ſelect force along with them ; who, when he ſent from his army to them thrice to abandon their

oppofition to the Great Dominator, and go
according to the Dominator's previous commands
to the ftations appointed, they, on the contrary,
fetting themfelves againft the faid Dominator's
commands, fo far from going to the ftations
appointed for them, did prepare for a conflict of
their army againft the military fervants of the
faid Dominator, and difcharging cannons and
fmall arms wounded very many, and fome of
thofe wounded did die.

Moreover, as they were about to proceed to
Mofcow, they were to halt in the field called the
Nun's field, in front of the monaftery, to deliver
a petition to Princefs Sophia Alexiowna, to call
upon her to go on directing them as before;
furthermore the foldiers on guard at that monaftery were to be maffacred, and after flaying thefe
they were to have gone on to Mofcow, difperfing
throughout all the black* fuburbs (*in omnia nigra
fuburbia*) copies of a certain feditious memorial,

---

* Black : the ferf clafs are in Ruffia called blacks, from their
fuppofed inferiority of blood. The old dynaftic race, whofe
defcendants formed and ftill form the nucleus of the *haute nobleffe*
of Ruffia, fpring from Rurik, of Norfe or Normandic race, who
reigned over that vaft country, according to the common computation, from 862 to 878. From him derive no lefs than 34

and winning over the blacks (*nigros*), ſtating that the Great Dominator had died beyond ſea. They were thus to raiſe a ſeditious movement among the ſerfs, and take them with them to kill the Boyars, to deſtroy utterly the German ſuburb, to ſlay all foreigners and not to admit the Grand Dominator into Moſcow. But if the military regiments ſhould not allow them into Moſcow, they meant to write alſo to the regiments of javelin throwers now in his, the Grand Domi-nator's, active ſervice, and to be aided by them againſt the ſaid ſoldiers; and that when the latter javelin throwers ſhould have reached Moſcow, then that they, united with thoſe other javelin throwers, would call upon the Princeſs

---

exiſting princely houſes, all bearing their titles in virtue of their dynaſtic deſcent by immemorial preſcription, the *ſangre blu* of Ruſſia. The fair-complexioned Rurik (or Roderic) cannot have come alone to the country over which he ruled. His fair-ſkinned Norman courtiers, probably, were the progenitors of the Boyar families, who conſtituted the courtiers and *miniſteriales* of the princes his deſcendants, among whom Ruſſia was long par-titioned; and were the founts of the great untitled lords, inſcribed in the "velvet book," the "book of gold" of the Ruſſian ariſ-tocracy. Theſe fair-ſkinned Northmen doubtleſs gave the con-temptuous name of blacks (Czarni) to the dark aboriginal race, who became their hewers of wood and drawers of water.—
TRANSL.

Sophia to direct them, and would flay the said
soldiers, murder the Boyars, and would in like
manner deftroy the German fuburb, maffacre the
foreigners, and would not admit the Dominator
into Mofcow. Of all which things aforefaid
thefe men have in the examinations and under
forture confeffed themfelves guilty.

"And the Grand Dominator, on account of
their having taken matters into their own hands,
hath decreed that thefe plunderers, traitors, and
tranfgreffors and rebels, fhall be punifhed with
death, in order that by their example others may
henceforward learn not to take affairs into their
own hands in this manner."

The fentence being thus framed fo as to include
all the Strelitz fo no tardy repentance was attended
with impunity for the crime. For before the
Czar's Majefty had fet out on his travels a mutiny
of the fame Strelitz had taken place, on the ap-
peafing of which they were pardoned on condition of never daring to attempt fuch a courfe
again. This condition was recorded in a public
written inftrument, by which they bound themfelves, even if no law were in force for treafon
againft Majefty, to every torment that could be

thought of, to the moſt cruel tortures, and to
the penalty of death itſelf, in caſe by renewed
contumacy towards the Sovereign's weal they
ſhould admit of anything contrary to their ſworn
allegiance, and their debt of moſt humble reſpeɛt.
All confirmed this ſanɛtion of the Czar with
their own ſignature, &c. ; thoſe who did not
know how to write marking with a croſs in
token of their approval. This was an aggrava-
ting faɛt which cloſed up the avenue of mercy,
and appointed rigorous juſtice the avenger of
treaſon.

THE FIRST EXECUTION.

10TH OCTOBER, 1698.

To this exhibition of avenging juſtice the
Czar's Majeſty invited all the ambaſſadors of
foreign ſovereigns, as it were to aſſert anew on
his return that ſovereign prerogative of life
and death which the rebels had diſputed with
him.

The barracks in Bebraſchentſko end in a bare
field which riſes to the ſummit of a rather ſteep
hill. This was the place appointed for the exe-

cutions. Here were planted the gibbet ftakes, on which the foul heads of thefe confeffedly guilty wretches were to be fet, to protract their ignominy beyond death. There the firft fcene of the tragedy lay expofed. The ftrangers that had gathered to the fpectacle were kept aloof from too clofe approach; the whole regiment of guards was drawn up in array under arms. A little further off, on a high *tumulus* in the area of the place, there was a multitude of Muf-covites, crowded and crufhing together in a denfe circle. A German Major* was then my com-panion; he concealed his nationality in a Mufco-vite drefs, befides which he relied upon his military rank and the liberty that he might take in confequence of being entitled by reafon of his being in the fervice of the Czar to fhare in the privileges of the Mufcovites. He mingled with the thronging crowd of Mufcovites, and when he came back announced that five rebel heads had been cut off in that fpot by an axe that was fwung by the nobleft arm of all Mufcovy. The

---

* Supremus-Vigiliarum-præfectus, *i.e.*, *Oberft-nvachmeifter*, or Major.—TRANSL.

river Jaufa flows paſt the barracks in Bebraſch-entſko, and divides them in two.

On the oppoſite ſide of this ſtream there were a hundred criminals ſet upon thoſe little Muſco-vite carts which the natives call Sboſek, awaiting the hour of the death they had to undergo. There was a cart for every criminal, and a ſoldier to guard each. No prieſtly office was to be ſeen ; as if the condemned were unworthy of that pious compaſſion. But they all bore lighted tapers in their hands, not to die without light and croſs. The horrors of impending death were increaſed by the piteous lamentations of their women, the ſobbing on every ſide, and the ſhrieks of the dying that rung upon the ſad array. The mother wept for her ſon, the daughter deplored a parent's fate, the wife lamenting a huſband's lot, bemoaned along with the others, from whom the various ties of blood and kindred drew tears of ſad farewell. But when the horſes, urged to a ſharp pace, drew them off to the place of their doom, the wail of the women roſe into louder ſobs and moans. As they tried to keep up with them, forms of expreſſion like theſe beſpoke their grief, as others

explained them to me : " Why are you torn
from me fo foon ? Why do you defert me ?
Is a laft embrace then denied me ? Why am I
hindered from bidding him farewell ? " With
complaints like thefe they tried to follow their
friends when they could not keep up with their
rapid courfe. From a country feat belonging to
General Schachin one hundred and thirty more
Strelitz were led forth to die. At each fide of
all the city gates there was a gibbet erected,
each of which was loaded with fix rebels on that
day.

When all were duly brought to the place of
execution, and the half dozens were duly diftributed at their feveral gibbets, the Czar's Majefty,
dreffed in a green Polifh cloak, and attended by
a numerous fuite of Mufcovite nobles, came to
the gate where, by his Majefty's command, the
imperial Lord Envoy had ftopped in his own
carriage, along with the reprefentatives of Poland
and Denmark. Next them was Major-General
de Carlowiz, who had conducted his Majefty on
his way from Poland, and a great many other
foreigners, among whom the Mufcovites mingled
round about the gate. Then the proclamation

of the fentence began, the Czar exhorting all the byftanders to mark well its tenor. As the executioner was unable to difpatch fo many criminals, fome military officers, by command of the Czar, came under compulfion to aid in this butcher's tafk. The guilty were neither chained nor fettered; but logs were tied to their legs, which hindered them from walking faft, but ftill allowed them the ufe of their feet. They ftrove of their own accord to afcend the ladder, making the fign of the crofs towards the four quarters of the world ; they themfelves covered their eyes and faces with a piece of linen (which is a national cuftom) ; very many putting their necks into the halter fprang headlong of themfelves from the gallows, in order to precipitate their end. There were counted two hundred and thirty that expiated their flagitious conduct by halter and gibbet.

SECOND EXECUTION—

13TH OCTOBER, 1698.

Although all thofe that were accomplices of the rebellion were condemned to death, yet the

Czar's Majefty would not difpenfe with ftrict inveftigation. The more fo as the unripe years and judgment of many feemed to befpeak mercy, as they were, as one may fay, rather victims of error than of deliberate crime. In fuch cafe the penalty of death was commuted into fome corporal infliction—fuch as, for inftance, the cutting off of their ears and nofes, to mark them with ignominy for life—a life to be paffed, not as previoufly, in the heart of the realm, but in various and barbarous places on the frontiers of Mufcovy. To fuch places fifty were tranfported to-day, after being caftigated in the manner prefcribed.

THIRD EXECUTION—

17TH OCTOBER, 1698.

Only fix were beheaded to-day, who had the advantage of rank over the others, if rank be a diftinction of honour in executed criminals.

FOURTH EXECUTION—

21ST OCTOBER, 1698.

To prove to all the people how holy and

inviolable are thofe walls of the city, which the Strelitz rafhly meditated fcaling in a fudden affault, beams were run out from all the embrafures in the walls near the gates, on each of which two rebels were hanged. This day beheld about two hundred and fifty die that death. There are few cities fortified with as many palifades as Mofcow has given gibbets to her guardian Strelitz.

FIFTH EXECUTION—

23RD OCTOBER, 1698.

This differed confiderably from thofe that preceded. The manner of it was quite different, and hardly credible. Three hundred and thirty at a time were led out together to the fatal axe's ftroke, and embrued the whole plain with native but impious blood : for all the Boyars, Senators of the realm, Dumnoi, Diaks, and fo forth, that were prefent at the council conftituted againft the rebel Strelitz, had been fummoned by the Czar's command to Bebrafchentfko, and enjoined to take upon themfelves the hangman's office. Some ftruck the blow unfteadily, and with trembling hands affumed this new and unaccuftomed taſk. The moſt unfortunate ſtroke among all the Boyars was given by him * whoſe erring ſword ſtruck the back inſtead of the neck, and thus chopping the Strelitz almoſt in halves, would have rouſed him to deſperation with pain, had not Alexaſca reached the unhappy wretch a ſurer blow of an axe on the neck.

Prince Romadonowſki, under whoſe command previous to the mutiny theſe four regiments were to have watched the turbulent gatherings in Poland on the frontier, beheaded, according to order, one out of each regiment. Laſtly, to every Boyar a Strelitz was led up, whom he was to behead. The Czar, in his ſaddle, looked on at the whole tragedy.

SEVENTH EXECUTION—

27TH OCTOBER, 1698.

To-day was aſſigned for the puniſhment of the popes—that is to ſay, of thoſe who by carrying

* That this was probably Prince Galizin, ſeems from the entry in the Diary under 27 Oct., 1698 ; though there is here a ſlight diſcrepancy as to the preciſe day on which the magnates performed as *executeurs des hautes œuvres* in this terrific tragedy. —TRANSL.

images to induce the ſerfs to ſide with the Strelitz, had invoked the aid of God with the holy rites of his altars for the happy ſucceſs of this impious plot. The place ſelected by the judge for the execution was the open ſpace in front of the church of the moſt Holy Trinity, which is the high church of Moſcow. The ignominious gibbet croſs awaited the popes, by way of reward in ſuit with the thouſands of ſigns of the croſs they had made, and as their fee for all the benedictions they had given to the refractory troops. The court jeſter, in the mimic attire of a pope, made the halter ready, and adjuſted it, as it was held to be wrong to ſubject a pope to the hands of the common hangman. A certain Dumnoi ſtruck off the head of another pope, and ſet his corpſe upon the ignominious wheel. Cloſe to the church, too, the halter and wheel proclaimed the enormity of the crime of their guilty burden to the paſſers by.

The Czar's Majeſty looked on from his carriage while the popes were hurried to execution. To the populace, who ſtood around in great numbers, he ſpoke a few words touching the perfidy of the popes, adding the threat,

"Henceforward let no one dare to aſk any pope to pray for ſuch an intention." A little while before the execution of the popes, two rebels, brothers, having had their thighs and other members broken in front of the Caſtle of the Kremlin, were ſet alive upon the wheel: twenty others on whom the axe had done its office lay lifeleſs around theſe wheels. The two that were bound upon the wheel beheld their third brother among the dead. Nobody will eaſily believe how lamentable were their cries and howls, unleſs he has well weighed their excruciations and the greatneſs of their tortures. I ſaw their broken thighs tied to the wheel with ropes ſtrained as tightly as poſſible, ſo that in all that deluge of torture I do believe none can have exceeded that of the utter impoſſibility of the leaſt movement. Their miſerable cries had ſtruck the Czar as he was being driven paſt. He went up to the wheels, and firſt promiſed ſpeedy death, and afterwards proffered them a free pardon, if they would confeſs ſincerely. But when upon the very wheel he found them more obſtinate than ever, and that they would give no other anſwer than that they would confeſs nothing, and that their penalty was nearly paid in full, the Czar left them to the agonies of death, and haftened on to the Monaftery of the Nuns, in front of which monaftery there were thirty gibbets erected in a quadrangular fhape, from which there hung two hundred and thirty Strelitz. The three principal ringleaders, who prefented a petition to Sophia, touching the adminiftration of the realm, were hanged clofe to the windows of that princefs, prefenting, as it were, the petitions that were placed in their hands, fo near that Sophia might with eafe touch them. Perhaps this was in order to load Sophia with that remorfe in every way, which I believe drove her to take the religious habit, in order to pafs to a better life.

LAST EXECUTION—

31ST OCTOBER, 1698.

Again, in front of the Kremlin Caftle two others, whofe thighs and extremities had been broken, and who were tied alive to the wheel, with horrid lamentations throughout the after-noon and the following night, clofed their miferable exiftence in the utmoft agony. One of them, the younger of the two, furvived amidft his enduring tortures until noon the following day. The Czar dined at his eafe (*commode*) with the Boyar Leo Kirilowicz Narefkin, all the reprefentatives and the Czar's minifters being prefent. The fucceffive and earneft fupplications of all prefent induced the monarch, who was long reluctant, to give command to that Gabriel who is fo well known at his court that an end might be put with a ball to the life and pangs of the criminal that ftill continued breathing.

For the remainder of the rebels, who were ftill guarded in places round about, their refpective places of confinement were alfo their places of execution, left by collecting them all together this torturing and butchery in the one place of fuch a multitude of men, fhould fmell of tyranny. And efpecially left the minds of the citizens, already terror-ftricken at fo many melancholy exhibitions of their perifhing fellow men fhould dread every kind of cruelty from their fovereign.

But confidering the daily perils to which the

Czar's Majefty was hitherto expofed, without an hour's fecurity, and hardly efcaping from many fnares, he was very naturally always in great apprehenfion of the exceeding treachery of the Strelitz, fo that he fairly concluded not to tolerate a fingle Strelitz in his empire,—to banifh all of them that remained to the fartheft confines of Mufcovy after having almoft extirpated the very name. In the provinces, leave was given to any that preferred to renounce military fervice for ever, and with the confent of the Woivodes to addict themfelves to domeftic fervices. Nor were they quite innocent : for the officers that were quartered in the camp at Azow to keep ward againft the hoftile inroads of the enemy, told how they were never fecure, and hourly expected an atrocious outbreak of treafon from the Strelitz ; nor was there any doubt but that they had very ambiguous fympathies for the fortunes of the other rebels. All the wives of the Strelitz were commanded to leave the neighbourhood of Mofcow, and thus experienced the confequences of the crimes of their hufbands. It was forbidden by Ukafe, under penalty of death, for any perfon to keep any of them or afford them secret harbour, unless they would send them out of Moscow to serve upon their estates.

Others have already stated that the Russians are sprung from the Roxolans, the name being only slightly altered. More recently the river Moskwa, which flows past the metropolis of Muscovy has given rise to their name of Muscovites. Nor have there been wanting men of genius to describe the times when this race, whom some will have it came from beyond seas, grew to their mighty strength from small beginnings, from their first royal seat in Novogrod to Kiew, then Wlodomir, and lastly Moscow. By the tyranny of Ivan Basilowicz which served him to subdue to himself so many vast neighbouring regions, the kingdoms of Casan and Astracan, either by the death of their rulers or their imprisonment, Muscovy grew to its present immensity of empire, the very hugeness of which has often already proved a source of misery, and the incurable wounds of which the restless minds of the people are constantly tearing open before they heal.

In the year 1682 civil dissensions, kept up by an ambitious woman, wreaked fearful internecine cruelties in rapine, and flaughter, and pillage. They attribute thefe great misfortunes to the wily machinations of Princefs Sophia. For when the late Grand Duke Feodor Alexiowicz, feeling his malady growing worfe every day, forefaw that death was at hand, he commended the affairs of the realm of Mufcovy to his elder brother Ivan Alexiowicz, an exceedingly mild prince, but one who appeared almoft imbecile, and who, on account of many other corporal defects was little fuited to the cares and anxieties of fovereignty. But when the Grand Duke was dead the Czarine Nathalia Kirilowna, a princefs of moft fubtle tact, ftudied very cleverly to perfuade the Boyars and Magnates of the realm that it would be better to crown her fon Peter Alexiowicz, the prefent Czar, paffing over Ivan ; and to appoint his kinfman Narefkin, his guardian until he fhould grow to maturity of intellect—alleging, that his noble nature, the vivid force of his genius, and the patience of labour that fhone forth in his tender years, were a fufficient demonftration of his greatnefs of foul and his kingly qualities.

Meanwhile, Princefs Sophia, a woman of no lefs artifice and cunning, having difcovered the defign of the Czarine Nathalia, laboured to explode it with countermines. It feemed to her that a deadly thunderbolt would be to perfuade the foldiers that the Czar, her own brother, had fallen a victim to the treafon of the Boyars, and perifhed by poifon they had brought to him. To give fupport to her affertion, fhe planned a more perilous deceit. It was the cuftom time out of mind to diftribute brandy—a breakfaft of the Ruffian fafhion—to the foldiers of the guard who had to be prefent in full numbers at the funeral and burial fervice for the deceafed Czar. With this beverage fhe mixed a moft noxious poifon; and, by an additional atrocity, contrived to turn againft the Boyars the odium of the crime fhe had perpetrated herfelf. She gave warning to the foldiers not to drink the brandy that would be diftributed,—for that it was poifoned and would be deadly to any that would tafte it,—that the fame dark fate menaced the foldiers as had befet the Czar; that all the Boyars were poifoners; that the lives of the foldiers were in imminent danger; that their only chance of fafety was in daringly avenging at once the murder of their fovereign and the

fchemes laid againft themfelves. The fate of
one Strelitz, who after fwallowing the poifoned
brandy became fwollen up and died, perfuaded
them that Sophia warned them truly and loyally.
Hence they began to mutter dark things againft
the Boyars, and invoke the fpirit of their dead
Czar. It feemed but juft to be angered with
poifoners, and the whole people was filled with
the magnitude of the danger, and was in a ftate
of wrathful fermentation againft the magnates.
Sixty thoufand rioters in the firft outbreak of
their fury feized upon the two perfonal phyficians
of his Majefty the Czar, Doctors Daniel and
Guthbier, and with tortures, the cruelty of which
is utterly beyond defcription, urged them to
confefs the crimes touching which, mifled by
the reprefentations of Sophia, they rather upbraided than interrogated them. One of the
doctors thought to hide himfelf in the German
fuburb until the fury of the populace who thirfted
for his blood fhould have worn itfelf out. But
with the true inftinct of the favage mob they
gueffed that the perfons who were concealing
him muft be Germans. Steel, fire, and maffacre
were threatened to all of German blood if they

fhould dare to afford further harbour to a man guilty of *leze* majefty.

The Germans became greatly alarmed that they would all have to pay the penalty from which they were endeavouring to fave one : and left all fhould perifh on his account, the doctor, difguifed as a beggar, got off into the fields to free the innocent from the contagion of his evil fortune. But, being betrayed into the hands of the ferocious populace, he was fhortly after hacked to pieces by the fwords of thofe madly raging men. When the doctors had been murdered in this horrible manner, the mob imperioufly demanded that the Boyars who were privy to the poifoning and to the Czar's death, fhould be given up to them for punifhment, and that a fum of 500,000 ducats* fhould be paid to them for arrears of their pay. The tolling of the great bell was the fignal agreed upon for the commencement of a violent onflaught. They battered the caftle with cannon, they broke open the gates, rufhed in, and hurled all the magnates

---

* The ducats known in Ruffia and Poland, were thofe of Holland for the moft part, and were equivalent to about ten fhillings of Englifh money.—TRANSL.

they could find out of the windows upon the lances beneath, and put them to death with the moſt cruel butchery. Nothing was held ſacred, no reſpeƈt was had to the majeſty of the dead ſovereign whoſe manes they had reſolved to appeaſe with theſe cruel offerings, the apartments were devaſtated, the treaſury plundered, everything holy profaned, the property of thoſe maſſacred ſold to the higheſt bidder, the very monaſteries vexed and exhauſted with a moſt iniquitous exaƈtion of ſeveral millions. Rebellion even raiſed the ignominious gibbet which ſhould have been its own meed, and here the maſſacred Boyars were regiſtered as traitors to their country—for all the rights of government were uſurped. They had already come to the reſolution of turning their wrath upon the Germans in the ſame way, when one of the Strelitz, whoſe hoary and aged locks had won authority over them, diſcouraged his companions by aſking them : "Why attack the Germans? Why attack innocent people? It would be a crime to injure theſe people, for they have done nothing againſt us. Beware; you will have to pay dearly for repentance that comes too late.

Sweden protects them, and her fierce fword
will avenge their wrongs as if they were her
own." Thefe words converted them to more
wholefome counfels, and they abftained from
the intended maffacre. Many thoufands of
men without diftinction of guilt or innocence
were fwept away in this peftilent outbreak. In
the part of the city called Kitaigorod alone,
five thoufand men who retreated thither to defend
their lives from maffacre, perifhed in various
ways.

At length the two princes, Ivan and Peter,
being raifed jointly to the fupreme fway, the difcords of the reft fubfided. Then an edict was
publifhed againft the rebels, penalties decreed
againft them, execution followed, and the ignominious gibbet that was raifed by unrighteouf-
nefs, was laid proftrate by lawful authority. But
the tranquillity of the realm was not of long
duration. In the year 1688 a fearful ftorm
fwept fiercely upon the Mufcovites. Several of
the Boyars were put to death, and the rebels
were ravening for the blood of the Czars who
had fled to the monaftery of Troycza for fafety.
On that occafion Mr. Lefort, with a very fmall

band of foldiers whofe loyalty was greater than
their numbers, was the firft to fet out for the
monaftery of Troycza, and thus acquired in the
higheft degree the favour of the Czar, by the
propitious gales of which he rofe rapidly to the
envied rank of General-in-Chief and Admiral,
which had never before been conferred upon a
foreigner, and recently he was the Czar's ambaffador to feveral European crowned heads.
The moft ferene Czar Peter Alexiowicz incurred
feveral other dangers from the perfidy of his
fubjects, but overcame all fnares, treafons, and
frauds with prodigious good fortune. Only a
few days before he left Mofcow, a plot of fome
great perfons was discovered againft his life, a
criminal defign which was very near to have
fucceeded, and when thefe were brought to
punifhment others followed in their footfteps,
who expected to perpetrate evil againft him in
his abfence with greater impunity.

THE CZAR'S GENEALOGY.

HE defcends from that moft ancient and noble flock of the Princes Romanowicz, which was clofely allied with the line of the Grand Dukes that became extinct, as is known, in the perfon of Feodor Ivanowicz the fon of the great tyrant Ivan Bafilowicz. His great grandfather was Knez Feodor Nikitiz, a man who had followed war from his youth, who had been fuccefsful and had won renown and very high general efteem. When of reverend years he was made patriarch, exchanging thus the helmet of military glory for the purple of high priefthood, and took the name of Philarete Nikitiz. He died in 1633.

His great grandmother was Iconomafia, daughter of the tyrant Ivan Bafilowicz. The fon of this marriage, Michael Feodorowicz, was the grandfather of the prefent Czar; and, on the expulfion of the falfe Dmitri, in 1613, fucceeded, by the fuffrages of the Mufcovites, to the government of the State. After twenty-three years of a profperous reign over the Mufcovites, during which he earned great applaufe, he died on the 12th of July, 1645. He had, by his firft wife, Iconomafia, two Princes: Alexis Michaelowicz, born the 17th of March, 1630, who fucceeded him upon the throne; and Ivan Michaelowicz, born the 1ft of June, 1631, and who died on the 8th of January, 1639. By Eudoxia Luka-nowna, who died within eight days after him, he left an only daughter, Irene, who was be-trothed to Count Waldemar, natural fon of King Chriftian IV., of Denmark, but who died before marriage.

Alexis Michaelowicz the very next day after his father's death, being then in his fixteenth year, was folemnly inaugurated Grand Duke; and fhortly after chofe for his wife Ilia Daniel-owa, of the noble family of Miloflawfki. She bore him four Princes and three Princeffes. The eldeft, born in 1653, was baptized Alexis Alexiowicz, who, in 1667, when King Cafimir abdicated the throne of Poland, was propofed, with great and exceedingly rich offers, as a candi-date for the crown of that country : but he died, in 1670, before his father. The fecond, Feodor

Alexiowicz, born in 1657, fucceeded to his father's fceptre.

The laft-mentioned Prince was twice married. His firft wife, Euphemia Rutetzki, died in childbirth together with her infant in 1681. He married, fecondly, Maria Euphrofina Marveona, of the moft noble Polifh family of Lupropin— an alliance which was hateful to his people, and which drew upon him the deteftation of the Boyars, and at laft death by poifon upon both himfelf and his wife on the 27th of April, 1682.

The third fon of Czar Alexis Michaelowicz, was Michael, who died in 1669.

The fourth was Ivan Alexiowicz, born in 1663, who was raifed to the throne, jointly with his brother, in 1682, and died in January, 1696.

The eldeft Princefs, Irene, died in 1670. The fecond, Sophia, is the torch and trumpet of the many dangerous feditions that have hitherto taken place in Mufcovy. The third Princefs was Marina.* Thefe two laft are ftill

---

* Elfewhere and ufually called by our author, Marpha.— TRANSL.

living, but were forced into a monaſtery in 1688, on account of the rebellion they had raiſed.

Thoſe above named were the iſſue of Czar Alexis Michaelowicz, by his firſt marriage. By his ſecond union, with Nathalia Kirilowna, of the Nareſkin family, he had two children: Peter Alexiowicz, the now happily reigning Czar of the Muſcovites, born on the 11th of June, 1672 ; and Nathalia, his cheriſhed ſiſter, who up to this has not been privy to any plot.

Peter and his brother Ivan Alexiowicz ſucceeded jointly to the ſceptre of Muſcovy, on the death of their father, in 1682 ; but on the outbreak of the freſh revolt in 1688, Ivan Alexiowicz, who was a lover of quiet, ceded of his own free will the whole ſovereign power to his brother.

HIS MAJESTY THE CZAR.

Thoſe brilliant gifts of nature and of ſoul which have ſpread his fame throughout almoſt every realm of the earth, pointed him out from

his infancy for kingly power and fovereign fway.
A well fet ftature, well proportioned limbs, the
vivacity of his youth, and an addrefs beyond his
years, fo conciliated the affections and good will
of his fubjects, on account of their expectations
of his natural qualifications, that he was openly
preferred by the contending fuffrages of numbers
of people to his brother Ivan Alexiowicz, who
was called to the throne of his progenitors by
that pre-eminence of primogeniture which is
held facred by the nations.   Ever felf-reliant, he
contemns death and danger, the apprehenfion of
which terrifies others.   Often has he gone quite
alone to traitors and confpirators againft his
life, and either from their reflection on the
greatnefs of their crime, or dread and remorfe
for their divulged treafon alone he has made
them quail by his Majeftic prefence ; and, left
this creeping and dangerous peft fhould fpread,
he has delivered them up to chains and prifon.
In 1694 he failed out of the port of Archangel,
into the North Sea, beyond Cola.   A ftorm
arofe and drove the fhips upon the moft perilous
rocks.   The feamen were already crying out in
defpair ; the Boyars, who had accompanied their

ſovereign, had betaken themſelves to their
prayers and their devotion of making thouſands
of croſſings—no doubt in terror at the contem-
plation of ſuch an awful ſhipwreck. Alone,
amidſt the fury of the wild ſea, the fearleſs Czar
took the helm with a moſt cheerful countenance,
reſtored courage to their deſpairing ſouls, and,
until the ſea ſubſided, found an aſylum for life
and limb on that very rock upon which, in rough
weather, many veſſels had been a prey to the
foaming brine.

A few years ago, before his two years' tour,
he told his magnates, at Szeremetow's, at whoſe
houſe he was dining, to what Saint, under God's
providence, he aſcribed his happy eſcape from
that tempeſt, "When," ſaid he, "I was ſailing
to Slowiczi Monaſtir from Archangel, with
ſeveral of you, I was, as you know, in danger
of ſhipwreck. How great was the horror of
death and the dread of what ſeemed certain
deſtruction that beſet your minds, I forbear to
record. Now we have eſcaped that danger, we
have got through our peril, but I hope you will
think with me, that it is but right to do what I
ſwore to do, and fulfil the vow I made to

heaven. I then proffered a vow to God and to my holy patron, the Apoſtle Peter, that I would go to Rome to pray at his tomb, leſs out of anxiety for my own ſafety than for all yours. Tell me, Boris Petrowicz," thus he addreſſed Szeremetow, "what are the country and the towns like? As you have been in thoſe parts you muſt be able to tell all about them." Szeremetow praiſed the amenity and beauty of the country, and the Czar ſubjoined: "Some of you ſhall come with me when I am going there; when the Turk has been humbled, I will acquit myſelf of my vow." His late moſt ſerene mother tried to diſcourage him from this projeƈt, and through her the Ruſſians ſuggeſted many figments againſt the Apoſtolic See. His anſwer to her was: "If you had not been my mother I could hardly reſtrain myſelf. My veneration for that name pleads your excuſe for what you have dared to ſpeak. But know that death is the penalty that awaits whoſoever henceforward ſhall preſume to blame my intention or reſiſt it." And to Rome aſſuredly he would have gone in performance of his vow, had not ſuch preſſing dangers ſummoned him back to Moſcow, on the breaking out of a revolt in his realm.*

With what fpirit, too, he laboured to introduce into Mufcovy thofe polite arts that had for ages been profcribed there, may be eafily gathered from his having fent into various countries of Europe,—into Germany, Italy, England, and Holland,—the more talented children of his principal fubjects, in order that they might learn, by intercourfe, the wifdom and arts of the moft

* Von Adelung (*Kritifch literärifche Überficht der Reifenden in Ruffland*) gives the following very curious extract, with reference to Peter's fuppofed propenfity at that time to Catholicifm, from the ambaffador von Guarient's fecond report from Mofcow, dated 12th Auguft, 1698, which remains in MS. in the Vienna Archives. That report bears the title : " Relation des Kais. " Gefandten Ignaz von Guarient and Rall über die Ankunft des " Erzbifchofs von Ancyra Petrus Paulus Palma zu Mofcau ;" at the clofe of which the ambaffador fpeaks of an unfavourable report about the war which had got abroad, but doubts its accuracy, and fays that he heard from well-informed perfons : "das derlei " Unglückfnachrichten von dem Minifterium aus fonderer Politik " darumben auffgefprengt worden, des Czaren Intention nach " Italien zu gehen ganz verhindern, und felbigen fich defto ehun" der in feinem Reich einfinden möchte, maffen alzugewifs, dafs " diefe unternehmende rayfs Ruffen, Calviner und Lutheraner in " groffe Beftürtzung und noch gröfferen Argwohn einer innerlich" guctführender Propenfion zu dem Catholicifmo täglich mehr " fetzen follte."—(See Von Adelung, *Kritifch literärifche Überficht der Reifenden in Ruffland.* St. Peterfburgh and Leipfic, 1845. Vol. II., pp. 392, *et feq.*).—TRANSL.

polifhed nations, and on their return be orna-
ments of Mufcovy, and in their turn excite their
juniors to the like deferts. He made known
his reafons for this plan, fome years ago, to his
Boyars, explaining its utility to them. They
all commended the monarch's prudence, but
infinuated that fuch immenfe good, however
defirable it might be, was unattainable. That
the genius of the Mufcovites was unfuited to
fuch purfuits ; that the money expended on it
would be wafted in vain ; and that he would
fatigue himfelf and his fubjects with profitlefs
labour. The Czar was indignant at thefe fay-
ings, which were only worthy of the profound
ignorance of thofe that gave utterance to them.
For they liked their benighted darknefs, and
nothing but fhame at their own deformity was
capable of drawing them into the light. "Are we
then born lefs bleft than other nations," the Czar
continued, " that the divinity fhould have in-
fufed inept minds into our bodies? Have we
not hands? Have we not eyes? Have we
not the fame habit of body that fuffices foreign
nations for their internal culture? Why have
we alone degenerate and rude fouls? Why

fhould we alone be left out as unworthy of the glory of human fcience? By Hercules! we have the fame minds; we can do like other folk if we only will it. For nature has given to all mankind the fame groundwork and feed of virtues; we are all born to all thofe things; when the ftimulus is applied, all thofe properties of the foul that have been, as it were, fleeping, fhall be awakened." The greateft things may be expected from fuch a Prince. Let the Mufcovites congratulate themfelves on the treafure they poffefs in him, for they are now really fortunate. He chofe his wife in the family of Lubochin,* and fhe bore him a fon named Alexis Petrowicz, a youth fplendidly gifted and adorned with ingenuous virtues, on whom reft the hopes of his father, and the fortunes and tranquillity of Mufcovy.

ESPOUSALS OF THE CZAR.

Different times call for different manners. It

---

* The family of Lapoukine, which ftill flourifhes, is of high race, infcribed in the velvet book, and dates from the 15th century. They were created princes in the laft century.—(*Notices des Princip. Fam. de la Ruffie.* Paris, 1845.)—TRANSL.

may, indeed, have formerly been the practice in Ruffia to affemble all the maidens of Mufcovy that were of comely form and remarkable beauty when the Czar was thinking of marrying, in order that he might felect whichever pleafed him beft. But the cuftom is become obfolete ; and the marriages of the Czars have of late been moftly decided by the advice of thofe who by official rank or favour were raifed to the honour of ftanding befide the throne. Polygamy, too, has fallen into defuetude, and they hold it to be finful to fhare the nuptial bed with a number of felect concubines. But fhould the Czarina be fterile, then the Czar may fhut· her up in a monaftery, and is at liberty to look out for a more fruitful union. Befides fterility there are other caufes of repudiation. We muft believe that other fovereigns do nothing rafhly, though we, as it often happens, cannot account for their motives. Thus, the wife of the prefent Czar, who, as fhe bore him a prince, could by no means be faid to be fterile, has neverthelefs been repudiated—a divorce which, no doubt, is grounded upon moft grave caufes, the weight of which we may perhaps conjecture from the fact that when the Czar was lying outfide of Azow he refufed to return until he fhould be certain that his wife's head had been fhaved, and that fhe had been fhut up in a monaftery called Suftalfki, about thirty miles diftant from Mofcow.

To feek for a wife among foreign princes has, up to this, been a perilous experiment for a Czar, the Boyars and leading people holding out vain apprehenfions that by foreign marriages foreign and new-fangled manners would be moft pernicioufly fubftituted in their country, that ancient ufages would become corrupted, the purity of the religion of their fathers be imperilled, and, in fhort, all Mufcovy be expofed to the utmoft danger. And the only reafon they allege for the poifoning of Czar Feodor Alexiowicz is that he had chofen a wife out of the Polifh family of Lupropin. At length fome hope is dawning that a gentler fpirit is beginning to breathe over Mufcovy, in order to the perfect development of which the Czar has taken fome new meafures of exceeding wifdom, for the purpofe of civilifing his fubjects by more frequent intercourfe with foreign nations; and they may thus come to like what they have hitherto perfecuted with fo much difguft ! They are beginning to defire marriages with foreign nations, now that they learn that there are no holier bonds to conciliate friendfhip between nations, and to fettle wars—nay, how often they give laws to the victors. Many believe that the Czar divorced the wife whom he has fhut up in a convent with the defign of marrying a foreigner.

MILITARY POWER.

None but the Tartars fear the armies of the Czar. Their fucceffes in Poland and Sweden, I think, muft not be attributed to their valour, but to a kind of panic fear and the evil ftar of the conquered. It is an eafy matter for them to call out feveral thoufand men againft the enemy; but they are a mere uncouth mob, which, overcome by its own fize, lofes the victory it had but juft gained. Yet if they were as ftout of heart, and as well verfed in military fcience, as they are numerous, ftrong of body, and patient of fatigue, their neighbours would have caufe to fear. But now, from a flothful genius and habits of flavery, they have neither ftomach for great things, nor do they achieve them. Count James de la Garde, general of the Swedifh militia, in the year 1611, with 8000 men put 200,000 Mufcovites to flight. When they firft beleaguered Azow, a fortrefs of the Perecop Tartars, fituated at the confluence of the Tanaij, near the Palus Meotides,* a cat jumping into the Czar's camp, out of the city, threw many thoufand Mufcovites with panic terror into a difgraceful flight; and having been caught afterwards, and brought when the expedition was over to Mofcow, is carefully kept to this day by the Czar's command in Bebrafchentfko. Although in the ftubborn defence of towns againft great befieging forces they have fometimes been worthy of praife, neverthelefs, in the field, againft the Swedes and the Poles, they were generally defeated, and often were put to great flaughter. What Charidemus faw wanting in the camp of Darius, is not to be found to this day among the Mufcovites—namely, a ftout body of veteran and

* The Sea of Azow.—TRANSL.

difciplined troops, men and arms, and banners
in regular array, intent upon the word of command of their officers, and drilled to keep their
ranks; where all obey, like one man, the word
to halt, wheel, charge, change order, and the
men know what they have to do as well as thofe
that command them.

THE INFANTRY.

The Strelitz were all mufqueteers, under the
name of javelin-men, and were the fame to the
Mufcovites as the Janiffaries are to the Turks.
The number of them in pay varied from 12,000
to 20,000. They were the moft dexterous of
the Mufcovites, and for that reafon the Czar's
body-guard; and the guards of his capital were
chofen from them. They prided themfelves on
the fignal privileges and great immunities that
had been conferred upon them, which were
nearly as great as thofe of the old Roman
foldier. Their annual pay was feven roubles
and fhekels and twelve meafures of oats; but
by the commerce which they were allowed to

exercife they often attained great and envied riches. In Mofcow their houfes occupied a vaft fpace in the Czar's own capital; but after the late rebellion had led to the condemnation of many thoufands of Strelitz to death, even thefe houfes, left they fhould remain a memorial of this impious faction, were, by the Czar's commands, uprooted from the foundations and broken to pieces.

When all the Strelitz had been put to death, or exiled, he fubftituted in their ftead four regiments, after the fyftem of the German armies, as regards officers and their rank. It is forbidden to call them Strelitz, as if, by inheriting the name, they might become alfo the heirs of the crimes that were perpetrated by thofe who bore it. There are only four of thefe regiments, but they conftitute a force of 8000 men. The firft was Gordon's; the fecond, Lefort's; the third Bebrafchentfko; the fourth, Simonowfki. That called Bebrafchentfko was lately broken up, all the men compofing it being drafted by the Czar into the fea fervice. When they were about to take the field there were as many armies as I have enumerated regiments. Thence it comes that the chief of a regiment is not a colonel, but a general. For to every general of thofe regiments a certain territorial diftrict is affigned, from which, according as the neceflities of war may demand, the ferfs are to be driven from their huts into the ranks, until the requifite number be filled up; and thus, what was a regiment in garrifon, fwells out of garrifon into an army in its huge proportions. They are then broken up into troops of a thoufand each, which receive the title of regiments, and are ufually put under the command of German colonels; for there are feveral German colonels without regiments living in Mofcow on half-pay, unlefs when on actual fervice. When a campaign has been decided upon, and preparations are being made to march againft the enemy, thefe officers are appointed as regimental commandants over a mob of the loweft and moft uncouth ragamuffins. When the expedition is over, the commanding officer has no further authority over his men, who go back again to the plough, alternate peafants and foldiers, at one time with arms in their hands, and next moment driving the plough.

It cofts but little to oppofe to the enemy an almoft incredible multitude of this tumultuary hofting of louts, efpecially as all thofe that are called upon to ferve are obliged to find their own provifions. Hence commiffariat officers are quite unknown, and the very name is incomprehenfible to the Mufcovites, who fay that it is not the Czar's bufinefs to look after provifions for private individuals, and that it is a matter which belongs to each one in his own particular; yet certain it is that more mifchief than advantage refults thence to the ftate. For how many die of famine—how many towns, villages, and hamlets, widowed of their inhabitants, degenerate into a wafte and folitary wildernefs. Befides which the changing from year to year, according to the fyftem by which thefe moft wretched peafants have to ferve in turn, is exceedingly pernicious to difcipline and the art of war. For thofe that are under arms this year being freed from fervice the next, the refult is that the troops are always frefh, raw, and inept foldiers. Nor can the fidelity of the recruiting officers be very great. They will be fure to ftudy their own pecuniary intereft, and not imprefs the moft fuitable, but the poorer or clofer-handed, who either will not, or cannot, purchafe their exemption.

A fhady army it is, good footh, and good fport for an enemy, unlefs by fome chance they fhould happen to meet with their peers. The Czar perceived what a ufelefs expenfe this inept militia was, and moft wifely refolved to correct the inveterate error of his nation. They were affembling in Bialogrod an army of four and twenty thoufand peafants, whom he abfolved from their military oath and fent back ·to till their fields, hoping for more profit thence; and impofing as their fole additional burden that they fhould pay a poll tax of a rouble per annum to the Czar. Prince Repnin, Colonel of Dragoons, fet out for Cafan and Aftracan to levy ten thoufand men, according to the German fyftem, which the Ruffians are unaccuftomed to, and others were fent off by the Czar with a fimilar commiffion to other regions and localities. He had made up his mind to raife a ftanding army of 60,000 infantry in his own pay, moft fagely confidering that it is only the veteran foldier who has been broken in by many years of training that is worthy of the glory of real warfare.*

THE CAVALRY.

The Muſcovite cavalry is compoſed of nobles and thoſe whom people of high rank are obliged to furniſh, and many of the latter claſs are domeſtic ſervants. When the Great General, or the Commander-in-Chief, who is ſo called in the armies of the Czar, is about to march on an expedition, he cauſes proclamation to be made by a herald† when the expedition is to take place, and has it intimated to the nobles to pre-ſent themſelves with a proper number of ſerfs fitted out for war. When this is done they all buckle on their weapons, and, with hearts full of diſmay at the chances that may await them, haſten to the appointed rendezvous. For their minds are filled with a double fear ; in the firſt place, that of the Czar's indignation if they ſhould be ſlothful in fulfilling his beheſts ; and,

---

* While theſe regular levies were as yet freſh recruits they were utterly routed, in 1700, by Charles XII. at Narva.—TRANSL.

† " Præconis voce."—ORIG.

in the fecond place, that of the rifk which hangs
over men about to engage in mortal ftrife with
the enemy.   Nor do they confider it any dif-
grace to purchafe at great coft the permiffion to
live fluggifhly at home and deprecate the perils
of war.   Nay, they go the length of contending
that fome Germans of chivalrous mould muft be
demented when they ftrive and ˙ labour and
entreat to be allowed to follow the army into the
field, and into all the very manifeft dangers that
attend military fervice.   Such Germans as thefe
they confider either to have little wit, or to
entertain fraudulent defigns againft the ftate.
For what can they mean ?   What fane thought
could make them of their own accord expofe
themfelves deliberately to danger?   Good footh !
they wot not of that   heaven-born fomething
that lies hid within the man whom valour leads,
amidft wounds and death, by praifeworthy ambition to the palm of glory.   Their cavalry is
armed with bows and arrows ; their fpears or
lances are fhort; they are all arranged according
to the Turkifh manner.   The dragoons have
been armed for the laft two years with carbines
and piftols.   If we may form an eftimate of

thefe fellows from the rafh audacity of their crimes, they are fitter for robbery than for rightful war.

There is another defcription of infantry who ufe arms curved in the fhape of a half-moon, and which they call Bardifch. Thefe men, while the army is being arrayed, are fent forward as the ftrength and bulwark of the hoft, and are the firft to attack the enemy, and are fierce until the arrows of their opponents begin to fhower deadly wounds among them. Their defign is either to make a great impreffion by a fudden fhock or to fly; but when they fee their comrades ftruggling without duly propitious fuccefs, and preffed upon and being flain, they are quite overcome at the fight of the others that are perifhing, and fo lofe heart that, as it were, lifelefs with fear, they caft away their arms, bid one another farewell, and without the idea of refiftance, they ftretch out their necks to make the ftroke of their enemies' fwords more fure, and concede the victory to the foe by their cowardice. Should the enemy purfue them in their flight from battle they fo abandon themfelves to the victors as not even to afk for life.

As there is ftill no folid fettlement of peace between the Mufcovites and the Turk, through the fault of the ambaffador, who, without due confideration of future contingencies, made a pact for a mere truce for two years, the Czar is gathering, with great folicitude, foldiers and *matériel* enough to repulfe and overthrow the enemies' forces. A levy of every tenth ferf throughout all Mufcovy is being made, and the *Knes*, Boyars, and merchants are obliged alfo to furnifh provifions for every ferf that they fend from their refpective eftates.

ARTILLERY.

They mount their artillery on the fame defcription of carriages as thofe which other European States ufe for battering the walls, demolifhing the curtains, and breaching the defences of fortifications ; and as the Mufcovites themfelves are not fkilled in the proper management of artillery, fcientifically ufed, they entertain foreigners at great coft for the purpofe, who are fent to them as a proof of amity from various countries.

MILITARY MUSIC.

The found of Ruffian mufic in general is fo difpleafing to the ear that it is more calculated to fadden than to roufe valour to martial daring. It is more like the moan of a funeral wail; and they poffefs not the art of inflaming martial ardour with nobler ftimulants. Their chief inftruments are fifes (*jatumeæ*) and kettle drums.

THE CZAR'S REVENUE.

Befides the tribute and annual tax which all the provinces are bound to pay ftrictly in due proportion, there are many perquifites that flow in addition into the fovereign's public treafury. The firft of thefe fources of emolument is the toll of the ports of Aftracan and Archangel, from which the Czar is faid to derive ten millions of imperials per annum.

The fecond in importance are the *kakaba* or public inns; for the Czar has complete monopoly of the fale of beer, brandy, and hydromel;

a fource from which above two hundred thoufand imperials find their way into the treafury.
Any private individual, were he even a magnate,
that fhould without fpecial licenfe from the Czar
expofe for fale hydromel, beer, or brandy, would
be deprived of the merchandife in queftion, and
moreover punifhed with an arbitrary fine ; nor
are inftances wanting of fentences of fharper
penalties being inflicted upon perfons found
defrauding the fovereign of his royalties. They
have been flogged with the *knout* and tranfported to Siberia, where they are compelled
continually to hunt the fable.

The Germans, however, enjoyed the privilege
of brewing and felling beer among themfelves,
being in other refpects obnoxious to the fame
penalties fhould they fell it to Mufcovites. Now,
however, they have been deprived of that privilege. Tichon Nikitowicz Strefnow, whofe office
nearly correfponds to that of lord high fteward,
was of opinion that it would be more judicious
not to deprive the Germans of the right of
brewing; inafmuch as an eafier method might
be employed to obtain the profit which was
expected from that meafure,—to wit, the impofi-

tion of a heavier tax upon the licenſes to brew which they had to take out from the chancery: and beyond doubt they would prefer paying this to buying beer brewed by the Muſcovites.

3°. They collect great wealth from ſables, of which the beſt are trapped in Siberia.

4°. Sturgeon in incredible multitudes frequent the waters of the Volga, and are taken in great quantity in ſpring and ſummer: their eggs form the ſtaple of an opulent commerce with foreign countries; they are ſalted and packed in large veſſels and called caviar,—a famous delicacy with the Italians. One Dutch merchant pays eighty thouſand imperials per annum to the Czar, for the right of exporting caviar.

5°. A German merchant has in the ſame way the monopoly, which he purchaſed from the Czar, of rhubarb, which the Muſcovites prize exceedingly.

The Engliſh paid the Czar, when he was in England, twelve thouſand pounds ſterling, and eight thouſand more in Holland, for the monopoly of the ſale of tobacco in Muſcovy. Notwithſtanding the Muſcovite clergy have always

hitherto fuperftitioufly held the fmoking and
chewing of that weed to be an impious and dia-
bolical cuftom ; nay, even in our time a Ruffian
merchant, to whom the Czar previous to his departure had granted the right of felling tobacco
on payment of the fum of fifteen thoufand roubles
per annum, was excommunicated by the Mufcovite patriarch—himfelf, his wife, his children,
and grandchildren, and curfed all to infinity.

RUSSIAN MONEY.

The Czar has no mines of gold or filver:
they believe, however, that they have difcovered
rich veins at a place called Kameni in Siberia.
General de Carlowitz has juft brought fkilful
miners into Mufcovy, fo that in a fhort time it
may be known for certain whether the earth
affords hope of the difcovery of gold or filver in
quantity. Still the Ruffian money was always
coined out of pure and good filver, though now-
a-days it is fomewhat adulterated and falls much
fhort of the old weight. They give fifty or
fifty-five *kopeks* in exchange for the imperial
florin (*folidum*), and coin a hundred and fome-

times as much as a hundred and twenty kopeks
out of one imperial, as we experienced there
in our own time by weighing kopeks with an
imperial. Now the kopek or Mufcovite coin
is not round, but of an oblong and oval form,
bearing on one fide the effigy of Saint George
with his lance, and on the other the name of
the Czar and the date. The Mufcovites have
alfo another coin called a *denga*, two of which
are equal to a kopek. They have no larger
coin: but they ufe different words to exprefs
certain numbers of kopeks; for inftance, two
kopeks make a penny (*denarium*), three an altin
(*altinum*), ten a grifna (*grifnam*), fifty a poltin
(*poltinum*), and a hundred a rouble. In our
time there was a report about copper money,
on account of the want of filver, to pay the
foldiers and fupport the coft of the war; but
when news of the conclufion of peace arrived,
whatever may have been ftruck was carried to
the exchequer to be laid by for future wants. No
perfon is allowed to carry minted money with
him out of Mufcovy; any perfon detected doing
fo lofes all his goods; but any perfon may ufe
letters of exchange or employ them to purchafe

merchandife.   Marcelius, a Dutch merchant, was
the firft to difcover an iron mine ; his defcendants poffeffed it for fome time by tenure of
villenage, until the family becoming extinct it
fell to the Czar, who gave it as a fief to Narefkin.   In the year 1700, money was ftruck after
our fafhion by order of the Czar, and the firft
payment of the foldiers was made in it.

THE CZAR'S PHARMACY.

There are two pharmacies : one in the Kremlin
fortrefs itfelf, the other in the city.   They were
eftablifhed by the Czar at the advice of the Germans, and kept up at great expenfe.   Formerly
the people ufed to live to a great and reverend
age, ufing nothing except certain well-known
inexpenfive fimples : they now die in more coftly
fafhion, and, as fome complain, much earlier,
nature being debilitated by the ufe of medicines.
This, however, they ought rather to impute to
their inordinate debauchery, and the pernicious
abufe of medicines, rather than to the herbs and
juices prepared with real healing art.   Boxes,
glafs veffels, and inftruments catch the eye with

a certain exterior flaſh; but frequently there is little in them for healing, ſince for the moſt part theſe veſſels are empty, nor are freſh drugs bought as they ſhould be by thoſe whom the Czar has appointed inſpectors or directors. If we may truſt their pharmacopeia, the Czar's pharmacies were never better furniſhed than at the time when Mr. Vinnius was over them. Like a man of German race as he was, he was ever full of forethought and activity; and when the phyſicians and apothecaries gave him notice, his only thought was to maintain the neceſſary ſupply. But now the people who have ſucceeded him in this function are ſo proudly ignorant and ſlothful, that they will neither liſten to the phyſicians nor buy freſh medicines with due fidelity. Through their miſtakes and careleſſneſs things are fallen into ſuch a ſtate that as often as there is a preſſing caſe for cure the doctor can hardly preſcribe the remedy which he thinks beſt ſuited to expel the malady, but is obliged to give ſomething like an equivalent which he knows may be had in the pharmacy.

But Prince Feodor Alexiowicz Golowin, when director, gave an example of greater induſtry:

for he fent a certain Ruffian—who, to the great mortification of numbers, received the doctor's degree after two years' ftudy—into Holland to buy up carefully whatever medicines were wanting. With the exception of this man, almoft all the phyficians are foreigners and Germans. Mr. Carbonari de Bifenegg and Doctor Zoppot are the beft fkilled in the healing art, and have the largeft practice. But they revere Surgeon Dermond like another Efculapius, and fome call him by the invidious name of Doctor Empiric. Doctor Blumentroft and Doctor Kellerman alfo enjoy good repute. There are a great many apothecaries, all Germans : but they have Mufcovite apprentices a great deal older than the mafters. They enjoy a falary of two hundred roubles per annum ; nor are they wearied with much labour. They take turn about: they are not in the habit of going to the pharmacy before eight or nine, and at two in the afternoon they go home to the German fuburb. Thefe are the bufinefs hours ; during the reft of the day no medicine is fold ; nor is it eafy to call thefe apothecaries, for Slowoda, the German fuburb, is an hour's diftance from the city.

TREASURES.

Theſe conſiſt of the regalia, the crown enriched with coſtly gems and ſtones. Secondly,
in a huge quantity of coined ſpecie, which moſt
people believed was exhauſted at this time by the
great coſt of arming ſuch an extremely numerous
fleet, the very name of which is terrible. But
the Czar will never want as long as he knows of
his ſubjects having any gold and ſilver remaining.
For their riches and private valuables are his only
mines of gold and ſilver. This abſolute maſter
uſes his ſubjects at his will, and their wealth in
what ſhare he pleaſes. He arrogates to himſelf
what part he likes of the ſpoils of the hunter;
he ſells their furs or makes preſents of them at
will. Air-dried fiſh are his munitions. At
market nobody can ſell unleſs the Sovereign's
merchandiſe has been firſt ſold. He rather dic-
tates than bargains the prices of what belongs
to him; and meaſures out for himſelf and takes
whatever there is either good or precious in his
dominions. Grand Duke Ivan deſpoiled almoſt
all Livonia of chalices, reliquaries, croſſes, and
ſilver; and it is never allowed to take gold or

filver of any defcription out of Mufcovy, unlefs for the redemption of captives loft in war, or of fuch as are carried off in the daily raids of the Tartars. But the Mufcovites are in the habit of difplaying their wealth in plate whenever the ambaffadors of foreign princes are, according to the national cuftom, fumptuoufly received at a princely and regal banquet. It is needlefs to fpeak of the large proportion which a variety of furs of almoft ineftimable price bear among the general wealth of the Czars.

THE CZAR'S COURT.

The former Grand Dukes made ufe of inefti-mable parade in their apparel and adornment, the majefty of the Pontiff being fuperadded to that of the King. On the head they wore a mitre, glittering with pearls and pricelefs gems ; in the right hand they bore an exceedingly rich paftoral ftaff; their fingers were covered with rings of gold ; and above the throne upon which they fat there was fixed, to the right, an image of Chrift, and to the left one of the moft Holy Virgin Mother. The prefence and ante-chambers were thronged with men clad in golden vefture and other precious infignia to the very feet.

But the prefent Czar, a great contemner of all pomp and oftentation about his own perfon, rarely makes ufe of that fuperfluous multitude of attendants. Nor do the Boyars or nobles about the court ufe the proud old garb, having learnt by the example of the Grand Duke that luxury in drefs is an empty thing, and that living in fine houfes does not conftitute wifdom. The Czar himfelf, when going through his capital, is often accompanied by two, and at moft three or four, of his more intimate attendants; feeling, even in the perilous time of the military revolt, a confidence in the fimple refpeᴄt of his fubjeᴄts for majefty. For in former times the Mufco-vites obeyed their fovereign lefs like fubjeᴄts than bought flaves, looking upon him more in the light of a god than a fovereign; fo that one often ufed to hear among the Mufcovites (what the vulgar ftill continually fay,) " *God only and the Grand Duke know that: everything that we have of health and comfort proceeds from the Grand Duke.*" This reverence of his people recalled Ivan Bafilowicz to the throne of his forefathers, when, after unheard-of atrocities, he had, out of fear of juſt vengeance, betaken himſelf to the retirement of a monaſtery; whether it be that reſpeét for the royal name which thoſe who live under monarchy revere as ſomething ſacred, or innate veneration for their ſovereign, or their truſt in one who had held the reins of government already, drove theſe men, born for ſubjeétion, into loyal obedience.

Sedition was almoſt utterly unknown in Muſcovy of old; now you would think the rebellions muſt be chained one to another. Hydra's head did not ſprout faſter than freſh rebellions ſpring out of the very graves of traitors. Hercules thoroughly ſubdued Hydra by fire; but the reſtleſs audacity of the Muſcovites feeds upon flames like a Salamander. Is it the iron age that has baniſhed olden fidelity and affeétion, and reverence for their ſovereign, even from among the dregs of the populace? Yet the cuſtom ſtill exiſts of proſtrating themſelves on the ground in worſhip of the Czar, as if his place were nearly as exalted in power as God's. As for the reſt, a throng of nobles—Sin-Boyaren, as they call them (that is, ſons of Boyars),

—perform the daily miniftrations. But there is nothing feemly in the fervice, no cleanlinefs among the fervers ; fo that the mere rudenefs of their unpolifhed manners and their filthy fervice would fuffice to diftinguifh this from every other court in Europe.

When the table is being laid for the Czar, no flourifh of trumpets fummons the courtiers to their functions ; but one of them cries out in a ftentorian voice, " *Gofudar Cufchinum, Gofudar Cufchinum*" (that is, " *The Grand Duke wants to eat* "). The cups in which drink is prefented to the Czar are made of gold and filver, in footh, but fo coated with filth that it is hard to difcover which precious metal lies hidden beneath the dirt. There is no order in the arrangements of the viands ; they are thrown higgledy-piggledy ; and they are generally torn afunder, not carved. There was a reverential old cuftom which forbade the admiffion of any perfon to the table of former Czars. They ufed to dine alone ; but they were accuftomed to fend fome difhes from their table to any of the Boyars that they wifhed to honour with an efpecial mark of favour. The prefent Czar, on the other hand, confiders it a decided affront to kings that they fhould be repelled from the pleafures of private fociety, arguing why fhould a barbarous and inhuman law be enacted againft kings alone, to prevent them enjoying the fociety of anybody? So that, neglecting the proud folitude of his own table, he is fond of converfing and dining with his advifers, with the German officers, with merchants, and even with the ambaffadors of foreign princes. Though this be fovereignly difpleafing to the Mufcovites, yet, as they muft needs obey, they had to adopt the fame fafhions, and often exhibit a fmiling countenance upon compulfion.

THE CZAR'S RESIDENCE.

It is called the Kremlin—is furrounded with a ftone wall two miles and nine hundred paces in circumference, and comprifes feveral very hand-fome ftructures belonging to the nobleffe within the ambit of its enclofure, feveral bazaars, feveral churches—as, for example, the Church of the Archangel Michaël, which contains the royal tombs. Blagavefine, or the Church of the

Annunciation, is remarkable for its nine towers, the roofs of which, as well as the whole church, are covered with gilt copper, and the higheſt tower thereof is ſurmounted with a croſs of pure gold, of immenſe value. Ivan Veliſkoy, or the Church of Saint John, the tower roof of which is gilt, has a number of bells, one of which, the largeſt in the world, weighs two thouſand two hundred poods, or ſixty-ſix thouſand pounds of our* weight. Within the ſame regal precinct, pre-eminent among the other chanceries, ſtands that called the *Poſolſki Pricas*, or Ambaſſadorial Chancery, wherein all affairs concerning the con-dition of the ſtate and negotiations with foreign princes are expedited. All ſtrangers, too, are dependent thereon. The chambers and apart-ments intended for the monarch's dwelling are ordained with ſumptuous pomp of decoration and hangings, and for ſize and ſplendour yield in nothing to the chief palaces in Europe.

In another part of the fortreſs there is a ſtud of various breeds of blood horſes, a kind of little Sybarite army, as it were. Horſes, to be prized

* 66,000 Vienneſe weight.—Transl.

by the Mufcovites, muft be tall and fhowy.
They like thofe of Arabia and Altenburgh.
Mufcovy poffeffes a native breed of horfes
exceedingly commendable for their fleetnefs ;
they call them *pachmaten.* The Czar's predeceffors ufed to appoint chafes of different
kinds in the various diftricts of their dominions,
the monarch referving hawking for his own
pleafure. The reigning fovereign, on the contrary, is attracted by other matters—the art of
war, fireworks, the roar of artillery, fhipbuild-
ing, the dangers of the fea, and fets the arduous
purfuit of glory above all pleafures and amufe-
ments. He went through the military functions
from the very loweft rank, and would not afcend
the throne of his anceftors, and mount the pin-
nacle of fovereign power, before he had paffed
through all the grades of military rank to the
higheft, that of General-in-Chief (Campi ducis),
fo glorious does he efteem it to have merited
dignity before poffeffing it.

Firſt. Left the religion of their forefathers
ſhould be changed, for they believe that three
ſigns have been predicted as prognoſtics of the
ruin of Muſcovy by one of their ſaints, whom
the ſupernal powers permitted to caſt a glance
far into the dark boſom of futurity.

Second. Change of dreſs. Third. Of money.
They formerly wore the ſame dreſs as the Tartars ; then they adopted the more elegant coſtume
of Poliſh faſhion ; now they imitate the Hungarian garb. For the moſt part they ſtill
obſerve with tenacious ſuperſtition the principal points of the ſchiſm by which they ſeparated themſelves from the univerſal body of the
Church. The true mode of making the ſign of
the croſs was changed in a council of the Greek
patriarchs, called at great coſt at Moſcow ; for
in former times there was no diſtinction in the
way in which clergy and laity made the ſign of
the croſs. All Ruſſians were taught to form it
with three fingers in honour of the moſt Holy
Trinity ; but after the council in queſtion the

ancient mode was allowed to priefts only, and all
laymen were enjoined by a public law to give
up that moft ancient cuftom, and form the crofs
with only two fingers held up.   How much of
innocent, noble and illuftrious blood was fhed on
account of that change the numerous wounds
ftill unhealed fadly fhow.

The old-fafhioned money was ftill in ufe in
our time, except that the public current value
was occafionally fomewhat diminifhed by wear
and tear ; yet it is certain that copper money,
which was coined to meet the excefs of war
expenditure, is referved in the Treafury, and the
laft letters brought hither out of Mufcovy
acquaint us that the coinage there has been
debafed.   Nor has the authority of the clergy
remained intaft ; for formerly they occupied
without difpute the firft places of honour in all
public affemblies, but now their dignity has
grown fo vile that they are feldom, or at leaft
only like laymen, admitted to table.   Methinks
fome old hag belonging to the popes muft have
dreamt thefe things inftinftively, for they are in
dread, and not without reafon, of being fhaken
from the axis of their fortune, and left they

fhall reign no longer than they can fucceed in keeping the populace and nation, by means of fuperftitious doctrine or contempt for fcience, in ignorance and benighted error; whilft it has ever been the fpirit of fhining virtue to ftruggle glorioufly to more arduous and better things.

Another thing of which they ftudioufly take care, is to guard their frontier towns and for-treffes with ftrong garrifons, that they may be prepared for the event of peace or war, and left fome chance of fortune fhould expofe everything to the intrigues of their enemies and the inteftine treafon of citizens.

Third. Left any of the magnates fhould rife to dangerous wealth and power, to the peril of the fovereign. He that boafts of his riches, or makes difplay of his wealth, runs the rifk of his life ; for perfons of formidable wealth are com-monly punifhed by being dragged to prifon upon a trumped-up charge of peculation, their goods are handed over to the Treafury, and they them-felves to exile or death.

Fourth. None of the provincial offices are perpetual ; governorfhips laft only a few years the duration of power being at the utmoft t hre years. They pretend that the fhort duration of honours is a great advantage to the country, for that governors who know that they will be ftripped of their authority in a year's time do not readily abufe their magiftrature, nor do the people grow too much attached to them, or dread a Prefident whofe authority will come to a fpeedy end. The powers of Feodor Madveowicz Apraxin, as Woivode of the port of Archangel, have been prolonged by the Czar for three years more, becaufe at the time when the Czar was ftaying there, to make a cruife on the White Sea, over and above the fidelity with which it was feen he had exercifed his fun{ctions, he went liberally to great expenfe to receive his Majefty with becoming honour.

Fifth. Formerly Mufcovites were not allowed to crofs the limits of their fovereign's dominions, left by beholding the happinefs of a foreign empire they fhould be excited to daring afpirations of innovation; but under the prefent Czar's reign it is required of them to vifit foreign countries, under the femblance of acquiring knowledge; and they are weakened in purpofe and power by this impofed neceffity of foreign

travel. Still, without the Czar's ſpecial per-
miſſion and command, nobody dare ſet foot with
impunity out of Muſcovy.

Sixth. Thoſe whom the requirements of commerce compel to croſs the frontiers for a time,
are puniſhed with confiſcation of goods, the
knout and exile, ſhould they fail to return home
within the time preſcribed.

Seventh. The Coſſacks are a great element of
ſtrength for the Czars. The Muſcovites conciliate them with annual gifts, and ſtudy to keep
them faithful with the fatteſt promiſes, left they
ſhould take it into their heads to paſs over to
the Poles, and by their defection draw off
the whole ſtrength of the military power of
Ruſſia; for this ſtout race excels the Muſcovites, both in the art of war and in bravery of
ſoul.

Eighth. In like manner, with civility, promiſes,
largeſſes, and multiplied artifice, they retain under
their aſcendency their neighbours the Tartars,
Circaſſians, Nogai, Samoiëds, and Tingoës ; for
they ſcarcely burden them with any tribute—
nay, theſe people rather expect an annual gift,
the delay of which beyond the uſual time, in

our day, made Ajuka, the Prince of the Calmuck Tartars, defert with 20,000 to the
Turks.

Ninth. It is an old habit of the Czars to fow
and fofter difcords among their very magnates,
whom they find it eafier to opprefs each and all
with more fecurity and under a greater mafk of
equity, when they are divided by mutual hate,
and ftriving in favage plots to get the better of
one another; in accordance with the old faw—
divide et impera.

Tenth. The Czar when upon his departure
from Mofcow puts feveral perfons at the head
of affairs, taking care to choofe thofe that he
knows to be by natural antipathy in difcord
with one another: left any one fhould abufe
the power entrufted to him or arm it againft his
prince.

OF THE ROYAL CITY OF THE CZARS.

Mofcow is the metropolis of Mufcovy, and it
takes its name from the river Mofkwa that flows
through it. The city is almoft circular, and is
divided into four parts each furrounded with its

own walls, or a vallum. The innermoft part, or as it were marrow of the city, is called Kytaygorod; next this lies the caftle or royal refidence, feparated from the former by walls, and is called *Kremelina gorod.* Thefe two parts are furrounded with a ftone wall. The part which encompaffes thefe on the eaft, north, and weft, is called Czargorod, which means the royal city, and this is encompaffed with a wall built of white ftone and a rampart of earth. The part round this outfide is named Skoroda, and is only encompaffed with hedges. The fouthern part bears the alias name of Strelitza Slowoda, becaufe it was inhabited by the foldiers or prætorians of the Grand Duke. But as all the houfes of the Strelitz have been torn down and razed to the earth fince the late rebellion, and the Czar wifhes the very name of Strelitz to be buried in oblivion, I believe that quarter will foon have a new name and deftination allotted to it. As for the reft, moft of the private houfes are built of wood, a very few of brick, and none but people of rank and opulent merchants live in houfes of ftone. Hence thofe frequent fires that often deftroy houfes by thoufands.

This city is three German miles in circumference, is grandly adorned and fair to behold, with its more than two hundred goodly churches, and a multitudinous variety of towers, for every church has its five towers. The high church is that of the moſt Holy Trinity, into which in days of yore, on Palm Sunday, the patriarch ſeated upon an aſs uſed to be led by the Czar : but ceremonies of this kind in the preſent Czar's time are either abandoned or are neglected and going out of uſe. The merchants, according to the nature of their wares, have different and ſeparate marts, and places, and ſpaces, in which alone they may expoſe their wares for ſale.

Firſt, in front of the Kremlin Caſtle there is a ſeries of ambulatories round about, with ſtalls behind ; for there is neither room nor allowance here to put up regular ſhops.

The ſecond mart is that in which ſilk and everything made of ſilk is ſold.

In the third, all kinds of cloth are expoſed for ſale. The fourth is for the goldſmiths ; the fifth, for the furriers ; the ſixth, for the ſhoemakers ; the ſeventh, for linen tiſſues ; the eighth, for pictures; the ninth they call the loufe market, from the number of barbers' ftalls there, where the Mufcovites go to have their locks clipped, and where the hair is thrown out into the ftreet; in the tenth, garments of all defcriptions are on fale; the eleventh is the fruit market; the twelfth, the fifh market; the thirteenth, the bird market. Befides thefe there is a public building which they call the Gaft-Hoff, near the palace of the Ambaffadors, in which Perfians, Armenians, and other foreigners, for the moft part expofe their wares. Independent of which there are many other feparate marts, according as the claffification of merchandife requires; and everything is arranged fo diftinctly and with fo much order as to be eafy of accefs and paffage from one to the other. There are cellars too for the fale of wine, which is brought by fea to Archangel and thence to Mofcow.

In the part of the city which as has been faid they call Czargorod, there are certain open fpaces called Pogganabrut: in thefe are fold wheat, meal, flefh, cattle, beer, hydromel, and brandy. The city is in a moft flourifhing ftate in refpect of the variety of trades in which its inhabitants are engaged.

It is indeed clofed with gates ; but not duly
provided againft the attacks of an affailing
force.

Nearly all that the natives make ufe of, or
that is fuitable for trade, is comprifed in the
following enumeration :—

1°. The fkins of various animals, which ferve
to protect the natives from the extreme rigour of
the climate, and which are fold in great quantities
to foreign merchants. Of thefe fkins the moft
prized are fables, the fineft of which are furnifhed
by the province of Petchora, upon which the
female fafhion of our day has fet fuch an extra-
vagant value in Europe. The others are black
and red fox, in which Siberia abounds, and alfo
white marten, beaver, the charming little ermine
fkins, wolf, lynx, and fo forth. 2°. Such a
quantity of wax, that in fome years as much as
two myriad pounds are faid to have been
exported. The greateft amount ufually comes
from Plefcow, though other provinces alfo abound
in wax. 3°. Such a profufion of honey, that
though a great quantity be confumed by the
natives in drink, a confiderable amount is
exported every year into the neighbouring

countries. 4°. Jaroſlaw and Wologda furniſh tallow. 5°. The whole country produces hides of oxen and deer. 6°. Oil produced by boiling down the carcaſes of ſeals. 7°. Caviar, of which a vaſt quantity is prepared on the banks of the Volga, the roe of the ſturgeon and other* deſcriptions of fiſh, and in which a lucrative export trade is carried on with foreign countries, eſpecially Italy. 8°. Flax and hemp are produced in great abundance and of excellent quality ; the former in the province of Volſko, and the neigh- bouring regions ; the latter in Smolenſko, Doro- gobuſa, and Viaſma. 9°. Comes ſalt, the greater part of which is gathered from ſalt ſprings in Stara-Ruſſa, and elſewhere ; but near Aſtracan it is caſt on ſhore in high floods. 10°. Tar, a vaſt quantity of which from the province of Carelia, and on the banks of the Dwina, towards the North Sea, exudes from the rock. They call what they uſe, inſtead of glaſs, *ſtude ;* it is what is commonly uſed for lanterns under the name of Ruſſian glaſs, and alſo *Marien glaſs.* 11°. Iron, for of other metals Ruſſia is almoſt barren.

***

* " *Bello-uginae,* ſturionis, *feverigæ,*" for the firſt and third of which I have not found the Engliſh name.—TRANSL.

They think, however, that they will find a vein of a different metal in Siberia.

OF THE RUSSIAN RELIGION.

Touching the alteration in the manner of making the fign of the crofs I have already fpoken. Who could imagine it to be of fo great moment for the worfhip of the true faith whether one fhould make the fign of the crofs with two or three fingers, or with the whole hand raifed. Neverthelefs, the Ruffian patriarch's doubt about the manner of making the fign of the crofs feemed a matter of fuch weight to the Mufcovites, that at great coft they invited the Patriarch of Conftantinople, and two others from Alexandria to Mofcow, to decide the queftion. True, indeed, the Mufcovites make the main part of their religion, and their only means of faving their fouls, confift in the mere fign of the crofs ; for it is extremely rare to find any among them that know by heart the two ordinary little prayers, the *Our Father* and *Hail Mary*. Nor have they fchools where thofe points are taught which it is becoming and neceffary for an adult

to know, as eſſential to ſalvation. But I cannot
imagine, nor will, or can, the Muſcovites when
queſtioned upon the ſubject, ſay what motive
chiefly induced the above-mentioned ſpiritual-
rulers to abrogate, contrary to the expreſs wiſh of
the people, and prohibit under the ſanction of ſuch
a cruel penalty the ancient mode of forming the ſign
of the croſs, which had been in uſe and allowed for
centuries. The lower orders thought that heaven
and eternal glory was torn from them by that
prohibition, and that thenceforward none but the
popes would enjoy the bliſs of heaven, as they
alſo were allowed to make the ſign of the croſs
with three fingers. Many ſtruggled againſt the
patriarch's law, as impious and irreverent towards
the Almighty; and numbers preferred to fall
beneath the axe of the executioner, rather than
abandon the ancient way of forming that ſacred
ſign. It would have been far more uſeful and
far more wholeſome labour to organiſe ſchools,
to appoint maſters for the inſtruction of the
youth, to teach the ignorant, to lead back the
erring to the right road to ſalvation. But as
they are, to the laſt degree, unſkilled in divinity,
and haughtily deſpiſe all learning from abroad,

they envy that enlightenment to thoſe that are to come after them, into which they themſelves are aſhamed to emerge out of their benightedneſs.

BAPTISM.

The Ruſſians deny that perſons are truly baptiſed who are regenerated, according to the Roman rite by the mere ſprinkling with water in the name of the moſt Holy Trinity ; but contend, with moſt obſtinate ſuperſtition, that baptiſm ſhould be performed by immerſion; that the old man muſt be drowned (*ſuffocari*) in the water, which is to be done by immerſion, and not by aſperſion. Inſiſting pertinaciouſly upon this error, they admit reiteration of baptiſm, and baptiſe anew, either by immerſion or, as the preſent uſage is, by pouring water over the whole body from head to foot, any perſons, no matter what religion they may have previouſly belonged to, who embrace the Ruſſian ſchiſm, either of their own free will, or, as is generally the caſe, upon compulſion. And becauſe there are three perſons in the Godhead, ſo they require a triple immerſion.

SACRIFICE.

They celebrate according to the Greek rite ; they uſe leavened bread and red wine ; they diſtribute the confecrated bread and wine together out of the chalice with a ſpoon. Though they commonly make uſe of red wine for the ſacrifice, yet if it is not to be had, they do not deny that white wine may be confecrated.

They hardly or with difficulty permit ſtrangers or thoſe that are not of their religion to enter their churches. For Catholics, however, they are leſs particular than for Lutherans and Calviniſts. Perhaps becauſe they are aware that we venerate the images and relics of ſaints, and that the others ſpurn them.

OF IMAGES.

They venerate only painted images, and not ſuch as are ſculptured or wrought in any other manner ; for they will have it that it is forbidden by the commandment of God in the Decalogue to adore any graven thing, which precept, however, in the way in which *adoration* ought to be underſtood, equally prohibits the painted and the graven.

SERMONS.

The Ruſſians, up to the preſent, have always condemned the function of preachers, ſaying that profeſſed preachers affect rather a uſeleſs elegance of language than earneſtneſs in proclaiming the word of God. Yet in the preſent age the practice of expounding the Goſpel has met with the approval of the Ruſſians. For there are even ſome to be found among them who, confident of their own learning, are not content with merely reading the Goſpel or holy Scripture aloud in the church (which was the old faſhion), but prefer a poliſhed and rhetorically laboured diſcourſe of their own compoſition.

THEIR VENERATION FOR THE MOTHER OF GOD.

They venerate the Mother of God with the moſt devout piety, and they hold it to be right and uſeful to reverence God's ſaints. They hold Saint Nicholas in principal veneration and honour, on which account they celebrate that ſaint's feſtival twice a year.

PURGATORY.

They believe in a third place, wherein all are detained until the Day of Judgment, holding that nobody is admitted into heaven unleſs upon ſentence paſſed in that public and final tribunal which has to decide upon thoſe that are worthy of the reward of heaven. They ſay that ſuffrages are beneficial to ſouls in this condition, and for that reaſon eſteem it very profitable and very meritorious to pray or perform good works for the faithful departed.

THE PATRIARCH.

He is the viſible head of the Ruſſian church. Under him he has metropolites, archbiſhops, biſhops, and archimandrites. The cuſtom prevails of carrying the paſtoral and croſs before theſe dignitaries wherever they go. None of them can marry, for they are all ſelected out of the monaſteries.

MONASTERIES.

They have monks and nuns who, in auſterity of life, in frequency of faſts, in rigour and poverty, exceed the diſcipline of our religious in ſeverity, but not in piety. For in the ſeaſon of their faſts they macerate the fleſh to ſuch a degree that it is held ſinful to give even medicine to the ſick ; but when the time of the faſt is over, they make uſe of every licenſe ; and, more like debauchees than monks, they are rampant drunk in the public places ; and, devoid of all ſhame, they are often found in laſciviouſneſs in the open ſtreets. They wear a 'ong black gown, with a cowl at the neck. They are all meanly dreſſed, except thoſe that bear the higher offices in the monaſteries, who are more expenſively clothed. They alſo make the three vows of chaſtity, poverty, and obedience. They are not imbued with letters. Sometimes Poles, deſerting to their ſchiſm, are mixed up in theſe monaſteries. Such a one I found in the monaftery called Jerufalem, which lies fix miles diftant from Mofcow.

THE POPES OR PRIESTS.

Orders are conferred by the impofition of hands. Round the head of the new ordained they bind a *vitta*, or, as they call it, a *fkuffia*, which is bleffed by the patriarch, and muft be kept with the greateft care ; for whoever fhould happen to lofe it, even by accident, would be deemed unworthy of the facerdotal office. If a layman fhould chance to get into a row with a pope, he muft beware not to fully the *vitta*. If he is going to beat the pope, he muft remove it from his head with due refpect, and in the mean-time lay it afide in a decent place, after which he may ftrike the prieft with impunity as much as he pleafes. No law, no penalty or excommuni-cation can take hold of him, provided that after the blows and buffets he replace the *vitta* with due veneration on the head from which he re-moved it. Thus the character of the honoured *vitta* is faved ; nor does he ftrike at the inftigation of the devil, who venerates the prieftly dignity in that manner, and only avenges his quarrel on the perfon of the man. All popes muft have wives; and the prieftly function is not allowed to be exercifed by one that is not bound in wedlock. But he muft marry a maiden or the widow of fome pope. Should he marry any other widow he would be rendered irregular and incapable,* *ipfo facto.* A pope may not marry again when his wife dies, nor is he capable† of celebrating or enjoying a facerdotal benefice without a wife: he may fing vefpers, indeed, and perform other minor ecclefiaftical acts, but may not offer at the altar. So that a wife is a fubftantial requifite for the exercife of the priefthood at prefent in the Ruffian Church : fave for monks, whofe rule it is to live in folitude and companionlefs. To the latter may be added the patriarch, metropolites, archbifhops, bifhops, archimandrites, and others, who are all chofen from among the monks. The popes may, however, marry a fecond time, provided they renounce the priefthood. So that it often happens that the fame

---

* " *Irregularis et inhabilis,*" &c.—ORIG.
† " *Idoneus,*" &c.—ORIG.

men whom you revere one year as popes,
you ſee next year as ſhoemakers, tailors, and
butchers.

When the common people meet the popes in
the public highways they aſk for their croſs and
their bleſſing, which the popes, ambitious of the
ſanctity of their character, publicly impart to
thoſe that ſolicit it. Yet they are ſcarcely better
behaved than the populace; for they often
ſtagger drunk through the thoroughfares of the
city, worſe than thoſe whom they are bound, in
virtue of their ſtate of life, to excite, by their
example, to virtue and piety. They are in the
habit of carrying a croſs with them everywhere:
how often that all-precious badge of our Redeemer, which theſe moſt baſe ſcoundrels carry
about, muſt be rolled in the gutter when they
are helpleſs and ſtaggering, after drinking brandy
to exceſs at ſupper. I do believe that there is
no people that ſhines ſo much in outward ſigns,
that counterfeit real piety, and in ſuch ſpecious
maſks of uprightneſs of heart, as this race which,
nevertheleſs, in diſſimulation, fraud, falſehood,
and in the moſt unbridled audacity in the com-
miſſion of every crime, ſurpaſſes far and wide

all other nations of the univerſe. Nor is this aſſertion made out of hatred, but from true and genuine experience ; as any perſon ſhall infallibly come to underſtand, who may happen to have the opportunity of frequent dealings with them. There are as many as four thouſand popes in the metropolis of Muſcovy, who can all live decently upon their revenues.

FESTIVAL DAYS.

There are almoſt as many feſtivals in Ruſſia as there are days in the year : but the feſtivals alternate between the different quarters of the city ; ſo that while one quarter is keeping holiday, the other is working. But the major feſtivals of the Nativity, the Reſurrection, the Aſcenſion, &c., they all keep holy together, which they indicate by a continual and annoyin jangling of a bell. If bell-ringing and the outward piety of making the ſign of the croſs be ſufficient to conſtitute true Chriſtian devotion, Muſcovy, at this preſent day, can preſent us with multitudes of exceedingly Chriſtian folk. On feſtival days they only reſt from labour in the forenoon ; at a very early hour in the morning, generally before daybreak, they get through their ſacred funćtions in the dark, and the day itſelf they conſecrate, if not to work, at leaſt to debauchery: ſo that one muſt always be in fear of a conflagration as often as the Ruſſians celebrate a feſtival, or, as they call it, *braſnick.*

BURIAL.

They uſe a number of ceremonies in the burial of their dead. They bring ſuperſtitious and profane women for thoſe occaſions, who follow the funeral with mercenary ſobs. In the coffin they hide letters of recommendation to Saint Nicholas, whom they believe to be the doorkeeper of heaven: and in theſe letters the Patriarch aſſeverates that the deceaſed led the life of a Chriſtian, and at length died with praiſe-worthy conſtancy in the orthodox Ruſſian faith. When the corpſe is laid in the grave, a pope, after a ſhort ſermon upon the neceſſity of dying, throws in the firſt burial earth. Beſides the prayers for the dead after the bodies have been committed to the ground, they have women at the grave, who ſet up a loud howling and wail, and aſk the deceaſed, with mighty vociferation, after the manner of the pagans, " *Why did they die ?* Why did they ſo ſoon deſert their dear ſweet wives?—their darling offspring? What did they want for? Meat? Drink?" Finally, they place upon the grave various deſcriptions of food, to be divided among the poor who are in the habit of gathering in crowds there. This they often repeat during the year, out of affection and charity towards the departed.

MASLANIZA.

The Italians call it *Carnevale;* the Latins, *Bacchanalia;* our Germans, in Muſcovy, *die Butterwochen* (butter* week) : becauſe during that week it is forbidden to eat fleſh, but it is ſtill allowed to eat butter : for during the reſt of the lenten faſt they uſe only linſeed oil.

---

* This is alſo the ſenſe of the Ruſſian word *Maſlaniza* from the Sclavic root *maſlo,* butter.—TRANSL.

ABSTINENCE AND FASTING.

They abſtain from fleſh on Wedneſdays and Fridays. They have, moreover, four other faſts during the year. The firſt, from Quadrageſima Sunday to Eaſter ; the ſecond, from the Sunday after Pentecoſt to the feaſt of the Holy Apoſtles Peter and Paul ; the third, from the firſt of Auguſt to the feſtival of the Aſſumption of the Bleſſed Virgin ; the fourth, from the tenth of November until Chriſtmas. The firſt of all is the ſtricteſt, and, from its laſting longer than the others, they call it the long faſt. In faſting-time it is not allowed to eat eggs, or butter, or cheeſe. No exception is made in favour of age or ill-health: they deem it better to die of faſting than preſerve life by eating eggs or fleſh. Nay, the very phyſicians, before they are ad-mitted to practice, have to bind themſelves, by oath, never to employ any medicines in faſting time for ſick Muſcovites, for the diluting of which eggs, fleſh, milk, or butter might be neceſſary, even though they may clearly foreſee that the ſick perſon muſt ſpeedily die without

the help and ufe of fuch a medicine. From
which aufterity and indifcreet obfervance of the
precept of fafting, I juftly take occafion to pronounce the Ruffian Church not to be a true
and genuine mother, but a ftepmother and an
adulterefs.

PUBLIC GOVERNMENT.

The cities are not under the jurifdiction of
mayors or the worthieft of their citizens; but a
diak is appointed by the Czar to adminifter the
law. With his ftaff of fcribes he conftitutes a
Pricas, or chancery, and cafes of every defcription
are tried by this tribunal. Except a little index
upon which are the judicial forms, and fome
legal axioms that have the force of precedent,
they have no written law, the will of the monarch
and the *ukafe* of the fenate being the fupreme
law. They fay, indeed, that one of the diaks has
compiled a book of the rights, ftatutes, decrees,
fentences, decifions, and the cuftoms which he
found to be obferved in Mufcovy from a very
remote period. But that collection of laws has
not, fo far, legal force and weight, nor are the

judges called upon to pronounce in accordance with it. In the year 1647, Grand Duke Alexis Michalowicz had the laws collected and reduced to order by his councillors, in a book they call *Soborna Ulafienia.** But each new monarch makes new laws ; for in a country governed defpotically, nothing but the fovereign's pleafure has force of law.

They begin their law-fuits nearly in this manner : the plaintiff fets forth by petition by whom and to what extent he has been injured ; and having obtained leave by *wepis*, which is an indult of the judge, he has an apparitor (*prifta-fillis*) fent to fummon the accufed, who is obliged to promife on his fealty to appear on the appointed day, otherwife the apparitor has power to detain him by every means in his power. Now, both plaintiff and accufed plead their own cafe, without the affiftance of either attorneys or advocates. If the cafe cannot be cleared up by evidence, it is terminated by fwearing. For when the judge cannot clearly fee which party is

---

* Thefe laws may be found tranflated into Latin by the Baron de Mayerburg, in his narrative of his Embaffy in Ruffia. They occupy 126 of the folio pages of that work.—Transl.

in the right, it is ufual for him to afk one of the
parties if he be willing to fwear upon the crofs
that he alleges the truth. If he confents to this,
he is forthwith conducted to church, and gains his
caufe by kifling the crofs. This crofs-kifling
they call *Chreflinam Cheloveniam*, and confider it
the fame as an oath. Hence they call traitors,
perjurers, and thofe that break treaties, tranfgreffors of the crofs. Should both be prepared to
fwear, they decide the cafe by lot. Should the
lofing party not fatisfy his creditor forthwith, he
is led into the public fquare, where condemned
perfons of this category are fuftigated in a deplo-
rable way, every morning from eight o'clock to
eleven. But if after being thus fuftigated for the
fpace of a year, they are not paying, they muft
fell their wives and children until the creditor
has been paid back to the laft farthing.

The complainant who firft gains the ear of the
judge is in general triumphant, even though his
fuit be unjuft, for there is no favourable confideration for the accufed; in fact, there is no great
difference between an accufation and a condemnation. Whatever the accufed may fet forth in
his own defence is feldom believed, or meets with

no attention. Their cuftom is to prove their
ftatement by witneffes, whom they bribe at a
trifling rate; and, moreover, he is confidered to
have the better cafe who has a ftronger body of
witneffes than his adverfary. Prefents, too, and
gifts, and largeffes, are a great help to a fuit:
nothing is expedited in a *Pricas,* unlefs the diaks
and fcribes have firft been put in good humour
with gold or filver. They beat the Harpies
hollow in rapacioufnefs; and by a moft corrupt
ufage, nobody can contrive to extort his annual
falary unlefs he firft propitiates all the officials
in the *Pricaffa,* from the diak down to the
vileft of the fcribes, by a percentage upon it.
He that has not the means of bribing witneffes, or gaining the diaks and fcribes with
gold, has the worft of ill-luck to be at law: the
caufe of juftice is oppreffed, and the iniquity of
corrupt judges can eafily make white black and
black white.

Debt is proved by writing fignature and feal,
and not by witneffes. If a dilatory debtor fhould
defer payment of the fum lent, the creditor prefents himfelf before the *Pricas* to the jurifdiction of which the debtor is fubject, as the com-

petent tribunal, and by petition, addreffed to the Prefident of the *Pricas*, prays that his debtor may be cited. If he appear upon citation, he is coerced by the efficacious legal remedy to pay at once the debt which his creditor has legally proved ; but if he do not appear on citation, he is feized wherever he may be found, and hurried by force before the tribunal. He who is the more liberal in his prefents has the beft cafe at law ; juftice and injuftice are up at auction ; as there is no fixed price, they are ufually bought by the higheft bidder. Wretched is the debtor's lot if the points of his defence be not gilded with plenty of money. Money, not argument, conftitutes the proof ; when that falls fhort, he is condemned to fomething nearly as bad as death. His knees tingle with the moft exqui- fite pain under the ftrokes of flender little canes (*tenuibus baculis*), in a tower which is the prifon for dilatory debtors. The beating is often re- peated every day until he pays or gives fecurity; but when he cannot afford to do either, he is often adjudged to his creditor, along with his wife and children, after he has undergone an abundant amount of beating proportionate to

the amount of his debt—for the ſlavery laws are
ſtill unrepealed in Ruſſia.

Pecuniary mulcts, *battoks*, and knouting, are
the puniſhments and penalties in civil caſes.
The money fines, unleſs when defined by cuſtom
or *ukaſe*, vary according to the judge's choice,
and are often greater or leſs. Battoks are two
ſlender ſticks, wherewith the condemned perſon
is often flogged to death; for his coat is taken
off, he is thrown down on the ground with only
his ſhirt on; one ſits upon his head, another on
his feet, ſo that his body may not move; and
then, thus ſtretched out on the ground, they
flog him, until the official ſtanding by, by word
or ſign, puts an end to the blows. The knout
is a ſcourge ſo ſavage that at the firſt ſtroke on
the naked ſkin the blood ſtarts forth, and it
leaves a wound of the breadth of a finger in
depth. This puniſhment, when applied to a
perſon in a civil caſe, they call the Czar's grace
(*Tzaream gratiam vocant*), and he that has
been thus caſtigated is bound to return thanks
for his paſtime, nor does he lie under any
note of ignominy, ſo that any perſon that
dares at any time to upbraid one with having

been ſo caſtigated becomes liable himſelf to the
ſame penalty.   But the puniſhment is penal and
criminal, if the perſon flogged be tranſported to
Siberia.

Thoſe accuſed of libel have to pay *Biszeſtia*—
that is, to redeem the injury they have done to
the perſon's reputation by a pecuniary mulĉt.
Every rank has its *recalde*, or fixed ſum, eſta-
bliſhed by tariff, which the libeller has to pay. He
that uſes libellous language to a boyar, a colonel,
or a phyſician, is liable to a fine of 2000 imperials; for the honour of all theſe three claſſes is
protećted with preciſely the ſame *occlade*, though
the authority of neither colonels nor phyſicians
is always maintained ſcatheleſs.   The defamer of
the wife of a Boyar is condemned to twice the
uſual penalty.   One uſing opprobrious language
to children expiates his crime with half the fine
which the laws have appointed to guard the fair
fame of their parents.

OF THE MANNERS OF THE MUSCOVITES.

The whole Ruſſian race is rather in a ſtate of
ſlavery than of freedom.   All, no matter what

their rank may be, without any refpect of perfons, are oppreffed with the harfheft flavery. Thofe that are admitted to the dignity of the privy council, affume the lofty name of magnates, and come next in rank after their fovereign, have merely more fplendid bonds of flavery ; they are chained in golden fetters, being liable to all the more bitternefs in that they ftrike the eye more infolently, and by their very flafh upbraid the vilenefs of the lot in which they are held up before the world.

He that fhould happen to fubfcribe his name in the pofitive degree to petitions or letters to the Czar would be publicly tried for treafon. Diminutives muft be ufed. Thus, for example, one whofe name may be James, fhould write himfelf *little James* (*Jacobulum*). For they deem it greatly derogatory to the fupreme rank of majefty not to revere their fovereign with all refpect by thefe humble diminutives of name. This was a crime imputed to the military engineer Laval, by which the Minifters contended that he had deferved the Czar's hatred ; for that he ought to write and ftyle himfelf the Grand Duke's *cholop*, or moft abject and vileft flave, and acknowledge that all the goods and chattels he poſſeſſed were not his, but the monarch's. And in this opinion they have a capital practical hand in their ſovereign, who uſes his native country and its inhabitants (*patriâ civibusque*) as if power abſolute, unbounded, uncircumſcribed by any law, lay openly with him to diſpoſe as freely of the property of private individuals, as if nature had produced everything for his ſake alone. Let him trample upon theſe ſouls born for ſlavery, and let the Ruſſians bear the lot that the gods have appointed.

The people are rude of letters, and wanting in that virtuous diſcipline by which the mind is cultivated. Few ſtudy polite manners or imitate them. John Barclay, in his "Mirror of Souls," deſcribes at length how this race, born for ſlavery, becomes ferocious at the leaſt trace of liberty; placid if oppreſſed, and not refuſing the yoke, they of their own accord confeſs themſelves ſlaves of their prince. He has a right to their wealth, their bodies, and their lives. Humility more ſordidly crouching the very Turks entertain not for their Ottoman ſceptre. They eſteem other races as well by their own character.

Foreigners whom chance or choice has led into Mufcovy they condemn to the fame yoke, and will have them be flaves of their monarch. Should they catch and bring back any of them departing furtively, they punifh them as runa-gates (*ut fugitivos*). As for the magnates, though they be flaves themfelves, towards their inferiors and the plebeians, whom they ufually call, out of fcorn, *black men* and *Chriftians*, their arrogance is intolerable, and the vulgar dread their frown extremely.

Devoid of honeft education, they efteem deceit to be the height of wifdom. They have no fhame of lying, no blufh for a detected fraud : to fuch a degree are the feeds of true virtue pro-fcribed from that region, that vice itfelf obtains the reputation of virtue. Yet I would not have you underftand that all the inhabitants of that monarchy, without any exception, are alike igno-rant and proud in their eftimation of virtue. Among fuch a quantity of tares fome wholefome plants do grow ; and the rofe that ftruggles into bloffom among this rank crop of fetid leeks, blufhes all the more fair, and fheds a perfume all the more grateful. Few indeed are they that juft

Jupiter hath loved, or fhining virtue raifed to the
fkies: but thofe few really ftand fo pre-eminent
that thefe rare torches can remain unremarked
only by the inexperienced, or fuch as are crufhed
beneath a mountain of vices. The reft are of
an incult, flow, and ftupid difpofition, fo ab-
forbed fometimes in ftaring at ftrangers, that
with their jaws and eyes wide open they quite
forget themfelves. Among thefe, however, are
not to be reckoned fuch as are fmoothed
down by the tranfaction of affairs, or bufinefs,
or that have learnt by recent travel that the
fun is not fhut up within the mere frontiers of
Mufcovy.

In their fchools pofitively the only labour of
the fchoolmafters is to teach the children how to
write and fhape their letters. The height of
learning confifts in committing to memory fome
articles of their creed.

They defpife liberal arts as ufelefs torments of
youth, they prohibit philofophy, and they have
often publicly outraged aftronomy with the
opprobrious name of magic. It is criminal to
introduce the calendar of Vogt the aftronomer
into Mufcovy, becaufe in this general propo-

fition, *Moscau wird feinem Ungluck auch nicht entgehen* (neither will *Mofcow efcape her ill-fortune*), he prefaged rebellion to the Mufcovites. They fay that evil fpirits, at whofe fuggeftion and fhowing aftronomers may fometimes guefs about the future what is beyond mortal ken, muft have helped him in this black art. The Czar is endeavouring, by means of various arts and fciences, to frame a better ftate of things in his kingdom. If fuccefs fhould crown the prudent efforts of good counfel, people fhall fhortly be aftonifhed at the fair edifice that will ftand where there was nothing but huts before ; unlefs fome misfortune fhould happen or a defection of the people, or perhaps even fimply the very barbarity of their inclinations fhould render them incapable of bearing their own good fortune, or fhould make them grudge to their pofterity a lot fo happy, and envy the labours of the prefent for the profit of future generations. It is but a fhort time ago that an enterprifing Pole fet up the firft printing prefs among them, but they only print in the Ruffian language. The Ruffian characters are not very diffimilar from thofe of the Greeks, by whom they were taught to

read and write. Their grammar and idiomatical
conſtruction too are not unlike the Greek.
In the ſame houſe with the printing preſs,
ſome Greek prieſts are maintained at the Czar's
expenſe, who teach Italian to any that wiſh to
learn it.

They add and ſubtract numbers differently
from other people : they have a board, with
ſeveral different deſcriptions of beads, by means
of which they calculate accurately, with ſur-
priſing quicknefs—juſt like the markers that
other nations make uſe of : they indicate various
numbers by the mode of collocation.

Though they are themſelves unſkilled in muſic,
they are fond of its harmonics. They have
foreign muſicians, whom they pet while they
are ſinging, but as ſoon as they are ſated with
their ſtrains, their ſtinginefs returns, and they
are diſcontent to be at a yearly charge for a few
hours' gratification. Nor are the exerciſes to
which the nobility of European Courts addict
themſelves in uſe in Moſcow : they take no
delight in the manly exerciſes of horſemanſhip
or boxing ; they take no pride in dancing, nor in
any other art that prevails in this age among

nations that are capable of a generous ardour for praife.

They tolerate no Jews in Mufcovy, unlefs they be baptifed :* for it feems abfurd to Muf- covites that men fhould differ from them in religion, whofe ideas, whofe craft, and whofe ex- ceedingly fubtle arts of deceit, they put in practice with equal fuccefs.

Plurimùm utuntur thermis et caldariis ; cum Turcis enim contractam ex concubitu maculam balneo abftergere confueverunt. Hæc hyemi inferviunt ; æftivis menfibus fœminis immixti mares fluminibus innatant toto corpore nudi, nullâ fexûs verecundiâ, nullâ fenii, aut inno- centis ætatis diftinctione habitâ.† Eâdem impu- dentiâ, nullâ fubuculâ tecti, ex aquis in gramina profiliunt, neminis afpectum veriti : quin ipfæ

---

* In thofe parts of the Eaft of Europe where there is a large Jewifh populace, you rarely hear a converted Jew called a Chriftian. A belief that, even after baptifm, they continue fecret practices of Judaifm, and diflike for their fordid nature, ftamps them with the name of *baptifed Jews*, or *Neophites;* and thefe names remain as a ftigma for generations attached to a family.—TRANSL.

† Not merely in Ruffia, but in Ruffian Poland in the heat of fummer, fuch fhamelefs promifcuous bathing ftill occurs in the ftreams and ponds along the very highways ; as the paffing traveller may have had to remark.

etiam puellæ nudi corporis fpeciem fine fronte
prætereuntibus objedant, non mediocre libidinis
incitamentum. Meritò porro ambigitur, utrum
major fit eorum fævitia, an luxuria et impro-
bitas: nam fcortationes, adulteria et ejufmodi
facinora omnem fuperant modum; cùm vix
pœna ulla legibus conftituta fit in ejufmodi
delinquentes. Indè Capitaneum quendam ob
nefarium cum filiâ suâ odenni commercium
ad capitis pœnam damnatum, hifce Campi
Dux objurgavit: " Cur libidinem tuam non
in alias exercuifti? Cùm tot fcorta et mere-
trices habere potuiffes, quot kopicas aut altinos
exfolviffes."

The flavery laws are in vigour among the
Mufcovites. Some become flaves by captivity,
others are fo by birth, many from being fold by
their fathers, or by themfelves: for if they be
manumitted by their dying mafters, fo accuftomed are they to flavery, that they make themfelves over as flaves to other mafters, or bind
themfelves flaves for a fum of money. Even
freemen that ferve mafters for regular wages
cannot leave their mafter's fervice at will; for
fhould fuch a one quit without his mafter's con-

fent, no other will take him into his fervice,
unlefs his former mafter or one of his friends
recommend him, and anfwer for his being truftworthy.

Paternal authority is ample enough alfo,
and preffes very feverely upon the fon, for the
father has the right of felling him four times
over. Thus, if after being once fold, he fhould
recover his liberty in any way, or be manumitted by his mafter, the paternal rights entitle
his father to fell him over and over again; but
after the fourth fale his father is allowed no
further power over him. However, in the
actual pofition of affairs, now that Mufcovy poffeffes a monarch whofe intellect is fo highly
gifted by nature, and who is urged on by the
wonderful ftimulus of glory, people opine that a
milder ftatute will be fubftituted for this very
crude authority of parents over their fons.
Though, in truth, the nation itfelf has fuch
a diflike of liberty, that it feems to exclaim
againft a happinefs for which it was not
created, and is fo inured to its flavifh condition that it will fcarcely endure the prudent
and kindly folicitude of the Prince for his

dominions and his subjects to be carried out to the full extent.

What they tell of the unconquerable stubbornness of this race under the most exquisite tortures is scarcely within the bounds of credibility. Before the Czar's travels abroad, one of the accomplices of the revolt of 1696 had already four times borne tortures of the most exquisite agony without the least confession of guilt; and the Czar, perceiving that tortures were of no avail, turned to enticements, and having kissed the person under the question (*osculo inquisito dato*) thus spoke to him—" It is no secret to me that thou hast knowledge of the treason attempted against me. Thou hast been punished enough; now confess of thy own accord out of the love that thou owest to thy Prince; and by that God, by whose singular grace I am thy Czar and Prince, I swear, not alone wholly to pardon thy guilt, but moreover, as a special testimony of my clemency, to make thee a colonel." This strange friendliness of such a mighty Prince bent the fierce nature of that iron man; and taking the freedom of returning the Czar's embrace, he thus began—" For me this is the greatest of all tortures; by no other ſhouldſt thou have ever vanquiſhed my determination," and thereupon he proceeded to unfold at great length the whole ſeries of the treaſon.

The Czar, carried away with wonder, that a man who had remained ſilent under ſuch awfully cruel tortures, ſhould be ſo ſoftened with one little kindneſs, having aſked him how he could have borne ſo many ſtrokes of the knout and the dreadful torture of fire applied to his back, he began another and more ſtupendous tale. He ſtated that he and his accomplices had founded a kind of aſſociation ; that nobody was admitted into it without being previouſly tortured ; that he that was found capable of bearing the moſt pain was afterwards decreed higher honours by the others; that a perſon who was only once tortured was a ſimple aſſociate and participator in the common advantages; that anybody who aſpired to the higher grades of diſtinction was not to receive them until he had undergone freſh tortures, and had proved that he could bear more in proportion to the eminence of the dignity ; that he had been tortured himſelf ſix times, and was the preſident of the whole ſociety;

that the knout was a mere nothing; that the
roasting of the flesh after knouting was nothing;
that he had had to go through far more cruel
pains among his associates: "for," continued
he, "the sharpest pain of all is when a burning
coal is placed in the ear; nor is it less painful
when the head is shaved, and extremely cold
water is let to fall slowly drop by drop upon it
from a height of two ells." He said that in all
these things he had surpassed himself and his
associates; and that those who, after being aspi-
rants for membership, were found unable to go
through the first tortures, were made away with
by poison, or in some other way, for fear they
should betray. That as far as he could remember, at least four hundred such inapt candidates
had been killed by himself and his comrades.
Thus this fellow bore ten times the most unheard
of tortures; six times from his associates, and
four times in the inquiry before the Czar. He
is still living, and, as I have set down above, is
now by the Czar's clemency a colonel and away
in Siberia.

A case of similar stubbornness occurred when
the Czar was returning to Moscow from Vienna.

He had already paffed Smolenfko and was approaching his capital, when one of his fuite, terrified at having committed fome flagrant act, fought fafety in flight. The inquirers could find no indication of the direction or road he had taken : when at length a peafant from the next hamlet came and faid that indeed he knew no particulars about the fugitive, but that he had feen a horfe in a neighbour's houfe. The Czar detained the informer, and fent off Mr. Adam Weyd to the houfe defignated, to obtain more pofitive information. He faw the horfe, and on his return confirmed the peafant's ftory to the Czar. So the owner of the cottage was brought up, and the Czar inquired civilly of him about the man and the horfe. But the hind denied any knowledge of a horfe being at his houfe. The Czar repeated the queftion in a grave tone : but the fellow perfifted in his denial. The Czar urged him to remember that he was fpeaking to his fovereign, the lord of his limbs, in whofe power were life and death. But the thick-fkulled clown was not in the leaft moved by the threat. The Czar in confequence commanded him to be thrown down on the ground and

dreadfully beaten from head to foot with a great
knotty ftick. When on further interrogation he
ftill would confefs nothing, he was again moft
violently thrafhed from top to toe. Still the
fellow remained contumacioufly filent. They
rolled him over again and almoft beat him to a
mummy. But ftill at every invitation of the
knotty club, the mangled ruftic lay like a block
and ftubbornly denied. To fuch obftinate ftub-
bornnefs are the fouls of thefe Mufcovites
hardened, that no torments—nay, not the very
prefence of their fovereign—can bend them to
confefs the moft manifeft truth. For it was
found out fhortly after by true and indubitable
proof, that this very ruftic had kept the horfe,
and had fent off the fugitive, with his brother
as guide, by fecret paths beyond Smolenfko.

OF FEMALE LUXURY.

The women of Mufcovy are graceful in figure,
and fair and comely of feature : but fpoil their
beauty with needlefs fhams. Their fhapes, unim-
prifoned by ftays, are free to grow as nature bids,
and are not of fo neat and trim figure as thofe of

other Europeans. They wear chemifes inter-
woven with gold all through, the fleeves of which
are plaited up in a marvellous way, being eight
and fometimes ten ells in length, and their pretty
concatenation of little plaits extends down to the
hands, and is confined with handfome and coftly
bracelets. Their outer garments refemble thofe
of Eaftern women : they wear a cloak over their
tunic. They often drefs in handfome filks and
furs, and earrings and rings are in general fafhion
among them. Matrons and widows cover the
head with furs of price : maidens only wear a
rich band round their forehead and go bare-
headed, with their locks floating upon their
fhoulders, and arranged with great elegance in
artificial knots.

Thofe of any dignity or honourable condition
are not urged to be prefent at banquets, nor do
they even fit at the ordinary table of their
hufbands. They may be feen, neverthelefs, at
prefent when they go to church or drive out to
vifit their friends; for there has been a great
relaxation of the jealous old rule which required
women only to go out in carriages fo clofed up,
that the very ufe of eyefight was denied to thefe

creatures made bond-flaves to a mafter. More-over, they hold it among the greateft honours that can be paid if a hufband admits his gueft to fee his wife or daughters, who prefent a glafs of brandy, and expect a kifs from the favoured gueft; and, according to the manner of this people, duly propitiated with this, they withdraw in filence, as they came. They exercife no authority in their houfeholds. When the mafter is abfent from home, the fervants have full charge of the ma-nagement of the affairs of the houfe, according to their honefty or caprice, without afking or acquainting the wife about anything. But the more wealthy maintain great crowds of hand-maidens, who do fcarcely any work, except what trifling things the wife may require of them; meantime, they are kept fhut up in the houfe, and fpin and weave linen. With fuch a lazy life one cannot blame the cuftom which condemned the poor creatures to fuch frequent ufe of the bath, fo that their idlenefs may be at leaft varied from time to time with another defcription of floth.

Whenever the wife of a man of the higher claffes is delivered of a child, they fignify it without delay to the *employés* and tradefmen, with rather a beggarly kind of civility. Thofe who dread the hufband's power, or are ambitious of his patronage, on receiving notice of the new birth, come to offer their congratulations in return ; and giving a kifs to the mother, they prefent fome offering as a token for the new-born babe. They had better beware not to give lefs than a gold piece, for that would be a kind of vilipending ; but everybody is free to be more generous in his gift. He that is found to be the moft liberal will be deemed the beft friend. What the poet fang of the populace, I apply with greater juftice to the Mufcovites—the Muf-covite tefts friendfhip by its utility. It is a fable that they value the affection of their hufbands for them by the amount of blows they receive from them ; for they know how to diftinguifh between ferocious and gentle characters better than words can tell. If any perfon of weight were to make a beginning of abandoning the old ufage, they would certainly ftruggle from beneath that moft vile bondage in which they are held towards their hufbands.

The Mufcovites hold it finful to marry a

fourth wife; in confequence of which the third is in general treated famoufly, although her two predeceffors are treated like bond-flaves; for the thoughts of a new wife, and their inordinate defires, induce them to wifh for their fpeedy death, and render the charms of the firft loathfome, perhaps even within the brief fpace of a year. It is quite a proverb, that a pope may have one and a layman a third wife. Becaufe when thefe die it is unlawful for them to marry again, and the Mufcovites treat thefe with true marital affection, as they never can expect to marry again when thefe die. Neverthelefs, fome of the more powerful extort a difpenfation from the Patriarch to marry a fourth time; and the Patriarch, even though he does not refufe it, ftill blames them as facrilegious nuptials, that are null in virtue of the immutable authority of the prohibitive law. The Don Coffacks have another cuftom. They may repudiate women *ad libitum*, provided it be in the circle of the whole community, which affembly they call a Krug. In prefence of the *Atamann** and the entire community the man

---

* "*Coram Ottomanno*," *i.e.*, the Hetmann.—TRANSL.

leads his wife into the middle of the circle, and proclaims that fhe pleafes him no longer; this faid, he twirls his wife round about, and letting her go, pronounces her free from his marital authority. The byftander who takes hold of the difcarded woman is compelled to keep her as a wife, and protect and maintain her until the next affembly day. Still the laws of thefe bar-barians have eftablifhed rules for repudiations; fo that they are not valid, except in circle and with the whole community as witneffes.

Thefe cuftoms differ but flightly from that whereby men of free condition, in Turkey, join in wedlock with their female flaves before the Woivode: an affociation of man and woman which is the next thing to concubinage: for the bond may be diffolved at the man's caprice. One intending to take a wife in this way goes before the Woivode and acquaints him with his intention. The latter, when about to join thefe perfons, afks them for a belt (*cingulum*) and a little chaplet of flowers (*ftrophiolum*) from the woman, and the propofal being made to the woman, and a certain dowry promifed,—for example, fifty imperials,—he gives the belt to the woman and the chaplet to the man, then takes note of the date and what takes place, and writes down ſome particular marks of the parties. When the man becomes tired of the woman, he has to call again on the Woivode, before whom the affair muſt be laid again ; and he, for a fee of two or three imperials—having firſt exacted the promiſed dowry for the woman—demands back from the man the chaplet he formerly received, and the belt from the woman, and, returning the belt to the man and the chaplet to the woman, he diſſolves the marriage, and pronounces both free.

OF MARRIAGES.

The faſhion of their marriage differs in no ſlight degree from the mode which a long ſeries of ages has ſanctioned in other countries. For among them the men are not accuſtomed to ſee or ſpeak to the girl they want to marry ; the queſtion is popped through the mother, or ſome other old woman, when the parents, without whoſe conſent they conſider marriage to be illicit, have agreed about the dowry, which is ſometimes proportioned to the wealth of the old people. For it is not ufual among them for the hufband to promife anything, nor have they any word to exprefs a donation on account of marriage. But if the hufband die without iffue of the marriage, the widow receives as much as fhe brought, provided the hufband has left property to that amount. If, however, fhe has had children by him, fhe takes the third part of the goods, or more, according to her hufband's will. Finally, they draw up the marriage articles, in which the girl's parents warrant her undefiled ; whence many lawfuits arife, if the hufband fhould have the leaft fufpicion that fhe was previoufly feduced. When thefe are completed, the betrothed girl fends the firft gift to her intended, which he reciprocates. Still, they are neither allowed to fee nor fpeak to one another. When the promife of marriage has been given, the father fummons his daughter, who comes covered with a linen veil into his prefence ; and afking her whether fhe be ftill minded to marry, he takes up a new rod, which has been kept ready for the purpofe, and ftrikes his daughter lightly once or twice, faying, " Lo ! my darling daughter, this is the laft that shall admonish thee of thy father's authority, beneath whose rule thou hast lived until now. Now thou art free from me. Remember that thou hast not so much escaped from sway, as rather passed beneath that of another. Shouldst thou behave not as thou oughtest towards thy husband, he in my stead shall admonish thee with this rod." With this the father, concluding his speech, stretches at the same time the whip to the bridegroom, who, excusing himself briefly, according to custom, says that he "believes he shall have no need of this whip;" but he is bound to accept it, and put it up under his belt, like a valuable present.

Now, towards the evening which precedes the solemn nuptials, the bride is conducted by her mother and other matrons in a carriage, or, if it be winter, in a sledge, with her marriage *trousseau* and a nuptial bed, elegantly appareled, to the bridegroom's house, and there she is guarded over-night, so that she may not be seen by her husband. Early in the morning of the day appointed for the marriage ceremony the bride, with a linen veil which covers her from the head to below the middle, is conducted to church by

her parents and friends; the bridegroom, on his
part, being accompanied by his friends; even
poor men uſing horſes, though the church may
be cloſe to their door. The ceremonies and
words which the prieſt makes uſe of hardly differ
from thoſe uſed among other Chriſtians. It is
with a ring that the pledge of fidelity is ratified,
and the hand of the bride is put into the hand
of the bridegroom, which done, the bride falls to
the bridegroom's feet and touches his ſhoes with
her forehead, in token of ſubjection; and the
bridegroom, in his turn, puts his tunic over her,
in teſtimony that he undertakes to protect her.
Then the kinsfolk and friends bow to both bridegroom and bride, as a pledge of mutual willing-
neſs to oblige and of friendſhip to be cheriſhed.
Finally, the bridegroom's father preſents a loaf
to the prieſt, who forthwith hands it to the
bride's father, begging him to pay the dowry he
has promiſed to the bridegroom on the day
appointed, and henceforward to maintain invio-
late friendſhip with him and his friends. In like
manner, too, he breaks the bride's loaf into
many pieces, and diſtributes a bit to each of the
relations and connections preſent, to ſignify that

they fhould henceforward be kneaded together like a loaf.

Thefe ceremonies being at an end, the bridegroom leads the bride by the hand to the church porch, and pours out a cup of hydromel for her, which fhe fips beneath her veil, and thus both return with their friends to the houfe of the parents—Ubi fub ingreffum farre afperguntur in fignum fœcunditatis et opulentiæ. Hofpitibus convivantibus, neonuptos confumare oportet: poftquam duabus, aut tribus circiter horis foli in lecto acquieverint, ex convivarum numero aliqui ad eos delegantur, ut fcifitentur ex fponfo, num fponfam adhuc incorruptam invenerit; fi fponfus affirmat exuberenti hofpitum gaudio, multis que tripudiis neonupti ad caldarium deducuntur, diverfis floribus, herbifque odoriferis exornatum. Ex quo ad fufficientem amœnitatem loti reducuntur ad templum continuandæ benedictionis uberiorem cumulum percepturi. Si verò ante vitiatam fuiffe fponfus conqueratur, ad parentes fponfa remittitur repudiata. Quo judicio probetur virginitas, addere non patitur temporis noftri caftitas.

THE QUALITIES OF THE SOIL AND CLIMATE:
FERTILITY AND RIVERS.

The foil of this region is for the moft part light and fandy : the proportion of fand being, however, more or lefs according to the different provinces. The region to the north, towards Siberia and the Samoiëds, is nearly barren ; the extent of the forefts, and the extreme rigour of the cold, condemning the land to fterility. The foil along the banks of the Volga is commendable for its grateful fertility ; but as the country there is obnoxious to the conftant inroads of the Crim Tartars, the land lies untilled, and that region is almoft quite uninhabited. All the regions fouthward are pleafant and fertile : rich paftures and corn lands lie there, and are watered by feveral rivers. The face of the country is the fame from Refon to Grate Novogrod ; nor is that which lies between Mofcow and Smolenfko very different, though frequent and denfe forefts give it a peculiar charaĉter. But the feafon of the year makes a vaft difference in the appearance of all thefe provinces ; for in the winter

months they are covered with exceedingly deep
fnow, efpecially northwards ; all the rivers are
imprifoned in very thick ice, and that for feveral
months together—generally during five—beginning with the month of November, and lafting
until the end of March, and often of April;
for then the fnows firft begin to melt, and the
ice to thaw.

The climate during thofe months is cold
beyond imagination, fo that drops of water
thrown upwards congeal before they fall.
They remember a cold fo penetrating, that
many in the very markets, and all who were
out in the fields, either utterly perifhed, or
hardly efcaped with the lofs of their extremities.
We did not experience fuch extremely fevere
cold in our time ; and, therefore, I only affirm
what was ftated by others, the length of whofe
ftay in Mufcovy fhould, I think, obtain for
them fomewhat of authority and credence.
Such is the real ftate of thefe regions in winter.
When fpring commences again, a change fo rapid
takes place, that fuddenly the woods are green
again, the grafs burfts forth, the flowers bloffom,
the crops germinate, the birds, particularly night-

ingales, fing everywhere fo fweetly that it feems as if nothing could be added to fuch magic enchantment.

The earth of thefe regions is confidered to derive a kind of advantage from the fnows, which are exceedingly deep, and cover the earth like a garment that protects it from being parched up with the froft; and again, on the other hand, at the beginning of fpring, thefe fnows are diffolved and liquefied in a very brief fpace, and the foil, which, as we have faid, is light and fandy, imbibes the humidity largely and very fpeedily, and when ftruck by the fun's rays, fends up every defcription of vegetation with great rapidity. Moreover, in proportion as the cold of the winter months is intenfe, fo the heat of the fummer in June, July, and Auguft, is beyond meafure ; fo that the fruits of the earth are by that means brought to maturity very rapidly. Moreover, the greater part of Ruffia abounds in fprings, and is watered with rivulets, lakes, and ftreams.

In fine, an advantage of the country refulting from its being permeated by vaft and very deep rivers, has been that Ruffia is rendered apt for

commerce even into the depths of her moft remote provinces. The principal of thefe rivers are
—1ft, the Volga, anciently called the Rha, and
by the Tartars named the Edel, which rifes forty
German miles above Jaroflaw out of lake Volgo,
and after receiving a great many tributary ftreams
from either fide, fpreads to a mile in width at
Jaroflaw, and after having moreover received
the river Occa at Nifinovogorod, rolls itfelf,
by many huge mouths, into the Cafpian Sea.
2nd, the Boryfthenes, now the Neper, or Dneper,
which, rifing not far from the metropolis of
Mufcovy, clofe to the hamlet of Dneperfko,
feparates Ruffia from Lithuania, near Oczakow,
a town belonging to the Perecop Tartars, and
difcharges itfelf into the Black Sea. 3rd, the
Tanais, commonly called the Don, the ancient
boundary between Afia and Europe, which,
rifing in Refan Ofera, takes a ftraight eafterly
courfe at firft through the lands of the Perecop
Tartars, and falls, not far from the river Volga,
into the Palus Meotides, near Azow, after being
fwollen by fome tributary ftreams. By this river
they go by water from the city of Mofcow to
Conftantinople, defcending by the river Mofkwa

into the Occa, the veffel being dragged acrofs
a narrow ifthmus, and again fet afloat upon the
latter ftream. 4th, the Dwina, which has its
fource in the province of Vologda, takes a great
bend, defcends right towards Arctum (*Aretum
verfus*), and lofes itfelf by fix mouths in the
gulf of Saint Nicholas; it is formed by the
junction of two ftreams, the Jug, and the
Suchana, whence its name of Dwina, which
means double in Ruffian. 5th, the Duna, which
rifes in the province of Novogrod, flows through
Livonia, and falls by Riga into the Baltic Sea.
6th, the Onega. 7th, the Suchana. 8th, the
Ocka. 9th, the Mofkwa. 10th, the Wichida,
befides feveral leffer ftreams, whofe beds are of
vaft extent, divide various provinces of Mufcovy.

Out of thefe rivers they bring to Mofcow a
vaft quantity of the fineft fifh, and of the kinds
that are moft rare elfewhere; and there for the
mereft trifle are fold, the fifh of which I have
already mentioned the names. Partridge, wild
duck, and other wild fowl, which the luxury of
numbers of people render exceedingly coftly in
other countries, are here fold for almoft nothing;
a partridge can be bought for two or three

kopeks—one kopek being the equivalent of two
kreuzers—and other birds are cheap in proportion. The Mufcovites confider hares to be
unclean, fo that they cannot eat them themfelves ; but they fell them to the Germans for
three or four kopeks; and venifon is quite as
cheap. An ox may be fometimes had for four or
five imperials ; a calf for ten or twelve kopeks.
They have learnt from Germans how to fow,
cultivate, and propagate lettuce, cabbages, and
feveral other garden products. Aftracan produces melons; Kiow, nuts and grapes; and
Mufcovy produces in profufion moft beautiful
tranfparent apples, which many of the warmeft
countries might envy, and which they call *Nolivas.*
Although in our time there was fome fcarcity of
bread in the remoter provinces of Mufcovy, ftill,
fo great is the plenty in ordinary feafons, that
there is more than is wanted for confumption.
The land is naturally fertile enough, if it were
not left in uncultivated fterility by the lazinefs of
the people.

The moft illuftrious lord* Francis, Jacobeïdes
Lefort, is the firft general and admiral of the fleet.
Of the reformed religion in Mufcovy, a native
of Geneva, he came along with two or three
companions more than twenty years ago, by way
of the White Sea, into Mufcovy, to feek his
fortune ; and he found what he fought. For in
the year '88, on the outbreak of a revolt, their
Czarifh Majefties had betaken themfelves to a
monaftery, called Droyza, as a place of fecurity,
in confequence of the open and fanguinary in-
fanity of the archers, otherwife called Strelitz,
which was not only raging againft the Boyars
with a blind and promifcuous cruelty, without
the leaft confideration for perfonal worth, but
was alfo athirft for the blood of their youthful
princes.

In this day of peril, when the loyalty of a
great many was fhaken, and deliberating which

---

* Illuftriffimus Dominus Francifcus Jacobeides Lefort, *i.e.*,
Francis, *fon of James*, according to the Ruffian fafhion of adding
the father's Chriftian name.—TRANSL.

fide to take, for the ftorm menaced an uncertain
iffue,—while fortune was, fo to fpeak, in doubt to
whom thofe vaft dominions were due,—in that
hour of direful danger, this Mr. Lefort ftarted
for Droyza, with a very fmall number of his
foldiers, marching refolutely in advance of fortune's decree, and not lagging behind it. This
loyalty, that never flinched for an inftant in the
very face of peril, raifed him to that high place
in the Czar's affection which even perverfe envy
cannot deny he deferved. Often hath fortune
fhaken off from her wheel, in the long run,
many a one that long flourifhed in royal favour.
The ftormy waves have fometimes reached this
man too ; but ftill we faw the Czar's attachment
to him live through them, unaltered by the fates,
to the envy of all the natives. Four years
before his death he fent his only fon to Geneva
to receive a polite education. The Grand Duke
himfelf was pleafed, along with his chief minifters, to accompany this youth fome miles on his
way. When Lefort's nephew was coming into
Mufcovy, his majefty went three miles out to
meet him, and gave him a valuable drefs of his
own. Perhaps he would have preferred to ex-

perience the greatnefs of the Czar's love and affection for him by fome other kind of proof, but he could not have defired a more certain one than that which he received. He exhibited his real merit towards the Czar, when, notwithftand-ing the refiftance of the entire council of the Boyars, he quickened his foul with the ftimulus of glory to warlike virtue. Hence it was by the Czar's aufpices, and not by the general's, that Azow, that ftronghold of the *Palus Meotides,* was wrefted from the Perecop Tartars. For though General Lefort, out of a horror of danger, never went near the works of the foldiers himfelf during the fiege, ftill he judged contempt of danger to be the ftamp of a great foul. It was he that was the caufe of the recent grand embafly of the Czar, and he began it at a happy moment ; for it was a great matter for Mufcovy to conclude a league with the moft auguft Emperor, which was an ample fecurity againft foreign enemies. The Perecop Tartars would affuredly have been driven as exiles out of their peninfula, and have been caft out of the Crimea, without a place to pafture their flocks, and the Mufcovite arms, after the ftorming of the fortrefs of Oczakow, might have carried terror with a victorious fleet beneath the very walls of the Conftantinopolitan Porte, if at the opportune moment of the league they had attacked the enemy with force equal to their fame. No Mufcovite can deny that the public fervice and the advantage of his prince were always his foremoft anxiety.

Freedom of coming and going was formerly denied to foreigners by a rude law, but has been allowed at his fuggeftion by the prefent Czar. He marvelloufly promoted the interefts of commerce to the no fmall increafe of the public wealth; nor is it lefs to his praife, that foreigners, whom they were in years gone by in the habit of coercing to embrace their religion, often with hunger and imprifonment, threats and tortures, are now left free in their own religion; on account of faith being a gift of God, which the Almighty beftows, and which force cannot inculcate. What will be the confequence of this fending of youth into foreign countries? If by their idlenefs they do not cheat the hopes preconcevied of them, they will adorn the greatnefs of Mufcovy with their counfels, will add to it by their experience, will guard her with their prudence and fortitude. How ftoutly he bore the anger of his prince when ftorming againft him, thofe who were prefent at what happened at Pilaw and Königfberg are never tired of proclaiming. Attached to the reformed religion, he could not conceal his inborn hatred of the orthodox, indulging even in feverity towards his own wife on that account, until the Czar, with the greateft and moft praifeworthy good temper fet bounds to the cruelties which he exercifed towards her. Stumpf, the paftor of thofe of the reformed opinions, publicly inveighed from the pulpit againft his inordinate defires. In other refpects, conciliating the good will of his prince by his loyalty, his equals by his obligingnefs, and all by his courteoufnefs, he ufed with moderation the authority to which he had attained. When he died, of an inflammatory fever, the regrets of numbers, and the tears of Majefty followed him to the grave. His annual falary was a thoufand roubles.

The moft illuftrious Sir Patrick de Gordon, a fcion of an exceedingly noble ftock in Scotland, ferved firft in the Swedifh and afterwards in the Polifh armies. Taken prifoner by the adverfe fate of war, he confented, on being preffed, to ferve under the Mufcovite ftandard, and gave fuch noble proof of his valour, that he was raifed to the fupreme military command, and ftood long without a rival. At length, the envy of Bafil Galizin burft out againft him—the fame Galizin who was the minifter of Sophia's ambition when fhe trampled on the tender years of the Czar by a haughty ufurpation of the fovereign power, and who now, punifhed as he deferved, pays the penalty of his attempts upon authority, in Siberian exile. He would have driven Gordon from the very apex of military rank down to the laft grade of a non-commiffioned officer ; but, trying his envious bite upon the very fharp knotted club of Hercules, he only gored his own jaws. For being convicted of an illegal correfpondence with the lily-bearing folk,* againft the ftate interefts of Mufcovy, he would, beyond all hope, have loft both life and fortune at one blow, if the Czar, who was then about laying the foundations of his power and his clemency together, had not fent the convict into exile.

---

* The French : from the Bourbon *fleur de-lis.*—TRANSL.

Galizin found out how eafy is the way from home into; banifhment ; while Gordon, on the other hand, who had bravely borne for a while his undeferved lot, and the fevere oppreffion of envy, being reftored by the Czar's clemency to his former rank as General, learnt, to his profit, that many are raifed by emulation above others, and that envy makes the fortune of many. He performed his military duties with prudence ; nor will the Mufcovites deny him, when dead, the honour they owed him living. Always cautious, he had the care and welfare of his prince fo much at heart, and with fuch circum- fpect fidelity, that he never could be reproached with a rafh act. Still, Mufcovy liked his counfel better than his perfon ; ufing the man's fagacity as often as they had in hand any matter of peculiar difficulty to decide upon. He is faid to be the originator of the fcheme, when his prince was going to travel for awhile abroad, of dividing the authority of the Regency between three rivals, fo that through the ardour of mutual rivalry they fhould adminifter everything per- taining to the tranquillity of the ftate with the more loyalty, and that none fhould reach that power of which all were ambitious. Nor would the honour of the Crofs of Malta have been purchafed at fuch coft,* if the popular favour, inclining too much towards a certain perfon, had not given rife to a fufpicion of danger, fuch as often transferred kingdoms; for fometimes it has been rather a punifhment than an honour to be fent on foreign embaffies and into ftrange countries. What, for example, is more common than to banifh from a capital, under the deceitful mafk of honour, thofe whofe power or popularity gives grounds for apprehenfion? Simple, indeed, but ftill, fhould a fortunate occafion offer, ready to dare; prudence of counfel, ripenefs of judgment, and a folicitude that prepared beforehand for every contingency, adorned Gordon. He had fo won the Mufcovites, who are by nature hoftile to ftrangers, and hate a diftinguifhed foreigner, by his heedleffnefs of his own renown, and his charming fociability, that when an inteftine tumult arofe, his houfe afforded a fafe and fecure afylum to the very natives. Often called *Father* by his fovereign, honoured

* Szeremetow.

by the Boyars, worſhipped by the Dumnoi, dear
to the nobles, and loved by the people, he
gained ſuch authority with them all, as a native
could hardly have aſpired to. A great artiſt
in pretexts and diſſimulation, conformably to
Ariſtotle's admonition, ſaying nothing to the
ruler of Muſcovy except what he knew would
pleaſe, left, while he ſtudied the advantage
of others, he ſhould damage himſelf and his
family.

My aſtoniſhment knew no bounds when, upon
my complaint of ſervants of the Imperial Lord
Envoy having been inſulted by ſoldiers, and
demanding ſatisfaction in the Lord Envoy's
name, when I touched upon the immunity of
ambaſſadors, which is ſanctioned by the common
law of nations, he replied that an ambaſſador
was not free in Muſcovy, and that delinquents
might be carried off to puniſhment from the
ambaſſador's court by lictors. No caſe, however,
occurred in our time to afford us experience of
what truth there may be in this. What happened to the Swediſh marſhal was limited by
peculiar circumſtances; nor am I of opinion that
that immunity of ambaſſadors, which is every-

where maintained with fo much jealoufy by thofe
who are fent abroad in that dignified capacity, is
abrogated by any pofitive decifion to the contrary
in Ruffia; for if fo, the natural confequence
would be that the Ruffians would place themfelves beyond the pale of other nations by a law
fo barbarous and uncivilifed.

In fine, Gordon, who was a man advanced in
years, died moft devoutly at eight o'clock in the
morning of the 9th of December, 1699, after
our departure from Mufcovy, on which occafion
he had accompanied us as far as Filli. His
Majefty the Czar vifited him five times during
his laft illnefs, and on the laft night was with
him twice, and with his own hands clofed his
eyes after his fpirit had fled. His Majefty the
Czar knew how great was the lofs of fuch a
man to him, and therefore gave orders that the
funeral of General Gordon fhould be conducted
with the fame pomp as had been appointed for
General Lefort. Three regiments of the Guards
accompanied it in mourning, the trumpets and
drums refounding fadly, the Czar occupying his
ufual place in the regiment; four-and-twenty
great guns were fired, giving a character of grief

or applaufe to the funeral. The fervice, facrifice, and fermon were duly performed by the Imperial miffionary, Mr. John Berula, by command of the Czar. The Czarewicz and the Czar's favourite fifter, Nathalia, were prefent at the devotions in the Catholic church, the day before. Gordon's annual ftipend was alfo fixed at a thoufand roubles.*

* " Patrick Gordon, of Achleuris," fays Von Adelung (*Kritifche-Liter. Ueberficht der Reifenden in Ruffland,* vol. ii.), " a fcion " of a diftinguifhed Scottifh family in the county of Aberdeen, " was born on the 31st May, 1635. In the year 1651 he was " fent to Braunfberg, to complete his education in the Jefuits' " College there. But after three years he ran away fecretly from " that inftitution to return home to his own country. Arrived in " Hamburgh he was induced to enter the Swedifh fervice, and then " began that feries of martial adventures in which five diftinct " times he was a prifoner of war, paffed into Polifh and Bran- " denburg fervices, and finally, in 1661, into Ruffia; where he " entered as major into the fervice of Alexis Michaelowicz. In " 1667 he was fent on a miffion to England, returned in the " following year back to Ruffia, and from that time until his death " remained in the home of his adoption. Peter the Great had " learnt to value and efteem the brave and clear-fighted warrior, " and beftowed upon him his entire truft. On the 9th of " December, 1699, Gordon died General-in-Chief, in Mofcow, " where Peter the Great vifited him feveral times during his ill- " nefs, and was with him at the moment when his foul departed " from its mortal coil."

" Gordon left him," adds Von Adelung, "an autograph " journal in the Englifh language, wherein he wrote his life from " the time of his birth until the year 1699, and which is preferved " in MS., in fix quarto volumes, which are in the Imperial

Adam Weyd, born in Muſcovy of German parents, diſliking the profeſſion of phyſic, entered the army. By his own induſtry he learnt ſo well from books the art of conſtructing mines, that he became known and eſteemed by his ſovereign. But all his ſedulous labour in conſtructing mines, at the ſiege of Azow, with the conſent of his prince,

"archives at Moſcow. A copy, in five quarto volumes, belongs "to the Imperial Hermitage, and one volume has been trans- "lated into Ruſſian by Herr von Kohler, junior. Müller has "printed ſeveral extracts from this MS. journal in the ſecond "volume of his Samml. Ruſs. Geſch. ; and among others, the "narrative of Gordon's campaign againſt the Tartars in the "year 1687." (*See Bd. II.*, pp. 441—178).

"Gordon left three ſons and one daughter who later was mar- "ried ſecondly to Major-General Alexander Gordon. The laſt- "mentioned is author of an account of Peter the Great, which "was printed under the following title :—

"'The Hiſtory of Peter the Great, Emperor of Ruſſia, to "'which is prefixed a ſhort General Hiſtory of the Country from "'the riſe of that Monarchy. By Alexander Gordon, of Achin- "'toul, Aberdeen. 1755. 2 vols. 8vo.'"

A German tranſlation of this work, by C. A. Wichmann, was publiſhed in 1765. 2 vols; 8vo.

Gordon's Biography may be found in Dr. Benj. Beckmann's Peter der Groſſe, als Menſch und Regent. Mittau, 1830. B. vi. pp. 175—185 ; alſo in Neues St. Peterſb. Journ. 1778. Bd. iv. April ; Korbs Diarium, p. 214 ; Beckmann's Lit. der Altern Reiſen. Bd. ii. p. 387 ; Müller's Samml. Ruſs. Geſch. Bd. ii. p. 141, &c.

What an intereſting publication would not Gordon's journal be at this moment ! How many curious details muſt be locked up in thoſe ſix quarto volumes of MS. which he left behind him ? —TRANSL.

turned out fo unfortunately, that inftead of hurting the enemy, againft whom they were directed, they only proved damaging to the Czar's foldiers, blowing fome hundreds of them that were on guard in the trenches into the air. He had the rank of Major when he was fent to announce the late grand Mufcovite embaffy to the Emperor's court. He was in the Imperial camp and accompanied the expedition when the moft auguft Emperor's General, the moft Serene Prince Eugene of Savoy routed the Turks with fuch dire flaughter at Zenta near the Theifs. He is never tired of acknowledging what an amount of experience of the art of war he drew from that *paleftra* of fo many heroes and moft gallant men. He piques himfelf on the moft Serene Prince Eugene of Savoy's having, with that innate politenefs which he fhows to everybody, even afked his advice. While we were ftill in Mofcow he folicited the title of brigadier-general, which is about the equivalent of major-general. They fay that now the two Generals, Lefort and Gordon, are dead, he afpires to the higheft military rank. He has felt the light-nings of wrathful Jupiter, nor will he ever forget the giddy and infecure freak that fortune played him at Veronaifch to teach him equanimity in adverfity as well as in fuccefs.

General Mengden has a falary of 600 roubles. The two brothers Riman are alfo Generals in Mufcovy; one of them, Charles, was flogged almoft to death (*pené ad mortem cæfus est*) for refufing to give up a German coat that he had, for theatricals.

There are a great number of colonels in Ruffia. Of thefe, Cafimir de Grage, a Catholic, an Imperial colonel of artillery, was fent by the moft auguft Emperor, about four years ago, to ferve the Czar. Next in rank to him are thofe who command the four regiments which they call the Guards: Baron de Blumberg, a member of the Courland nobility, of the confeffion of Augfburg; James Gordon, fon of General Gordon, a Catholic; Lima, a Catholic, whofe annual pay is two hundred roubles; Schambers (Chambers?*) is of the confeffion of Augfburg. There are feveral other colonels, but without

---

* Chambers was, I believe, a Scotch gentleman of the Chambers or Chalmers, Lairds of Balnacraig.—TRANSL.

regiments ; in time of peace, or when not actually engaged in war, they merely bear the name
of colonels, ſatisfied to live on half-pay as long
as they may live idly in Moſcow. Of this
number are Acchentowel,* from Scotland, a
Catholic; Palck de Werden, Meus, Brüſs
[*Bruce*], Junckmann, Jungers, Werner, Weſthof, Angler, Lefort, de Delden, Cimbier, Toubin.
Theſe are all ſectaries of the reformed or of the
Anglican confeſſion. The laſt-named, Toubin,
a man decrepit with age, ſpent thirteen years
miſerably in Siberia; his annual pay was not
above a hundred roubles, to which quite lately
twenty more have been added.

LIEUTENANT-COLONELS.

Of Germans† in the Muſcovite ſervice are:
Colom, Duprez, Levingſton [*Livingſton*], Bordwig [*Borthwick*], Rosſurm, Bogowſki, Salm,

---

* Alexander Gordon, of *Achintoul*, afterwards roſe to the
rank of Major-General, and left a hiſtory of Peter the Great,
which was printed at Aberdeen in two volumes 8vo. in 1755.—
TRANSL.

† As the reader has probably already remarked, our author
uſes the word *German* for all foreigners in Muſcovy. This probably ariſes from the fact, that the Ruſſians commonly uſe the
ſameword to expreſs a German and a foreigner.—TRANSL.

Brüſs [*Bruce*], Delden, Lipſdorf, Clemenz, Schlippenbach, Ronard.

MAJORS.

Meneſius [*Menzies*], Taurlaville, Straus, Schilling, Kleim, Niz, Oſtoja, Holſt, Goſt, Weber.

CAPTAINS.

Rickman, Gummert, Erckel, Baccho, Prinz, Gordon, Liman, Soes, Bock, Funck, Bordwig [*Borthwick*], Sawanſki, Frobes [*Forbes*], Weyd, Holſt, Polſt, Rosfurm, Kaldberner, Breyer, Grob, Zege de Manteifel, Weſthof, Meus, Goſt, Brand, Prinek, Hambel [*Campbell?*], Pablowſki, Berner, Winter, Engels, Robert, who was ſlain by the ſoldiers that he led to the nuns' monaſtery, two Müllers, Oſtrowſki, Fadenreich, Hochenrein, Edenbach, Elinhauſen, Kellinghauſen.

SEA CAPTAINS.

Bamberg, Kiehn, Meier, Reis, who alſo aċts as paymaſter.

LIEUTENANTS.

Prigen, who, for aſking for his diſcharge,

underwent the *battok* by order of Galizin, and is
banifhed to Cafan, Phograd [*Fogarty ?*], Lizkin,
Wud [*Wood ?*], Leiko, Faftman, Junger, Rickman ; the reft are Mufcovites.

Several of thefe officers are of Courland and
Livonian families. They come to Mufcovy
from thofe remote regions, and traverfe that
long and perilous route, induced to undertake
that long pilgrimage by the idea of fhaking off
the yoke of the Swedes, which they complain of
as intolerable and growing every day more op-
preffive. One of them, in familiar difcourfe
confidentially avowed to me that he had come to
Ruffia to find out whether the Grand Duke was
powerful enough and in a pofition to protect the
Livonians and defend them againft the violence
of the Swedes. He faid that there were others
for the fame purpofe of exploration in Poland :
for that Livonia wanted to throw off the yoke of
Sweden and transfer her allegiance to fome other
powerful neighbour, becaufe the king of Sweden
deprives the inhabitants of Livonia of all their
advantages, and every day burdens and oppreffes
them more and more with an almoft intolerable
amount of taxes and contributions. The fame

officer added, that after being a year and a half in Mufcovy he was unable to difcover that any help could be hoped for from the Mufcovites.

When his Majefty the Czar made war upon the Turks and Tartars, and defigned to caft them out of their ftronghold, he wrote friendly letters to the Imperial Court and fome other German powers, to afk for perfons fkilled in military engineering and the conftruction of mines. Thereupon, the following perfons were fent to him by the moft auguft Emperor of the Romans :—

Cafimer de Garge,* Colonel of Artillery ;
Baron de Borgsdorff,†
Laval,
Laurence Schmid,
Laurence Urban,
} Military engineers in chief;

and likewife fix miners with their non-commif-fioned officers.

---

* *Sic*, though elfewhere our author writes the fame officer's name De Grage.—Transl.

† *Sic*, though in other places throughout the book his name is written De Burckerfdorff, and De Burgfdorff.—Transl.

The moft ferene the Elector of Brandenburgh in like manner fent him :—

Rose,
Holtfman, } Military engineers ;

Johann-Jacob Schufter,
Elias Kober,
Samuel Hack, } Artillerymen.
Guftaf Gifewetter,

The moft puiffant the States of Holland fent the following individuals to Mufcovy :—

De Stamm,
Goufki,
Gordes [*Gorges ?*],
Schnid,
Sperreuther.

The merchants that live for the fake of trade at Mofcow, are moftly Englifhmen and Dutch. One Italian only has come to Mofcow, and ftill remains, Anthony Gufconi, a Catholic, from the dominions of the Grand Duke of Tufcany. There are a great many non-Catholics, fuch as Minder, Goll, Wolff, Brandt, Lipps, Popp, Leiden, Hackenbrandt, Ifenbrandt, Kannen-gieffer.

OF THE BOYARS AND PRINCIPAL STATESMEN
OF MUSCOVY.

Knes Bazil Galizin* was viceroy of the kingdoms of the Cafan and Aftracan, minifter of
foreign affairs,† and keeper of the Czar's feal.
A prime minifter indeed, and one whofe reputation for prudence and fortitude gave him fo
complete a fway over the minds of the youthful
Czars,‡ that he might be faid to reign in their
name. He combined political and military functions, contending with an exceeding powerful
army againft the barbarians, and fought to de-
ferve the fovereignty of Ruffia by counfel and
deed. Fortune flattered a hope fo impious, but

---

* The family of the Princes Galizin is ancient, very illuftrious
and ftill numerous in Ruffia. They are not, however, defcended
from Rurik, the grand progenitor of the old reigning dynafty of
Mofcow and its agnates, the majority of the prefent and extinct
princely families of the Ruffian empire. The Galizins, in common with the princely Polifh families of Wifzniowiecki, Czartorifki, and Sapieha, trace their origin to Guedemin, Grand Duke
of Lithuania, the anceftor of the Jagellon dynafty in Poland.—
(*Vide Notices des Principales Fam. de la Ruffie.* Paris, 1845).
—Transl.

† " *Negotiorum legatoriorum adminiftrator.*"—Orig.

‡ The brothers Ivan and Peter, who for a time reigned jointly.
The feeble Ivan refigned his fhare of authority to Peter in 1688,
and died in 1696.—Transl.

failed him at laft, when he daringly attempted
what was unlawful and too lofty, when coveting
that fovereign rank which he approached fo
nearly, and growing dizzy with the fatal defire
of poffeffing himfelf of the fceptre itfelf, he was
hurled by a fall moft grievous down to the
lowlieft lot of man in exile. Then were detected
the dangerous machinations of Horne, and the
peftilent counfels that had fo long been fold under
the pretence of the greateft friendfhip. This peft
was raging with irreparable damage at the time
when Bafil Galizin marched with an army againft
the Tartars. The Crimea contains a defert of
feveral hundred miles in extent by continual
devaftations; Galizin fet fire to the grafs of this
defert, under pretext of depriving the Tartars
of forage; but in reality, in order to celebrate
the obfequies of his troops amidft thofe moft
fatal pyres. For prefently, feigning that the
Tartars were rapidly approaching, he urged his
whole army to flight athwart the burning herb-
age. Many thoufands perifhed moft miferably,
ftifled in the black and peftilent fmoke. The
author of this immenfe difafter was foon clearly
known, and the councillor was found ftamped

upon the gold pieces which were diſcovered to
be the commoneſt coin among Galizin's treaſures.
He confeſſed himſelf that he was the fomenter
of that dreadful treaſon, and was ſtripped of all
that he poſſeſſed, and ſent at firſt to trap ſables
in Siberia. At preſent, through his prince's
indulgence and the commiſeration of ſome great
perſonages, he has had a reſidence nearer to
Moſcow aſſigned to him, and his daily maintenance, which in exile was fixed at one altin, is
now increaſed to ſeveral. He has another ſolace
in the company of his wife, the companion
of his misfortune, as ſhe was of his pro-
ſperity. His functions are now divided between
two.

Leo Kirilowicz Nareſkin obtained the adminiſtration of foreign affairs. His ſtepping-ſtone
to this eminent poſition was his ſiſter, Nathalia
Kirilowna, the mother of the preſent Czar.
There are ſome that envy him the name of
prime miniſter, becauſe, though young, he has
been ſet over the ambitious counſels of ſome
older men. But the eminence of the functions
which he performs, when compared with the
condition of his predeceſſors in that dignity,

ſeems to ſettle the whole diſpute. Always of an even temper, this man knows well the prerogative of the office which he bears, except when he happens to give ear to an evil counſellor. Ukrainzow is a man of conſiderable craft. Diak Boſnikow, too ſevere upon many. Nareſkin reckons ten thouſand ſerfs upon his property.

The ſupreme adminiſtration of the kingdom of Caſan and Aſtracan was given to Prince Boris Alexiowicz Galizin* upon the baniſhment of his brother Baſil, in conſequence of his being found perfectly innocent of his brother's crime. Theſe two great men, between whom the fortune of unhappy Baſil is divided, burning with mutual rivalry, cordially purſue one another with hatred, ſometimes without any diſguiſe. Each pretends that the other's office is an acceſſory of his own. Up to the preſent the Czar has not cared to give his attention to put an end to this ſtate of things, by taking his deciſion as maſter about their diſputations and quarrels—which are ſometimes ſlan-

---

* The Nariſckhins, who had then but juſt emerged from utter obſcurity, attained importance by marriage with the imperial houſe ; the mother of Czar Peter being of that family, and ſiſter of the prime miniſter ſo often mentioned in this Diary.—TRANSL.

derous. This Galizin has a ſaying that he eſteems *"the faith of the Ruſſian, the prudence of the German, and the fidelity of the Turk."* He is a moſt vehement zealot for the Ruſſian religion: he has earned the name of John the Baptiſt among the vulgar, for having induced ſo many foreigners to allow themſelves to be baptiſed again. Deſcended of a moſt ancient princely family, which traces its origin from a Poliſh ſtock, he keeps up a ſtately court, worthy of the exalted rank of his houſe. He maintains Italian architects in his ſervice, and has got them to build two moſt beautiful churches in his villages of Dobrowiza and Veſomba, everlaſting monuments to his renown and his prudence. Skilled in the Latin tongue himſelf, he has given his ſons Poliſh preceptors to teach it to them, conſcious of what advantage it will be to thoſe deſtined to have intercourſe with foreign nations.

Tichon Nikitowicz Streſnow was the Czar's guardian during his minority. He is now preſident of the Chancery of Ukaſes (*Cancellariæ ordinatoriæ*), and all ukaſes, decrees, orders, and commands concerning the ſtate of Muſcovy and political government, depend on him. Under the

name of *Rofferade,* he is the competent judge of
all cafes refpecting the nobles—a kind of function,
perhaps, not unlike that of Grand Conftable.
He is a man of fuch fpotlefs loyalty, that often
at public banquets, when toafts are drunk, his
name is the type under which all true men to
the Czar are comprehended, and the words
Tichon Nikitowicz mean the moft trufty of
minifters.

Knes Michaël Lehugowicz * Tzerkafki is a
man of fober years and manners, whofe blame-
lefs probity of life and honoured hoary locks
have gained the affections of everybody. In our
time, when the Czar was going to Azow, he
appointed him his vicar, and gave him authority
at Mofcow fecond only to his own.

Knes Feodor Inrowicz Romadonowfki, Boyar
and Generaliflimo of the four regiments of the
Guards, has the fupreme jurifdiction in civil and
criminal cafes. During the Czar's ftay abroad
he held the reins of power, with title of Viceroy

---

* The family of Tcherkafky, though long in Ruffia, and
intermarried with the imperial houfe, is not of Ruffian but of
Circaffian origin, having come originally into Ruffia from Grand
Cubardia, where one of its branches ftill reigns.—(*Vide Notices
des Principales Familles de la Ruffie.* Paris: 1845.)—TRANSL.

and Governor-General (*pro Regis et gubernatoris nomine*). The antiquity of his family, of which he is the head, adds to his confideration.

Knes Peter Ivanowicz Profarowfki, Boyar, and Treafurer of his Majefty the Czar, is of a diftinguifhed family, but more remarkable among his countrymen for the fanctity of the life which he leads. He never opens a door, for fear of contaminating his hand by the contact of what perhaps the touch of an unclean perfon, or of a foreigner,—all of whom he believes to be heretics,—may have fullied.

Befides thefe, the perfons of greateft rank are —Alexis Simonowicz Schahin, Boyar, General-in-Chief of the armies of his Majefty the Czar; Feodor Alexiowicz Golowin, Boyar,* Admiral of the Czar's fleet, and Governor of Siberia, who has laudably performed the functions of governor and of ambaffador, firft to the Chinefe, and

---

* Golowine. This family traces its origin to the Crimea, from whence it emigrated in 1488. It reckons thus among the illuftrious houfes of Ruffia, without being originally of Ruffian ftock. Golowin was created a Count of the Holy Roman Empire in 1702, a title which his defcendants ftill enjoy.—(*Vide Notices des Principales Familles de la Ruffie.* Paris : 1845.)

lately, with M. Lefort, to divers European
princes./ On the 20th of March the Czar conferred upon him the firſt crofs of knighthood of
the Order of Saint Andrew, which he had inſti-
tuted. Artemon Alexiowicz Golowin, General
of the regiment of Bebrafchentſko. Boris
Petrowicz Szeremetow,* Boyar, and General of
the army of Bialogrod. In the year 1695, in
conjunction with Ivan Mofeppa, chief of the
Coffacks, he inveſted the iſland of Tawan and
the Tartar city of Kirikirmini. He brought
home rich booty after its furrender, though fome
aſſert that he had bound himfelf by oath, after
the Ruſſian manner, by placing his hands upon
the crofs and kiffing images, to allow liberty to
every one to retire with as much goods as they
could carry off without carts. He was at one
time ambaſſador at the Imperial Court. He
lately vifited Italy and the fleet of the Knights
of Malta, and purchafed thus, at great coſt, the
crofs of Malta. Vehement in council, and ſtout
of hand, he is the terror of the Tartars—a main

---

* The family of Sheremetow is illuſtrious in Ruſſia, tracing
its origin up to the fourteenth century.—(*Vide Notices des Principales Familles de la Ruſſie.* Paris: 1845.)

ornament of Ruſſia. Feodor Madreowicz Ap-
razen, Boyar, and ex-Governor of the port of
Archangel. General Ivan Ivanowicz Butterlin.*
General Knes Dolgorugoy,† who was fome years
ago ambaſſador in France. Knes Ivan Ivanowicz Tzerkaſki. Knes Andreas Michaelowicz
Tzerkaſki. Feodor Fedrowicz Plefceow Tzarei-
wicz Melitinſki. Two Lubochins,‡ brothers of
the Czarine, one a lieutenant, the other a non-
commiſſioned officer. Troikurow, preſident of
the Chancery of the Strelitz. Boris Bovifowicz
Galizin. Maduei Brodawicz. Few of thefe
Boyars are fummoned to the meetings of
Council; the others retain nothing but the honorary name. I do not mean that all the Boyars
are enumerated above, for there are feveral others
away from the Czar's court as governors of
provinces.

---

* The family of Bouterlin is very ancient and famous in
Ruſſia. They were originally entitled Boyars, but in the laſt
century they were created Counts.—(*Vide Notices des Principales
Familles de la Ruſſie*   Paris: 1845.)

† The family of Dolgorouki, which is of princely degree, and
one of the agnate lines of the original reigning family of Ruſſia,
is both illuſtrious and important.—(*Vide Notices des Principales
Familles de la Ruſſie.*   Paris: 1845.)

‡ Lapouchin.

The Referendaries are next in rank to the Boyars. Some of them are Dumnoi-Diaks, and are in reality fecretaries of ftate (in time Cancellarii). The moft important of thefe are the following : Procop Bogdanowicz Wofnizin ; Emilian Ignatowicz Ukrainzow; Andrew Andreowicz Wignius, Artemonowicz.

Procop Bogdanowicz Wofnizin has filled feveral embaffies. Long ago he was ambaffador to the Turkifh Sultan, the Shah of Perfia, the King of the Poles, and to the illuftrious republic of Venice in the years 1697 and 1698. He was joined with General Lefort and Boyar Golowin in the magnificent embaffy that went to the Elector of Brandenburg, the moft puiffant the States of Holland, and the moft auguft Emperor of the Romans. He was prefent as plenipotentiary at the negotiations for peace with the Turks which were held at Carlowitz, where he managed the affairs of his prince wonderfully, if he can manage to explain away the fault of the two years' armiftice. Yet he feems to be quite pardoned for his fault, inasmuch as he has not only obtained the prefecture of the Czar's *Apotheca,* which it is not cuftomary to beftow upon any perfon whofe merits and loyalty are not clear, but moreover has been lately honoured with a new diplomatic miffion, being appointed to go to the Swedes.

Emelian Ignatowicz Ukrainzow Dumnoi-Diak, of the Ambaffadorial Chancery,* Privy Councillor and Secretary of State, Lord Lieutenant of Cargopol, and Envoy Extraordinary to the Ottoman Porte, has been brought up from his youth among public affairs. He was formerly ambaffador to the States of Holland, and has left behind him everywhere veftiges of fingular prudence, and tranfacted his bufinefs fo fuccefsfully and in fuch a praifeworthy manner, that he acquired fo much reputation as to provoke the envy of his rivals. Often was he brought into danger of lofing his life by the perverfe flanders which certain people told to his prince, but he was faved from their fnares by the mercy of God, and reconciled to his prince by demonftrating the purity of his actions, hatred of which had raifed him up enemies. Of all men in Mufcovy he was deemed the beft calcu-

---

* Foreign Office.

lated to redeem by his more wary folicitude the error of the two years' armiftice of Carlowitz, which another had committed. What the newf-papers have afferted with their ufual mendacious liberty, about his arrival in Conftantinople, the infolent falute of artillery, his captivity, and the Sultan's indignation, is contrary to the truth. He himfelf is a much more truftworthy autho-rity touching the whole of his journey to the Sublime Porte, and of his treatment, an account of which he wrote to the Lord Aulic Councillor of War, ex-ambaffador to Mufcovy, M. de Guarient.

Andrew Andreowicz Wignius, Privy Coun-cillor of his Majefty the Czar, and Chancellor of the kingdom of Siberia, was born of a German father, and, treading in his father's footfteps, embraced the Ruffian religion. He has filled feveral foreign embaffies and different offices in Mufcovy. Afk not with what fpirit everywhere he gave proofs of his prudence and his extraction. As Dumnoi of the Chancery of Siberia, not only he enjoys no falary, but even pays a thoufand roubles per annum to the Czar upon the con-dition that all the Woivodes of Siberia fhall be dependent on him : and he creates none of them without a profitable confideration. He is of a cultivated mind, and exceedingly crafty. He governs the Woivodes by the dread they have of him, and deters them from rapine. For he queftions the merchants who have come from China through Siberia, what they paid for toll to the Woivodes. When he learns that there has been either too much paid or too difhoneft a deficit, he threatens the Woivodes, by letter, with the knout, confifcation, death, and all manner of direful things, unlefs they refrain ; that he will fuborn fecret fpies who will acquaint him with every fingle act they do. Without making mention of the merchants, he feigns that other perfons have given information, left on their return through Siberia the Woivodes, athirft for revenge, fhould be ftill fharper on them. It is not two years fince he appointed a Woivode to a place where preceding Woivodes had been in the habit of collecting only fix hundred roubles per annum for the Czar, while this newly appointed man, driven to be more faithful by the dread of punifhment, and by conftant comminations, wrote fome time fince to his patron Wignius that he

had in hand ten thoufand roubles for the Czar
for one year's revenue : fo advantageous to the
ftate is it, that truftworthy men fhould be fet to
prefide over the public offices.

The very Viceroy of Siberia, the richeft of
the Mufcovite princes, the head of the Tzerkafki
family, was convicted upon being impeached by
Dumnoi Wignius. The Czar had appointed
that prince to be governor-in-chief of all Siberia,
from a belief that a man rolling in private wealth
would not covet his neighbours' goods, and would
be proud of attending faithfully to the interefts
of his fovereign. But thofe that have drunk
deepeft are the moft thirfty for water. Never
was there a man more rapacious, but not without
devices to efcape being accufed of direct robbery. He exacted nothing from the merchants :
he fubftituted his diligent domeftics for that purpofe. Thefe fellows, like harpies, let nothing
efcape intact. Whatever was commendable for
coftlinefs, rarity, or beauty that the merchants
had brought with them, this horde of fervants
drove and compelled them to leave behind, to
their great lofs, unpaid for in Siberia. If there
ftill happened to remain anything among their

wares, the fatal beauty of which was pleafing to the Woivode, accefs, hearing, and leave to depart were denied—the Woivode indeed being, as he ufed to pretend, ignorant of the whole affair ; but, in reality, being himfelf the author, and fuggeft-ing every mode of frefh exaction. Accufed there-fore of breach of truft, the Czar fummoned him to Mofcow, and when he could not wipe out the crime objected to him, he was condemned to be hanged, and he deferved it. The convict had actually mounted the gibbet, which was fet up in front of the Chancery, in the citadel, and had the halter about his neck, when he was gracioufly reprieved from the penalty of death, and dragged off to another; being compelled to bear more than a hundred ftripes of the knout at the hands of the executioner, previous to pafling the reft of his wretched days on board the Czar's galleys—a miferable warning of the exact fidelity with which the fovereign's affairs are to be performed.

Artemonowicz, Dumnoi-Diak, appointed am-baffador in ordinary to the moft potent States of Holland, has taken his wife and children along with him, and is to ftay for three years. Eight fons of Boyars follow him, at the Czar's prefling

command, to acquire fkill in navigation, and
matters connected with feafaring during that
period. He is well acquainted with the Latin
tongue, and ufes it more fluently than the others ;
he has won the Czar's good graces by his reputation for extraordinary prudence, is certainly
polite, and of a fociable and refined character for
a Mufcovite. The fortrefs of Riga, through
which he lately paffed on his way to Holland,
faw a fample of the eftimation that he fets upon
honours. Upon his arrival and entry within the
walls he was faluted with a difcharge of great
guns, which is one of the higheft marks of
refpect in European courts ; but to Artemonowicz it appeared an impertinence. "What
means that bellowing," cried he, "if my hungry
ftomach is barking :" fetting more ftore of honour in wine, brandy, and comeftibles, than thofe
marks of refpect that were paid to him.

The Diaks, a title which they interpret *cancel-
lifta*, but who in reality, if we confider their
function, are fecretaries of the ambaffadorial
chancery, are two in number—Bafil Bofnizin and
Boris Michalowicz, who have earned refpect by
the miffions which they filled abroad.

What cautions and precepts to be obferved they are in the habit of giving their agents upon foreign miffions, let this one inftruction given to the Marfhal of the great Mufcovite embaffy, which I here fet forth at full length, ftand as an example:—

> "*In our year* 1698 : *by command of the great Lord the Czar, and Grand Duke Peter Alexiowicz of all Great, Little, and White Ruffia, Autocrat, to Godfrey Briftaff.*

"You have written letters from Nimvegen to the grand ambaffadors, that you were obliged to pay tolls that were exacted in divers places in Holland; but that you went from Nimveguen as far as Cleves by water, or by fea. That potwoda, pofthorfes, and forage for your own horfes was very dear ; that the money given to you in ready imperials will hardly be fufficient, and that it will confequently be neceffary to fend you an order for more.

"As foon, therefore, as thefe orders fhall reach you, you fhall with all poffible diligence go on by the route which has already been recommended to you; proceeding without delay or uſeleſs ſtoppage as far as the frontiers of the empire.* If, as you admoniſh us, the imperials are inſufficient for you, you ſhall, in caſe of neceſſity, command that there be delivered to you by the ſcribe and the maſter of the ſables, five hundred ducats out of the treaſure; however, if a greater and extreme neceſſity preſs you, you ſhall cauſe a thouſand ducats to be conſigned into your hands; but of the careful cuſtody and uſeful employment of both ſums, the imperials as well as the ducats, you ſhall render an accurate account. Moreover, ſhould proviſions be cheaper in places there, you ſhall diminiſh the allowances, but ſhall give as much as you think neceſſary left there ſhould be any unſeemly want. Take care that all abſtain from drunkenneſs; pay leſs to thoſe that get drunk.

"Wherever ſovereigns give rations, or money inſtead of them, to your company, you ſhall totally withhold the uſual allowance. Moreover, from whatever city you may now be at, or ſhall arrive at henceforward, always adviſe thence the

* The Germanic empire. The original has *"fines Cæsareos."*
—TRANSL.

Grand Plenipotentiary Ambaſſadors at Amſterdam, or wherever elſe they may be, touching the
progreſs of your journey.

"Dumnoi Diak,

"Procop Wosnizin."

    "*In the year* 1698, 25 *March. By com-
mand of the Great Lord and Grand
Duke Peter Alexiowicz, of all Great,
Little, and White Ruſſia, Autocrat ; and
by directions of the Grand and Pleni-
potentiary Ambaſſadors, General and
Admiral and Governor of Novogrod,
Francis Jocowicz Lefort ; Commiſſary
General of the War Department, and
Governor of Siberia, Feodor Alexiowicz
Golowin ; and Chancellor and Governor
of Bochowia, Procop, Bogdanowicz,
Woſnizin : it is enjoined upon the
Chamberlain (aulico) Godfrey Briſ-
taff :—*

    " To ſet out from Amſterdam, through Hol-
land, to Nimveguen ; through the Brandenburg
cities, Cleves, Weſel, Lippſtadt, Münden, Hild-
eſheim, Acherleben, and Hall ; through the

Electoral Saxon cities to Leipſic, and thence through Bohemia to Prague, or by whatever ſhorter and more convenient road there may be, or the Electoral Saxon and Brandenburg commiſſaries and guides ſhall lead you, as far as the Emperor's frontiers. With him are ſent the court (aulici) ſervants and domeſtics of the Grand Embaſſy. With him alſo is ſent the Great Lord's money, his treaſure of ſables, the cloths, plate, and furniture of all kinds of the ambaſſadors, for the more ſecure and ſafe conduct whereof letters of paſſport have been delivered to him under the ſignatures and ſeals of the grand ambaſſadors. Before his departure the grand ambaſſadors wrote to requeſt the moſt auguſt the Emperor, the moſt ſerene the King of Poland, Elector of Saxony, and the moſt ſerene the Elector of Brandenburg, to receive in a friendly manner at their coming, the ſervants ſent on in advance, and to grant them *potwoda*, proviſions, and the other neceſſary aids and furtherance on the road. When Briſtaff himſelf ſhall reach Cleves, he ſhall requeſt a commiſſary, proviſions, and guides, and ſhall, with all precaution and circumſpection, go on by the road indicated to the frontiers of Saxony ; and he ſhall be careful to do in like manner when he ſhall have croſſed the limits of Saxony and entered thoſe of the Emperor. But at the Imperial frontier he ſhall await the arrival of the grand and plenipotentiary ambaſſadors.

"If in any cities *potwoda* and rations ſhould be refuſed, he ſhall hire horſes, and according to the ſcale inſerted in this inſtruction ſhall diſtri-bute an allowance in money among his company. For the neceſſaries of *potwoda*, proviſions, and other expenſes, in order to meet any extraor-dinary caſe, we have confided to the ſcribe of the ambaſſadorial chancery, Nikiphor Ivanow, the ſum of four thouſand imperial dollars (*ſolidonum imperialium**) to be employed only in caſe of abſolute neceſſity. He ſhall ſet forth in detail in his book of accounts the ſums expended and the purpoſes for which they were laid out, and

---

* I am not quite certain that the old dollar, or crown impe-rial is the coin meant. He has told us elſewhere that the Ruſſian *kopek* of his day was worth about two *kreuzers*; and, again in another place, ſpeaking of a new currency regulation which took place while he was in Ruſſia, he ſays that the Ruſſian treaſury received theſe imperial ſolidi at fifty-five kopeks, and made an enormous profit by coining them into one hundred and ten kopeks immediately after.—*See Antea.*—TRANSL.

ſhall exhibit his account book, together with the
remaining money, to the grand and plenipotentiary ambaſſadors; but ſhall, neither by himſelf
or in the name of others, incur any ſuperfluous
outlay. He ſhall make anſwer to thoſe that aſk
queſtions about the ſtay of the grand and plenipotentiary ambaſſadors, that they are ſtill detained at Amſterdam about weighty affairs of his
Majeſty the Czar; but that they will ſhortly
follow. To ſuch, however, as may inquire touching matters of greater moment, which it is
the buſineſs of the ambaſſadors to give anſwers
about, he ſhall reply that he is a ſoldier, and
ignorant of affairs of that nature. He ſhall
enjoin upon the domeſtics of the ambaſſadors to
comport themſelves with modeſty and compoſure,
to go nowhere without leave, to abſtain from
exceſs in drink, not to diſgrace themſelves by
brawls or altercations, or in any other way ſhow
themſelves uncivil. He ſhall take great care of
theſe particulars: thoſe who, contravening this
mandate, ſhall frowardly ramble or gorge themſelves with wine, he ſhall puniſh according as he
may ſee fit; but the clowns of the viler kind he
ſhall order to be chaſtiſed with *battok* and caning.

The ſcribe Nikiphor Ivanow and Theodore Bulaew, ſhall never quit the money and treaſure of ſables for an inſtant, and ſhall have the aſſiſtance of three of the Hayduks, turn about for twenty-four hours; and he ſhall take heed with the ſcribes, that the latter remain with the treaſure and guard it with careful vigilance. Finally, Briſtaff himſelf ſhall from every city at which he arrives certify the grand and plenipotentiary ambaſſadors touching his ſtay and the progreſs of his journey, leſt they ſhould not know where they are, to what cities they are going, and what day they may be about proceeding further."

OF THE MINISTERS OF FOREIGN PRINCES WHO IN OUR TIME WERE AT MOSCOW.

The moſt Illuſtrious and moſt Reverend Friar Peter-Paul Palma de Arteſia, Archbiſhop of Ancyra and Vicar Apoſtolic in the kingdoms of the Great Mogul, Golgonda and Idalkan, expoſed to His Majeſty the Czar, who was then in Holland, the route he was under the neceſſity of taking, and by his humble entreaty obtained from His Majefty a mandate to Knes Boris Alexiowicz Galizin, Viceroy of the kingdoms of Cazan and Aftracan, not only enjoining him to receive the Archbifhop with proper kindnefs on his arrival at Mofcow, but further ordering that he fhould be conducted in fafety to the frontiers of Perfia, free maintenance being by fpecial grace granted to him as long as he fhould be paffing through the kingdoms and provinces belonging to His Majefty the Czar.

On the 6th of July, 1698, the Archbifhop, accompanied by two priefts, Captain Molino, a doctor, a watchmaker, and fome other perfons, arrived in Mofcow. A houfe in Slowoda was at firft appointed for his lodging; but on the third day after his arrival, Knes Galizin, to fulfil the Czar's command, affigned a part of his own palace to the accommodation of the Archbifhop, his horfes, and conveyances, for as long as he fhould ftay in Mofcow. On the 10th of July he honoured the feftivity of the Octave of Corpus Chrifti with his prefence. On the 16th of the fame month, he fortified in the faith fifty Catholics with the facrament of Confirmation. Meantime, Knes Galizin had a fhip ftored with a variety of proviſions, fitted out, on board which the Archbiſhop, provided with the Czar's credentials, proceeded on his way down the Ocka and Wolga, and ſo on by the Caſpian Sea into Perſia.

The moſt illuſtrious Sir John Staniſlaus Boghia, Starof of Troki, Chamberlain of the moſt Serene the King of Poland, and his envoy extraordinary at the Court of his Majeſty the Czar. When the rebellious bands of the Sapieha faction, ravaging in every direction, were exciting great tumult throughout all Lithuania, he was ſent in quality of envoy to the Autocrat of Ruſſia to announce the election of the new king, and his ſubſequent coronation. He was alſo charged to examine accurately the numbers and ſtrength of the Czar's troops that were lying upon the confines of Lithuania, and to report the preciſe truth about them as ſoon as poſſible.

In conſequence of the pillages of the Sapiehas, and the manner in which the roads were every-where waylaid, it was by no means ſafe to travel with a becoming ſuite, ſplendid furniture, and the magnificence becoming his dignified character, for had the matter been diſcovered, he would have loft both his life and all his goods. So, more fagely, attended by a fingle fervant, unencumbered with any baggage, he efcaped through the fnares of the enemy, and fortunately reached the frontiers of Mufcovy. Knes Michael Gregorowicz Romadonowfki commanded the Strelitz towards Lithuania. The envoy could not affert the prerogative of his office to that prince, except by exhibiting his paffport and credentials, excufing himfelf from prefenting himfelf at the frontiers of Mufcovy without a proper fuite, by alleging the diforders in Lithuania. Romadonowfki, commiferating the envoy's lot, furnifhed him, at his requeft, with a fufficient fuite, horfes and conveyances, to continue his journey to Mofcow, the Czar's capital. Admitted, introduced, and accepted by the miniftry, he took poffeffion of the lodging that was affigned to him in the Palace of the Ambaffadors. He complained greatly of the dangerous craft of the Mufcovite miniftry, he very often bemoaned how he had given up his paffport and credentials to them, and how he had been captioufly circumvented by them. When he was dining, on the 1ft of July, 1698, with Boyar Leo Kirilowicz, he showed him letters which he had received from his most supreme king, lauding the dexterity of the imperial envoy, and censuring his too easy mode of proceeding, and his giving up the letters of credence. He fell into some nonsense and contentions with a certain Knes Dolgorugoi, and is said to have challenged him to a duel, and, Dolgorugoi not coming to the ground, to have fired a pistol into his window.

The Muscovites were so mortified at this, that from that moment out they were to a man against the Lord Envoy in everything, and left hardly any stone unturned by which they might increase his annoyance and disgust. Detesting, moreover, this excellent man, having given him an answer touching his credentials, they were trying to get rid of him, and this gave rise to a fresh altercation. For the Pole refused to go until he had seen the sovereign to whom he had principally been sent. The matter being in consequence laid before the Czar, who at the time happened to be staying in Holland, his Majesty, whose singular prudence and most laudable equanimity shines forth in everything, wrote back in favour of the Pole to the following effect :—" The

envoy is fent to me, not to you : let him remain
therefore until I return. Meantime do you furnifh him with a becoming maintenance." On
account of fome rather fharp words which re-
flected on his dignity, he, horrible to tell, ordered
a certain interpreter of the Ambaffadorial Chancery to be chaftifed with a fcourging, to the in-
citement of frefh hatred;—the Mufcovite miniftry
bearing it ill, that, without their leave afked,
their fubjects fhould be beaten by foreigners,
their minds were every day more eftranged from
the envoy; fo that the declarations of the Dumnoi
and others moft flatly pronounced him to be no
envoy, that he had brought doubtful credentials
—no certain name being expreffed in them. Oil
was poured on the fire when letters came from
the Mufcovite Refident at Warfaw, to the effect
that the Poles knew nothing of, and would have
nothing to do with, the envoy fent to the Czar.
To this the envoy ufed to reply, that he had
no doubt that fome of the Poles, who were his
private enemies, either knew nothing about the
matter, or pretended that they did not; that he
was fent by the king and the republic; that he
was not folicitous about the knowledge, igno-

rance, or malevolence of private individuals, but
that the chara&ter with which he was clothed was
known well enough to the Mufcovites ; for that,
though his name was not exprefled in one letter
of credence, it was to be found in another ; that
he had brought feveral letters of credence ; that
the obloquy was aimed at his moft ferene king,
and that he was purfuing infults addrefled to his
king, and not his own.   And, to fay the truth,
even had he brought no credentials whatever, I
have myfelf no hefitation in thinking that he was
quite right, and that the ufual entertainments
and honours of an ambaffador were due to him
from the very fa&t that the Mufcovites had not
hefitated to receive him folemnly in the chara&ter
of envoy ; for it cannot be open to their caprice
that the fame perfon be an ambaffador at one
moment, and the next not.   Neverthelefs, the
Mufcovites, almoft totally averfe to him, refufed
thenceforward to allow him the free maintenance
cuftomary in thofe countries, and, ftriving with
might and main to annoy him in every inftance
they could, they imputed all to his faftidious ambition ; by all which he could not help fometimes
being juftly excited. The Danifh Envoy pretended

to precedence over the Pole, becaufe, as he ufed to fay, " My king was born to the fceptre, but he of the Poles is only called to that eminence by free fuffrages ; "—difputes of which the Mufco-vites difapproved, as out of place. They tacitly took the fide of the Pole, and if the greater or lefs fplendour with which the envoys were honoured was not a matter of accident, it pronounced for the Pole. But they hated the man. He was difmiffed, without any ceremony, on the 2nd of November.

On the 6th of December, when he was about to ftart for Veroneje, to the Czar, the Miniftry ftopped him, on the grounds of his being already fully difmiffed, and that without frefh letters of credence there was nothing further to treat of. Still, he protefted, when Major-General de Car-lowicz, in confequence of frefh Lithuanian dif-turbances that were apprehended, folicited the Czar to fend 20,000 troops, as foon as poffible, to the frontier, and gave warning, moreover, that it would feem to him more judicious if His Majefty the Czar, inftead of this perilous often-tation of ftrength, fhould complain to the re-public of thefe infulting internal plots, as if it turned to his own disparagement that after the election and coronation of a new king had just been announced to him, they should wish to proceed to another choice. Meantime, the Muscovites, to whom the envoy's long delay after his dismissal was displeasing, gave him notice that he must quit his apartments within the space of three weeks, and leave Moscow, and make room for the Envoy Extraordinary of the Elector of Brandenburg. But when they perceived that he was not making the slightest preparation to go, fifteen *potwoda* were sent, on the 11th of January, to the Court of the Ambassadors for his use, to accelerate his departure and the speed of his journey.

The most illustrious Sir Paul Heins, Envoy Extraordinary of the most serene the King of Denmark to the Czar's court, made it his principal study to preserve the friendly relations existing between his King and his Majesty the Czar, and to draw them closer and more intimate by the sanction of a treaty of alliance. Contending with the Envoy of Poland touching precedency, he set hereditary kingdoms above elective. On the 9th of October, 1698, the

Czar's Majefty, out of fpecial condefcenfion, ftood godfather to a fon of his. On the 1ft of the following November, he went in chafe of greater honours, when at an early hour in the morning he went to the Danifh commiffioner Baudenand's, where the Czar was known to have paffed the night. But the ferenity of the morning was overcaft by fome clouds in the courfe of the day : thofe clouds being gathered on the Czar's countenance by a too free contradiction. In like manner he was near conjuring up a tempeft on the 15th of January of the year 1699. Under the pretext of bufinefs, having obtained leave to follow the Czar to Vcroneje, he took his way thither on the 4th of March, along with the envoy of Brandenburgh, on which occafion his arrival faved a courier of the Czar's half dead from the fury of an affembled mob of ruftics, and the pillaging clowns fled in terror at the fight of the new comers ; while he denounced a Woivode that was flow in furnifhing him with *potwoda* with fuch effect, that the man was cited to Vcroneje and flogged with the knout. On the 29th May, he returned to Mofcow, on the Czar's departure from Veroneje to Azow for a cruife.

The moft illuftrious Sir Marquard de Prinz, envoy extraordinary of Electoral Brandenburg, who, when his Majefty the Czar was in the Brandenburg States with his ambaffadors, had acted as his commiffary, made his folemn entry into Mofcow on the 24th of January of the year 1699, having come to congratulate the Czar on his return to his own ftates and provinces. On the 4th of March he ftarted, along with the Danifh envoy, to Veroneje, where he received a prefent of the Czar's portrait, enriched with gems and precious ftones; returned thence on the 16th; and, laftly, on the 26th, took his departure in ftate, the Mufcovites accompanying him with a folemn cavalcade beyond the gates. On leaving he appointed Sir Timothy de Zadora Kefielfki as Refident, to attend diligently to the interefts of the Moft Serene the Elector.

Denmark and Sweden have commiffaries here, of whofe fervices the ambaffadors of thofe countries not unfrequently avail themfelves. The Swedifh is named Knipper; the Danifh, Baudenand.

And thefe things I was able to obferve amidft

the diſtraction of more weighty affairs during
the time of the embaſſy; the which, as well to
feed the curioſity of the learned, as to give ſome
idea of this nation to perſons going into Muſcovy, have been committed to type. Be indul-
gent, gentle reader, and if ſome over-plain
ſpeech ſhould haply offend thy eyes, I intreat
of thee to be perſuaded that the ſtyle of writing
adopted lays no pretenſions to be hiſtorical, but
is merely familiar. And ſhould ſome errors,
beyond thoſe that have been noticed and cor-
rected, have eſcaped the pen, unleſs thou ap-
proacheſt with a cenſorious ſpirit, thou canſt
eaſily amend them.

APPENDIX.

APPENDIX OF ADDITIONAL NOTES.

——✦✿✦——

NOTE TO THE NAME KINSKY.

[See Vol. I., p. 3.]

KINSKY, of the well-known great Bohemian family (born 1634, died 27th January, 1699), firſt diſtinguiſhed himſelf in an Embaſſy to Poland in 1664. He was Chancellor of Bohemia when the Turks invaded Auſtria in 1683. He ſubſequently contributed greatly to the elevation of the Electtor of Saxony to the Poliſh throne, which had taken place juſt before the date of our Diary.—TRANSL.

NOTE TO THE NAME OF THE VENETIAN AMBASSADOR RUZINI.

[See Vol. I., p. 4.]

Carlo Ruzini, a noble Venetian, ſon of a Pro-curatore di San Marco, was the moſt illuſtrious

member of an ancient family, to which fome
afcribe an ancient Roman origin; but which
others with more probability believe to have come
from Conftantinople to Venice between the
twelfth and thirteenth centuries. Carlo was born
in 1653. His father Marco was an illuftrious
fenator of the Republic, and died in 1711. His
mother was Catherina Zeno : fhe died in 1704.
Carlo was ambaffador in various courts, and was
knighted. In 1692 he was ambaffador to the
Spanifh court, and made a pompous entry; in
1695 he paffed as ambaffador to Vienna; in
1697 he was plenipotentiary and ambaffador extraordinary at the Congrefs with the Turk, held
in Carlowitz; in 1701 he was fent as ambaffador
extraordinary to congratulate Philip V., of Spain,
in Milan; then he was fent to Conftantinople; and
while there, was in 1703 created a Procuratore di
San Marco, from which time he was continually
employed in diftinguifhed internal offices of the
Republic until 1712, when he was fent ambaffador to the Congrefs of Utrecht. Upon his
return thence he was again occupied in high
domeftic employments, being chofen in 1715 a
Sage of the Council. Finally, after other dignities, he was in 1732 elected Doge of Venice,
and died, aged 81, in 1734. He was a patron of

the painter, Longhi.—(*Capellari : Il Campidoglio Veneto. MS. in the Library of S. Marco, Venice.*)—TRANSL.

NOTE TO THE NAME OF LESCZYNSKI.

[See Vol. I., p. 19.]

Raphael Lefczynfki, Grand-General of the Crown of Poland, was the father of Staniflaus Lefczynfki, who was elected King of Poland in 1704, after a civil war, in which the Swedes turned the balance in his favour. After a few years King Staniflaus was again by civil diffen-fions driven out, and the Saxon, Auguftus the Strong, reftored. Staniflaus retired to Nancy, where he was the centre of an accomplifhed circle. His daughter Marie was the virtuous Queen of Louis XV. of France.—TRANSL.

NOTE TO THE NAME OF SAPIEHA.

[See Vol. I., p. 42.]

In 1695 the Bifhop of Wilna, irritated at the ravages which Sapieha had caufed his foldiers to commit in the diocefe, launched an excommuni-cation againft him, which Sapieha caufed to be burnt by the executioner. Some years later the

Pope arranged thefe differences. Sapieha, after the death of the heroic John Sobiefki, King of Poland, had great quarrels with the family of Oginfki and other Lithuanian nobles, who accufed him of arrogating royal authority, of having laid wafte the eftates of the nobles, of levying contributions, of having feized on the perfons of the deputies fent by the States of Lithuania to King Auguftus, and having countenanced the licentioufnefs of his foldiers. From that time Sapieha never went to diet or affembly without a ftrong and numerous efcort. In 1700 the two parties came to a pitched battle, where Sapieha's faction was utterly routed. The whole Sapieha family was profcribed by the States of Lithuania, and their poffeffions confifcated. In 1702 they were reconciled with the States through the intervention of King Auguftus; and, neverthelefs, the turbulent chief of the family, who had been created a Prince of the Holy Roman Empire in 1702, joined that King's enemy, Charles XII. of Sweden. In 1711 he was fortunate enough again to make his peace with King Auguftus. The princely family of Sapieha defcends from an Agnate of the Jagellon dynafty; and ftill fubfifts in Poland.—TRANSL.

NOTE TO THE NAME OF CAPTAIN MOLINO.

[See Vol. I., p. 129.]

More correctly *Da Molino*. The family is one of the moſt illuſtrious of Venice; ſome ſay it came from Ptolemais ; ſome ſay from Mantua. It was famous among the Cruſaders. Malfatti ſays of them : "furono huomini grandi di perſona, un poco cuffi, molto cattolici, elemoſinieri e di buona qualità, gran maeſtri di edificij, e maſſime di edificare Molini." They bore a mill wheel for arms. They built ſumptuous chapels in the Church of S. Giovanni e Paolo, and the Churches of S. Andrew and S. Agnes in their native city. The moſt diſtinguiſhed of this patrician ſtock, Franceſco da Molino, was elected Doge in 1645, and died in 1655. Perhaps the member of this family mentioned in this Diary as having accompanied the Archbiſhop of Ancyra on his way to the realms of the Great Mogul, was Philip (ſon of Mark) da Molino, who, in 1684, went with the Venetian Ambaſſador, Moroſini, to Poland, and who died a Senatore di Pregadì in 1714, aged 50.—(*Capellari: Il Campidoglio Veneto. MS. in the Library of S. Marco, Venice.*)— TRANSL.

NOTE ON THE RUSSIAN NOBILITY, ITS ORIGIN, HISTORY, AND CLASSIFICATION.

In virtue of a law promulgated in 1682, all Ruſſian nobles are in modern times entitled to equal rights, whatſoever may be their titles or origin. But in a merely honorary ſenſe the Ruſſian nobility is divided into five claſſes, viz., 1ſt, the Princes of the Ruſſian Empire; 2nd, the Counts of the Ruſſian Empire; 3rd, the Barons of the Ruſſian Empire; 4th, the untitled gentry whoſe nobility dates back beyond the reign of Peter the Great: 5th, the untitled gentry whoſe nobleſſe is poſterior to that reign.

In the category of untitled gentry whoſe nobleſſe is anterior to Peter I., there are families whoſe antiquity and hiſtorical luſtre place them far above moſt of the houſes of Counts of the Ruſſian Empire. Such* are the Boutourlins, the Szérémétews, the Saltykows, the Samarins,

---

* Some branches of the families here mentioned have, how-ever, been from time to time dignified with the title of Count: a line of Boutourlins, for example, created Counts in 1760; of Szérémétew, created Counts in 1706; a line of Saltykows are Counts ſince 1732, and raiſed to the rank of Princes in 1790; a line of Pouchkins are Counts ſince 1797; a line of the Golovins, created Counts of the Germanic Empire in 1707, were aggre-gated to the Counts of Ruſſia in 1709.

the Pouchkins, the Sabourows, the Golovins, and others. The eldeft line of the Saltykows, for example is untitled; the fecond line, Counts Soltyk of Poland; the third line, Counts Salty-kow fince 1732; the fourth and youngeft that of the Princes Saltykow, created in 1790.

The nucleus of the great Ruffian nobility confifts of the princely families defcended in the male line directly and legitimately from Rurik, the firft fovereign of Ruffia; and from Guede-min, Grand-duke of Lithuania, anceftor of the Jagellon dynafty of Polifh kings.

Rurik, a heathen, who was of Norman origin, reigned according to the ufual computation from 862 to 879. His great-grandfon St. Wladimir (who, having lived before the final feparation of the Greek and Latin Churches, is recognifed as a faint in both), converted all Ruffia to Chriftianity in 988; and died in 1015, dividing Ruffia into twelve principalities among his eleven fons and a nephew. For four centuries this fatal divifion weakened Ruffia, was the fource of conftant internal difcords, opened the way to the Mogul conqueft (1236-1240), and threw the civilifation of the whole country for centuries behind the reft of Europe. At length, however, the Grand Dukes of Mofcow (defcendants of Rurik) having, towards the clofe of the fifteenth century, attained fupremacy, the other branches of the fame race fell into comparative political infignificance. The Agnates were compelled to exchange their ancient fovereign appanages for rich private domains. Thofe who refufed to do fo were defpoiled of all, and caft into dungeons.

The fubjugation of the Agnates accomplifhed, the fuccefsful houfe fought to confound them with the Mufcovite ariftocracy. With this view two meafures were adopted under Ivan the Great (III.), who afcended the throne in 1462. Firft a genealogical record (*Rofdoflovnaia Kniga*) was compiled, in which fide by fide with the old ex-fovereign princely Agnates, were infcribed the Boyar families of Mofcow ; to wit, the Romanows (who became fubfequently the reigning family), the Szérémétews, the Saltykows, the Boutourlins, the Sabourows, the Pleftchéiéws, the Samarins, the Kalitchews, &c. &c. This book was recopied under Ivan IV., and two families only—viz. the Adafchews, and the Golovins—were added to it on that occafion. The fecond meafure taken under Ivan III. ftruck ftill more rudely than the firft at the political pofition of the defcendants of Rurik and of Guédemin. It eftablifhed that thenceforth political rank fhould be determined by the Court dignities held by the father, grandfather, and great-grandfather of each perfonage. This rule, which was in force until 1682, rendered the rank of *Boyar* hereditary *de facto*, if not *de jure*, and completed the fufion of the old princely Agnates with the *Boyar* families. Thus the defcendants of Rurik and Guédemin found themfelves on a level at Court with thofe of the old fervants of their kindred princes of Mofcow. The inftitution which had its fountain in this law was called the *Mefnitcheftvo*. When the *Mefnitcheftvo* was abolifhed in 1682, a complete equality of all nobles before the law was introduced was eftablifhed ; and, at the fame time, the ancient genealogical book was copied for the laft time. The copy being bound in red velvet, was called, and retains the name of the Velvet Book (*Barhatnaia Kniga*). This " Book of Gold" of the Ruffian nobility is depofited in the Heraldic Chamber of the Senate of St. Peterfburgh. Notwithftanding many intrigues, no new *Boyar* family fucceeded in obtaining a place in it : not even the Narifchkhins, ftrong in their recent intermarriage with the Houfe of the Czars.

Until the reign of Peter the Great, the title of Prince (*Knes, Kniaz*), was, if we may truft to

Prince Dolgoruki, borne in Ruffia by families of fovereign origin only.* Peter I. introduced the practice of *creating* princes, counts, and barons —thefe laft two titles totally foreign to Ruffia up to the eighteenth century. The firft created Prince was Alexander Mentfchikow (fo often mentioned in this Diary), the paftry-cook's boy, who became fucceffively Czar Peter's valet, favourite, and prime minifter. He was created a Prince of the Holy Roman Empire by the Emperor Leopold of Germany in 1705 ; and two years later Peter made him a Ruffian Prince. The two firft Counts were the fame Mentfchi-kow, and High-Admiral, Field-Marfhal Golovin,

*

* It has ftruck the tranflator, however, that Kord fometimes fpeaks of individuals, like Szérémétew, of illuftrious but Boyar rank, by the style of *Prince*, which properly fhould only be the equivalent of the Slavic title *Knez*. It has occurred to him that the title *Knez* may then have been occafionally more loofely but improperly given focially, if not officially, to the greater mag-nates. The Ruffians now invariably tranflate their word Knez by that of Prince. Moldo-Wallachian Boyars not unfrequently affume the higher title. Certainly, in the fouthern Slavic coun-tries, the title Knez was not always confidered ftrictly as the prerogative of princely dignity. It was frequently both given to, and ufed by, magnates like the great extinct Zrini and Frangipani of Croatia, as an equivalent of their Hungarian title of Count : a fact of which the tranflator of this Diary convinced himfelf by an examination and comparifon of contemporaneous Slavic and Latin original charters in private archives in Croatia. —Transl.

on whom the Emperor Leopold conferred the
rank of Counts of the Holy Roman Empire in
1702. The firſt Count of the Ruſſian Monarchy was Field-Marſhal Szérémétew (the diſtinguiſhed and dignified *Boyar*, ſo often mentioned
in this Diary as a Knight of Malta), whoſe title
of Count dates from 1706. The firſt Baron of
Ruſſia was created in 1710, in the perſon of the
Vice-Chancellor Schafirow. The title of Baron
of the Ruſſian Empire confers but ſlender ſocial
advantages. It was ſo little eſteemed, as to be once
conferred upon a Court dwarf (in 1726, Baron
Titſchinin). There are only eight families now
extant in Ruſſia with the rank of Ruſſian Baron.
Eight more are extinct. The poſterity of one
Ruſſian Baron exiſt however in England, the
Dimſdales, deſcended from Dr. Thomas Dimſ-
dale, an Engliſh phyſician to the Ruſſian Court,
who was created a Baron of Ruſſia in 1769.
Among his achievements was vaccinating the
Empreſs Catherine and the Grand Duke Paul,
afterwards Emperor.

In 1722, Peter the Great promulgated a law,
by virtue of which hereditary nobility was acquired
down to a few years ago (and ſtill with ſlight
reſtriction), as of right, by all civil ſervants of a
certain rank in the ſcale of public *employés*; and

by all officers of the land and fea fervice without
exception. Thus every Ruffian foldier may
hope to bequeath hereditary nobility to his defcendants. Under the operation of this law the
rank of noble is more eafily attainable in Ruffia
than anywhere elfe in the world. A flight
reftriction was however confequently introduced
of late years, requiring higher rank in the civil
and military fervices for the acquifition *ipfo facto*
of the right to hereditary nobleffe. The great
Souvárow, who died a Prince and a Field-
Marfhal, began life as a common foldier. The
late diftinguifhed Field-Marfhal Prince Pafkie-
wicz, Viceroy of Poland, was the fon of a man
who had earned his nobility in the army.

The Ruffian nobleffe of princely degree is conftituted as follows :—I. There are thirty-one
fubfifting houfes of the male legitimate race of
Rurik. II. One princely family reprefenting
by a female line a branch of his defcendants.
III. Two defcending illegitimately from him,
but in the male line. IV. Four that defcend in
the male legitimate line from Guedemin, Grand
Duke of Lithuania, who was the progenitor of
the Jagellon dynafty of Polifh Kings. V. Ten
houfes of foreign princely origin who have been
admitted as Ruffian princes. VI. Eleven

families of *created* princes—all of courfe made
fince Peter the Great's time.

Befides the above there is the category of
families of princely origin that are fettlers in
Ruffia; and again, many Georgian, Armenian,
Tartar, and Calmuck families who have affumed
and bear with impunity the title of Prince.

The rank of Count, unknown to Ruffia before
the time of Peter the Great, was conferred upon
—I. Sixty families that are ftill extant ; and
four more that are already extinct. II. Befides
which there are three families of Counts of the
Holy Roman Empire, who are not Counts of
the Ruffian Empire, though of Ruffian race.

With reference to *Boyar* families: There are,
I. Forty-three extant Ruffian families of un-
titled nobility, infcribed in the Velvet Book;
II. Three fuch families not recorded in the
Velvet Book.

Of Polifh Princes in the Ruffian Empire
there are fifteen families ; the lateft creation
being one by the Emperor Alexander I. in
1820.

There are eleven foreign families fettled in
Ruffia, who are of illuftrious princely rank.
Thefe, as well as families having foreign titles
of Prince, Count, &c., fettled in the Empire,

are recognifed as fuch and allowed to enjoy their titles : but unlefs they be princes, &c., of Ruffia, in the *official armorial* of the *Ruffian Empire,* they are ranked only among untitled nobles.—[See Dolgoruki, *Notices des principales Familles de la Ruffie, &c.*]—TRANSL.

NOTE ON SZEREMETEW AND HIS FAMILY.

[See Vol. I., p. 274.]

The family of Schérémétew, as their compatriot Dolgoruki writes their name, is one of the beft, moft hiftorical, and moft national houfes in all Ruffia. Its authentic derivation may be traced to the fourteenth century. Its founder was Andrew Kabyla (or as others have it Kambyla), from whom are likewife fprung the houfes of Kalytchew, Nepluiew, Barbarykine, Ladyghine, Konovtfyne, and, foremoft of all, the Romanows (whofe real name is Romanow-Youriew), that illuftrious Boyar houfe called to the throne of Ruffia by the voice of the nation in 1613. Among the Boyars of the Houfe of Szérémétew, feveral diftinguifhed themfelves in the wars of the fixteenth century. Boyar Theodore was eminent for his talents as a ftatefman, his valour and his uprightnefs. He was

married to a coufin-german of Czar Michael
Romanow, and to him the Houfe of Romanow
mainly owed their elevation to the throne of
Ruffia. Boyar Bafil was Commander-in-Chief
of the Forces under Czar Alexis, was made
prifoner at the Battle of Tchoudnovo, and fpent
thirty years of his life in harfh flavery in the
depths of the Crimea. His nephew Boyar and
Field-Marfhal Count Boris was the Szérémétew
fo often mentioned in this Diary as an honorary
Knight of Malta. He was one of the moft
remarkable perfonages ever produced by this
family, fo fruitful of eminent men. He conquered Livonia and Efthonia, and was Commander-in-Chief at the Battle of Poltawa, where
the army of Charles XII. was deftroyed. We
have feen how he was created an honorary Knight
of the Hofpital of St. John of Jerufalem.
Peter I. created him a Ruffian Count in 1706.
Count Boris was as eftimable for the qualities
of his charadter, as for his eminent talents for
command. Noble, upright, beneficent, his
death, which took place in 1719, was deplored
as a calamity alike by the Ruffian army, which
during twenty years he had led to victory, and
by the poor of St. Peterfburgh and Mofcow,
who faid: "We have now loft our adopted

"father." Such is the character given by Prince Dolgoruki, of this true Knight.

Field-Marſhal Szérémétew's daughter, Nathalia, was the wife of Prince Ivan Dolgoruki, he to whoſe ſiſter was betrothed the young Emperor Peter II., who died on the very day appointed for the celebration of the marriage.

The Empreſs Anne then aſcended the throne; power paſſed into the hands of her favourite the ferocious Biren, Duke of Courland; and Prince Ivan Dolgoruki was exiled with all his family to Siberia. His heroic and gifted wife Nathalia Szérémétew accompanied him thither; and when nine years later her huſband was brought back from Siberia to Novogorod, and cut into quarters, ſhe returned to Ruſſia and took the veil at Kiew. The day before pronouncing her vows, ſhe went to the ſteep bank of the Dniepr, and caſt into that broad fair river which flows paſt Kiew's walls the nuptial ring from her finger. This conſtant woman lived thirty years afterwards as a nun, and died in 1771.—[See Dolgoruki, *Notices des principales Familles, art. Dolgoruki.*]—TRANSL.

NOTE ON THE CZAR'S FAVOURITE, GENERAL LEFORT.

[See Vol. I., p. 162.]

Lefort was a native of Geneva, where he was born of a patrician family on the 2nd January, 1656. He entered the Swifs guards in the French fervice at the age of fourteen. Thence he went to the Netherlands, where he was at the fieges of Grave, 1674, and Oudenarde, 1675, under the Prince of Courland, who loft his whole regiment in thefe two fieges ; and Lefort, em-barraffed by the lofs of his equipment and bag-gage, accepted a Lieutenancy in the Czar's fervice, which he entered upon in the fummer of 1675, in his nineteenth year. He was hand-fome, bold and enterprifing, generous and difin-terefted, fpoke four or five languages well, and foon became advantageoufly known to the Danifh refident, De Horn, and to feveral Princes and Boyars. Early in 1677 he got the command of a company of infantry ; and with a view of fettling in the country, married the daughter of Colonel Souhay. In 1683 he became Major, in the following year Lieutenant-Colonel, and then was placed in command of troops and artillery for a confiderable expedition. In 1696 he con-

ducted the fiege of Azow; and there fhowed
fuch military fkill, that he became the Czar's
favourite. He was entrufted with the greateft
affairs, made Commander-in-Chief by land and
fea, Viceroy of Novogorod, and firft minifter of
State, with the rank of ambaffador and plenipotentiary to all foreign courts. At his death, in
1699, he left an only fon, Henry, then abfent,
who became Captain of the firft company of the
Czar's guards, and died aged about twenty, in
1703, at Mofcow. The general's nephew, Peter
Lefort, who entered the Ruffian fervice in 1694,
became a Lieutenant-General in Czar Peter's
fervice. He married, firft, in 1713, a daughter
of General Weiden; and fecond, in 1717, a
daughter of M. de Bœrner, of a principal family
in Mecklenburg. He was the fon of Ami
Lefort, who was created a Knight of the Holy
Roman Empire, by Leopold I. in 1698, and
filled the principal offices of his native republic
of Geneva till his death, aged 77, in 1719.

John, another nephew (often mentioned in this
Diary) of General Francis Lefort, was Pruffian
Chamberlain, and a Councillor of the Czar, and
was accredited as Ruffian Envoy to the Court of
France in 1717, where he regulated the cere-
monial for the Czar's reception. Later, he was

accredited to Poland, and was decorated with the *grand cordon* of Alexander Newſki.—TRANSL.

NOTE ON THE FAMILY OF NATHALIA KIRYLIOWNA NARISHKIN.

[See Vol. II., p. 125.]

She was the ſiſter of the Prime Miniſter, Leo Nariſhkin, ſo often mentioned in this Diary. The family, according to Dolgoruki (*Notices des princip. Fam. de la Ruſſie*) was of recent low extraction, deſcended from a Bohemian or Sileſian boor ; and, Dolgoruki adduces as a proof how jealouſly pure the official roll of the ancient nobleſſe of Muſcovy was kept, by adducing the fact, that when the Velvet Book—the book of gold of the Muſcovite nobility—was laſt tranſcribed in Czar Peter's time, the Nariſhkins, notwithſtanding their cloſe parentage with the autocrat, were unable with all their efforts to get admiſſion to its pages.—TRANSL.

NOTE ON THE FAMILY OF PETER'S CZARINE.

[See Vol. II., p. 132.]

Eudoxia, or Ottokeſa Feodorowna, was daughter of the Boyar Feodor Abramowitz Lapoukhin. Peter was married to her in his ſix-

teenth year, on the 29th of January, 1691. It
was upon the birth of his fon next year, that the
turbulent Princefs Sophia, feconded by Boris
Galitzin, fought Czar Peter's life, exciting the
Strelitz to a treafonable mutiny, from which
Peter found fafety in flight to the ftrong convent of the Trinity called Droicza, fome miles
from Mofcow. The infurgents and their leader
were racked alive ; Galitzin was banifhed by
the counfels of the Narifhkins, and Czar Peter
named his own uncle Leo Kirilowitz Narifhkin,
fo often mentioned in this Diary, to be his prime
minifter.—Transl.

NOTES ON SOME RUSSIAN EMBASSIES TO LONDON.

Evelyn makes mention of three Ruffian Embaffies that he faw in London. The firft of
thefe was in 1663, when he jots down in his
Diary :

" 27th Dec.—Went to London to fee the
" entrance of the Ruffian Ambaffador, whom
" his Majefty ordered to be received with much
" ftate, the Emperor not only having been kind
" to his Majefty in his diftrefs, but banifhing
" all commerce with our nation during the
" rebellion.

" Firft, the city companies and trained bands
" were all in their ftations : his Majefty's army
" and guards in great order. His Excellency
" came in a very rich coach, with fome of his
" chief attendants ; many of the reft on horfe-
" back, clad in their vefts, after the Eaftern
" manner, rich furs, caps, and carrying the
" prefents, fome carrying hawks, furs, teeth,
" bows, &c. It was a very magnificent
" fhow."

Two days later Evelyn notes :

" 29th.—Saw the audience of the Muscovy
" Ambaffador, which was with extraordinary
" ftate, his retinue being numerous, all clad in
" vefts of feveral colours, with bufkins after the
" Eaftern manner ; their caps of fur ; tunics
" richly embroidered with gold and pearls, made
" a glorious fhow. The King being feated under
" a canopy in the Banqueting Houfe, the Secre-
" tary of the Embaffy went before the Ambaf-
" fador in a grave march, holding up his mafter's
" letters of credence in a crimfon taffeta fcarf
" before his forehead. The Ambaffador then
" delivered it with a profound reverence to the
" King, who gave it to our Secretary of State :
" it was written in a long and lofty ftyle. Then
" came in the prefents, borne by 165 of his

" retinue, confifting of mantles, and other large
" pieces lined with fable, black fox and ermine;
" Perfian carpets, the ground cloth of gold and
" velvet; hawks, fuch as they faid never came
" the like ; horfes faid to be Perfian ; bows and
" arrows, &c. Thefe, borne by fo long a train,
" rendered it very extraordinary. Wind mufic
" played all the while in the galleries above.
" This finifhed, the Ambaffador was conveyed
" by the mafter of the ceremonies to York
" Houfe, where he was treated with a banquet,
" which coft 200*l.*, as I was affured."

On the 30th of May following, Evelyn faw
" the Ambaffador take leave of their Majefties
" with great folemnity."

This was the Embaffy fent by the Czar to
congratulate Charles II. on his reftoration :

" The Czar of Mufcovy fent an Ambaffador
" to compliment King Charles II. on his reftora-
" tion. The King fent the Earl of Carlifle as his
" Ambaffador to Mofcow, to defire the re-eftab-
" lifhment of the ancient privileges of the Englifh
" merchants at Archangel, which had been taken
" away by the Czar, who, abhorring the murder
" of the King's father, accufed them as favourers
" of it. But, by the means of the Czar's mini-
" fters, his Lordfhip was very ill received, and met

" with what he deemed affronts, and had no fuccefs
" as to his demands, fo that at coming away he
" refufed the prefents fent him by the Czar. The
" Czar fent an Ambaffador to England to com-
" plain of Lord Carlifle's conduct ; but his Lord-
" fhip vindicated himfelf fo well, that the King
" told the Ambaffador he faw no reafon to con-
" demn his Lordfhip's conduct."—[*Relation of the
Embaffy by G. M., authenticated by Lord Carlifle,*
printed 1669.]

Again, in 1667, Evelyn faw a Ruffian Embaffy at Court, of which he thus fpeaks in his
Diary on the 28th Auguft of that year :

" In the afternoon . . . to the audience
" of a Ruffian Envoy in the Queen's Prefence-
" Chamber, introduced with much ftate, the
" foldiers, penfioners, and guards in their order.
" His letters of credence brought by his fecretary
" in a fcarf of farfenet, their vefts fumptuous,
" much embroidered with pearls. He delivered
" his fpeech in the Rufs language, but without
" the leaft action or motion of his body, which
" was immediately interpreted aloud by a German
" that fpake good Englifh ; half of it confifted
" in repetition of the Czar's titles, which were
" very haughty and Oriental : the fubftance of
" the reft was, that he was only fent to fee the

" King and Queen and know how they did, with
" much compliment and frothy language."

Of the third Ruffian Embaffy in England which
Evelyn witneffed he thus fpeaks, A.D. 1682 :

" 24th [November].—I was at the audience
" of the Ruffian Ambaffador before both their
" Majefties in the Banqueting Houfe. The
" prefents were carried before him, held up by
" his followers in two ranks, before the King's
" ftate, and confifted of tapeftry (one fuite of
" which was doubtlefsly brought from France
" as being of that fabric, the Ambaffador having
" paffed through that kingdom as he came out
" of Spain), a large Perfian carpet, furs of fable
" and ermine, &c. ; but nothing was fo fplendid
" and exotic as the Ambaffador who came foon
" after the King's reftoration. This prefent
" Ambaffador was exceedingly offended that his
" coach was not permitted to come into the
" Court, till, being told that no King's Ambaf-
" fador did, he was pacified, yet requiring an
" atteftation of it under the hand of Sir Charles
" Cotterell, the Mafter of the Ceremonies ; being,
" it feems, afraid he fhould offend his mafter if he
" omitted the leaft punctilio. It was reported he
" condemned his fon to lofe his head for fhaving
" off his beard, and putting himfelf in the

" French mode at Paris, and that he would
" have executed it had not the French King
" interceded—but query of this."

At the fame time with this laft-mentioned
Ruffian Embaffy there were alfo in London an
Envoy from Morocco, with whofe appearance,
manners, and deportment, Evelyn was much
ftruck. He defcribes him as a handfome perfon,
well featured, of a wife look, fubtle, and extremely civil. It was he that brought as prefents
oftriches and lions ; which provoked the witty
monarch to laugh, and fay " he knew nothing
" more proper to fend by way of return than a
" flock of geefe." Evelyn tells how he was " at
" the entertainment of the Morocco Ambaffador
" at the Duchefs of Portfmouth's glorious apart-
" ments at Whitehall, where there was a great
" banquet of fweetmeats and mufic ; but at
" which both the Ambaffador and his retinue
" behaved themfelves with extraordinary modera-
" tion and modefty, though placed about a long
" table, a lady between two Moors, and amongft
" thefe were the king's natural children, namely,
" Lady Lichfield and Suffex, the Duchefs of
" Portfmouth, Nelly, &c., concubines, and
" cattle of that fort, as fplendid as jewels and
" excefs of bravery could make them ; the

" Moors neither admiring, nor feeming to re-
" gard anything, furniture or the like, with any
" earneftnefs, and but decently tafting of the
" banquet . . . did not look about or ftare
" on the ladies, or exprefs the leaft furprife, but
" with a courtly negligence in face, countenance,
" and whole behaviour, anfwering only to fuch
" queftions as were afked with a great deal of
" wit and gallantry." He tells further, how
the Moor " went fometimes to the theatres,
" where, upon any foolifh or fantaftical action,
" he could not forbear laughing, but he endea-
" voured to hide it with extraordinary modefty
" and gravity. In a word, the Ruffian Ambaf-
" fador, ftill at Court, behaved himfelf like a
" clown compared to this civil heathen."—
Transl.

THE END.

BRADBURY AND EVANS, PRINTERS, WHITEFRIARS.

No. 11, BOUVERIE STREET, FLEET STREET, E.C.

March, 1863.

WORKS PUBLISHED BY
BRADBURY AND EVANS.

THE ENGLISH CYCLOPÆDIA.

Conducted by CHARLES KNIGHT.

The ENGLISH CYCLOPÆDIA is published in FOUR DIVISIONS, *each Division being complete in itself and sold separately.*

THE CYCLOPÆDIA OF GEOGRAPHY.

Four Volumes, price 2l. 2s., or bound in 2 Vols., half-morocco, 2l. 10s.

This Cyclopædia embraces the Physical Features of every country, the Statistics of its department, and its Cities and Marts of Commerce; as well as recording its history to the most recent period.

THE CYCLOPÆDIA OF BIOGRAPHY.

Six Volumes, price 3l., or bound in 3 Vols., half-morocco, 3l. 12s.

The Cyclopædia of Biography may, without presumption, be stated to be the most complete Biographical Dictionary extant; unequalled in any language for the universality of its range, its fulness without verbosity, its accuracy, and its completeness to the present time. It possesses the new and important feature of giving notices of living persons, English and foreign, of contemporary celebrity. No work of a similar nature approaches the English Cyclopædia of Biography in cheapness.

THE CYCLOPÆDIA OF NATURAL HISTORY.

In Four Volumes, price 2l. 2s., or bound in 2 Vols., half-morocco, 2l. 10s.

The Cyclopædia of Natural History includes the contributions of the most eminent Naturalists. In BOTANY, those by Dr. Lankester, Dr. Lindley, and Dr. Royle; in GEOLOGY, those of Sir Henry de la Beche, Mr. Horner, and Professor Phillips; in MINERALOGY, those of Mr. R. Phillips and Professor W. Turner; in ZOOLOGY, those of Mr. Broderip, Professor Forbes, Mr. Ogilby, and Mr. Waterhouse; in COMPARATIVE ANATOMY and PHYSIOLOGY, those of Mr. Day, Professor Paget, and Dr. Southwood Smith.

THE CYCLOPÆDIA OF ARTS AND SCIENCES.

Eight Volumes, price 4l. 16s.; or bound in 4 Vols., half-morocco, 5l. 12s.

The Cyclopædia of Arts and Sciences, embracing as it does all subjects not belonging to either of the above Divisions, is necessarily the most importan and comprehensive. The following List mentions the principal subjects comprised in it :—

MATHEMATICS AND ASTRONOMY.	ARCHITECTURE ; CIVIL ENGINEERING.
PHYSICAL SCIENCES ; OPTICS ; ACOUSTICS;	MANUFACTURES AND MACHINERY.
DYNAMICS ; ELECTRICITY ; MAGNETISM ;	PAINTING ; SCULPTURE ; ANTIQUITIES.
METEOROLOGY.	ENGRAVING ; MUSIC, &C.
CHEMISTRY.	RURAL ECONOMY.
NAVIGATION AND MILITARY SCIENCES.	PHILOLOGY ; MENTAL PHILOSOPHY.
MATERIA MEDICA ; MEDICINE ; SURGERY.	GOVERNMENT AND POLITICAL ECONOMY.
	LAW AND JURISPRUDENCE.

Also, in 1 Vol. 4to, uniform with the Work, price 6s. cloth ; or 9s. half-bound, morocco.

A SYNOPTICAL INDEX TO THE FOUR DIVISIONS.

** *Subscribers are requested to complete their Sets without delay, as the Parts and Numbers can only be kept on sale for a limited period.*

LIST OF SOME OF THE

CONTRIBUTORS TO THE ENGLISH CYCLOPÆDIA.

Dr. ADDY, Cambridge.

G. B. AIRY, A.M., Trinity College, Cambridge, Astronomer Royal.

Dr. ATKINSON, F.C.S., Lecturer on Chemistry, Cheltenham College.

J. ATTFIELD, St. Bartholomew's Hospital.

W. AYRTON, F.R.S., (the late).

C. BAKER, Yorkshire Institution for the Deaf and Dumb, Doncaster.

Rev. F. BAKER, Bolton, Lancashire.

Rev. J. BEARD, LL.D., Manchester.

Sir FRANCIS BEAUFORT (the late), Hydrographer to the Admiralty.

Dr. BECKER (the late), of Berlin.

SAMUEL BIRCH, British Museum.

A. BISSETT, A.M., Barrister-at-Law.

T. BRADLEY, King's College, London.

E. W. BRAYLEY, F.R.S. JAMES BREESE.

J. BRITTON (the late), F.A.S.

W. J. BRODERIP (the late), F.R.S.

G. R. BURNELL, C.E. G. BUDD, M.D.

J. H. BURTON, Advocate, Edinburgh.

Rev. C. J. BURTON, Vicar of Lydd.

A. CAYLEY, F.R.S., F.R.A.S.

W. D. CHRISTIE, A M., Trin. Coll. Cam.

T. COATES, formerly Sec. to Society for the Diffusion of Useful Knowledge.

HENRY COLE, South Kensington Museum.

W. D. COOPER, F.A.S. W. COULSON.

EDWARD COWPER (the late), King's College.

G. L. CRAIK, A.M., Professor of History, Queen's College, Belfast.

Professor DAVIES, Woolwich.|

Sir J. F. DAVIS.

Dr. DAY, Professor of Medicine in the University of St. Andrew's.

J. C. F. S. DAY, Barrister-at-Law.

Sir H. DE LA BECHE, F.R.S., &c. (the late).

A. DE MORGAN, A.M., Trin. Coll. Cam. ; University College.

W. R. DEVERELL (the late).

R. DICKSON, M.D. GEORGE DODD.

Dr. DOMEIER (the late), Trin. Coll. Cam.

Rev. J. W. DONALDSON (the late).

Captain DONNELLY, R.E.

J. DOWSON, Sandhurst.

B. F. DUPPA (the late).

Sir C. L. EASTLAKE.

Sir H. ELLIS, late Principal Librarian of the British Museum.

T. FALCONER, Barrister-at-Law.

SAMUEL FERGUSON, Barrister-at-Law, Dublin.

E. FORBES (the late), Professor of Botany, King's College.

E. FRANKLAND, Ph.D., F.R.S., St. Bartholomew's Hospital.

T. GALLOWAY, A.M., F.R.S. (the late).

W. C. GLEN, Poor Law Board.

Dr. GILDEMEISTER, University of Bonn.

Rev. J. W. GLEADHALL, Cambridge.

C. W. GOODWIN, Barrister-at-Law.

Dr. T. GOLDSTÜCKER, Professor of Sanskrit in University College, London.

JAS. GRANT, Barrister-at-Law.

R. GRANT, A.M., F.R.S., Professor of Astronomy in the University of Glasgow.

Dr. GREENHILL, Trin. Col. Oxford.

E. GUEST, Master of Caius College, Cambridge.

Dr. GUTHRIE, F.C.S., Professor of Chemistry, University of Mauritius.

EDWARD HALL, C.E. J. O. HALLIWELL.

N. E. S. A. HAMILTON, Brit. Mus.

W. C. HAMILTON, State Paper Office.

J. A. HARDCASTLE, Trinity College, Cambridge.

SIR EDMUND HEAD. Rev. W. HICKEY.
GEORGE HOGARTH.
F. HOLME, Corpus Christi College, Oxford.
J. HOPPUS, Professor of Mental Philosophy, University College, London.
LEONARD HORNER, F.R.S.
W. HOSKINO (the late).
H. HOWARD, R.A. (the late).
Rev. J. HUNTER, F.S.A. (the late).
Colonel JACKSON (the late), Secretary to the Royal Geographical Society.
D. JARDINE, A.M. (the late), Police Magistrate, Bow Street.
C. J. JOHNSTONE, M.D. (the late).
R. M. KERR, LL.D., Barrister-at-Law.
T. H. KEY, A.M., Trin. Col. Cam., University College.
J. B. KINNEAR, Barrister-at-Law.
Dr. JOHN KITTO (the late).
CHARLES KNIGHT.
Count KRASINSKI (the late).
E. LANKESTER, M.D.
Colonel LEAKE (the late).
J. LE CHAPPELAIN, Actuary of the Albion Insurance Company.
E. LEVIEN, M.A., Baliol College, Oxford.
G. H. LEWES. Sir G. C. LEWIS, Bart.
Rev. G. F. LEWIS. Dr. LINDLEY, F.R.S.
GEORGE LONG, A.M., Editor of the Penny Cyclopædia.
J. J. LONSDALE, Barrister-at-Law.
CHARLES MACFARLANE (the late).
D. MACLACHLAN, Barrister-at-Law.
A. T. MALKIN, A.M., Trinity College, Cambridge.
T. MALONE, London Institution.
Mr. Serjeant MANNING.
DAVID MASSON, Professor of English Literature in University College, London.
T. E. MAY, Clerk Assistant of the House of Commons.
R. H. MEADE, formerly Lecturer at St. George's Hospital.
Rev. A. W. M. MORRISON, A.M., Trinity College, Cambridge.
J. C. MORTON. A. MUNOZ DE SOTOMAYOR.
Rev. R. MURPHY (the late), Caius College, Cambridge.
J. NARRIEN (the late) Professor of Mathematics, Royal Military College, Sandhurst.
E. NORRIS, Honorary Secretary to the Asiatic Society.
WM. OGILBY, Trinity College, Cambridge.
Rev. T. J. ORMEROD. JOHN OXENFORD.
J. PAGET, Bartholomew's Hospital.
J. PHILLIPS, F.G.S., Professor of Geology in the University of Oxford.
R. PHILLIPS, F.R.S. (the late).
J. R. PLANCHÉ, Rouge Croix Pursuivant.
W. PLATÉ, LL.D. J. C. PLATT.

Major PROCTOR, late of the Royal Military College, Sandhurst.
G. R. PORTER, F.R.S. (the late). Secretary to the Board of Trade.
A. RAMSAY. T. G. REEP.
Rev. W. L. RHAM (the late), Vicar of Winkfield.
CARL RITTER, Professor of Geography n the University of Berlin.
Lieutenant RAPER, R.N.
Dr. ROSEN (the late), Professor of Sanskrit, University College, London.
Dr. REINHOLD ROST, of St. Augustine's College, Canterbury.
Dr. J. F. ROYLE.
Rev. Dr. C. W. RUSSELL, President of Maynooth College.
S. M. SAXBY, Principal Instructor of Naval Engineers of Her Majesty's Reserve, Sheerness.
Dr. LEONARD SCHMITZ, Rector of the High School, Edinburgh.
Rev. R. SHEEPSHANKS, A.M. (the late), Trinity College, Cambridge.
Rev. T. SHORE. J. SIMON, M.D.
G. R. SMALLEY, King's College School.
Rev. E. SMEDLEY (the late).
H. SMITH (the late), Secretary of King's College, London.
Dr. WM. SMITH, Classical Examiner in the University of London.
T. SOUTHWOOD SMITH, M.D.
W. SPALDING (the late), Professor of Logic, St. Andrew's University.
J. STARK, Advocate-General, Ceylon.
G. G. STOKES, Lucasian Professor in the University of Cambridge.
W. J. TAYLER, A.M., Cambridge.
JAMES THORNE.
C. TOMLINSON, Lecturer on Physical Science, King's College School.
G. TUCKER, Professor of Moral Philosophy in the Virginian University.
W. TURNER (the late).
A. URE, M.D., F.R.S. (the late).
ANDRE VIEUSSEUX (the late).
G. R. WATERHOUSE, Keeper of Geology in the British Museum.
THOMAS WATTS, British Museum.
R. WESTMACOTT, R.A.
Rev. R. WHISTON.
WALTER WHITE, Assistant Secretary of Royal Society.
J. J. G. WILKINSON.
G. WILLMORE, A.M. (the late), Trinity College, Cambridge, Barrister-at-Law.
Cardinal WISEMAN.
Lieut. WOLFE, R.N.
R. N. WORNUM, Curator of the National Gallery.
W. YOUATT (the late).

THE ENGLISH CYCLOPÆDIA.—CONTINUED.
OPINIONS OF THE PRESS.

FROM THE TIMES.   OCT. 4, 1861.

"As regards the contents of this Cyclopædia, it is, however, impossible to give any sufficient impression of an aggregate which includes somewhere or other all the information generally required upon every conceivable topic. A good Encyclopædia, as every one knows, is a compendious library, and though students may require further information, upon some points, than its summaries contain, even students will be surprised in this instance to find the materials at their disposal when they once adopt the habit of resorting to its pages. For all practical purposes a large proportion of the articles may be said to be exhaustive; they are accurate to a degree which will strike even those who know what pains have been taken to render them so; and, as they are concise as well as full, every column being rammed like a sky-rocket, the owner has a reservoir out of all proportion to the library shelves it will occupy."

FROM THE SATURDAY REVIEW.   SEPT. 28, 1861.

"Upon the whole, then, we are able to speak very favourably of this new Cyclopædia. Its great recommendation is not its comparative cheapness (though the cost only averages about half a guinea a volume), but its originality, completeness, and general trustworthiness. We may express a hope that its enterprising publisher will have no reason to regret his considerable venture. He is not likely, we think, to have to complain of want of patronage, if it is sufficiently remembered that any one of his four great Divisions may be purchased separately as a work complete in itself. Few may be able to afford the whole series; but there are many who will be glad to procure, for example, a Biographical Dictionary, while others will require, for their peculiar tastes or studies, the Geographical Cyclopædia, or those of the Arts and Sciences, or of Natural History."

FROM THE SPECTATOR.   SEPT. 28, 1861.

"It is a work that may safely be consulted by the most advanced students, and is likely to hold its own as the most complete work of reference in the language, until some great revolution in science has taught us how blindly our wisest philosophers are still groping in the dark."

FROM THE EXAMINER.   OCT. 19.

"Mr. Knight completed a few weeks ago the two-and-twenty volumes of that excellent English Cyclopædia, into which the 'Penny Cyclopædia' has now been recast. The revised issue was planned in four divisions. Each is a complete work, having distinct claims on a large special class of readers, while the four together now constitute a general Cyclopædia, singularly accurate and full, of which the two-and-twenty volumes—eight given to Arts and Sciences, six to Biography, four to Geography, and four to Natural History—cost only twelve pounds. Now that its reprints may be on untaxed paper, this admirable work and others that preceded or are concurrent with it will, we trust, bring their late worldly reward to one who, having been for forty years a most unwearied labourer for the instruction of the public, toils yet with the determined vigour of youth when his years are three-score-and-ten."

FROM AN ARTICLE BY DAVID MASSON, IN MACMILLAN'S MAGAZINE FOR MARCH.

"Whoever wants an Encyclopædia, extensive and yet cheap, and compiled throughout on the principle of compendious and accurate information on all subjects rather than on that of collected individual dissertations, cannot do better than procure the 'English Cyclopædia' of Mr. Charles Knight. *   *   * As a digest of universal knowledge which shall serve for the popular and miscellaneous purposes of all, and at the same time furnish materials and abstracts for those who are studying special subjects, and aim at substantial and exact science, the 'English Cyclopædia' may be confidently recommended."

In Eight Volumes, large 8vo, price £3 16s. 6d., handsomely bound in cloth, illustrated with many hundred Woodcuts and Steel Engravings,

AND DEDICATED TO

HIS ROYAL HIGHNESS THE PRINCE OF WALES,

CHARLES KNIGHT'S
POPULAR HISTORY OF ENGLAND.

Extract from the Author's Postscript to Volume 8.—" In the Introduction to my First Volume I have stated the circumstances which led me to entertain the idea of writing a book that might be recommended for purposes of instruction, 'when a young man of Eighteen asks for a History of England.' With a pardonable pride, I may presume to mention that my desire to produce such a book has been welcomed in a manner far beyond my hope—I fear beyond my desert. Whilst the Prince of Wales was pursuing his studies at the University of Cambridge, my History was used as a text-book, and was quoted and recommended by the Rev. Charles Kingsley, the Professor of Modern History, in the course of Lectures which His Royal Highness attended. The exalted rank of the student—the literary eminence of the Professor—combine to render this compliment most grateful to me. It affords me the consolation of believing that, whatever may be the errors and deficiencies of my undertaking, it has been recognised by one whose opinion is of no ordinary value, as a well-meant endeavour to write the History of the Kingdom and of the People with a due sense of my responsibility to be just and truthful, and with a catholicity of mind that may be preserved without the suppression of honestly-formed opinions."

OPINIONS OF THE PRESS.

FROM THE ATHENÆUM.

" We very cordially recommend Mr. Knight's volumes to the readers whom they seek. We know of no history of England so free from prejudice, so thoroughly honest and impartial, so stored with facts, fancies, and illustrations,—and therefore none so well adapted for school or college as this 'Popular History of England.' "

FROM THE TIMES.

"This is the history for English youth."—Jan. 12, 1860.

FROM "ALL THE YEAR ROUND," IN AN ARTICLE UPON PARISH REGISTERS.

" So observes Mr. Charles Knight in his admirably comprehensive popular History of England, from which no topic that concerns the history of the English people—not even this question of the origin of parish registers—has been omitted ; that book of Mr. Knight's being, let us say here by the way, the best history extant, not only for, but also of, the people."

FROM THE EXAMINER.

" During the last five years Mr. Knight has been labouring at the *magnum opus* of his literary life. His ambition has been to advance liberal thought and right knowledge in England by a History of England, so written as to engage popular attention, giving the succession of events in the detail necessary to their full perception, and with his own high interpretation of their relative importance. He is the last man who would see in English History the kings and queens instead of the people."

FROM THE WESTMINSTER REVIEW.

" So far as we are acquainted with this comprehensive history we cannot hesitate to commend the results of Mr. Knight's seven years' labour. He has probably done all that talent, industry, uprightness, and an enlightened sympathy could do. His history is probably the most available, and the most informing history of England that we possess. It has one cardinal moral merit ; it is a thoroughly patriotic history—the production of an educated Englishman who loves his country, without concealing his country's faults, and without hating the country of a neighbour. It has the merit of being readable, and presenting a complete and often graphic narrative of nearly two thousand years of England's fortunes and of England's action."

** *The work is sold separately in Volumes.   Vols. I. to VI., price 9s. each ; Vol. VII., 10s. 6d. ; and Vol. VIII., 12s.   Also in Parts.   Parts 1 to 54, price One Shilling each.   Parts 55 to 58, price 3s. 6d. each.*

WORKS BY W. M. THACKERAY.

THE VIRGINIANS.

Illustrated by the Author. Two vols. 8vo, cloth. 26s.

Also, a Cheap and Popular Edition, price 7s.

THE NEWCOMES.

Illustrated by RICHARD DOYLE. Two vols. 8vo, cloth, 26s.

** Also, a *Cheap and Popular Edition, with-out Illustrations, uniform with the Miscellanies, in crown 8vo, 7s.*

VANITY FAIR.

Illustrated by the Author. One Vol. 8vo, cloth, 21s.

** Also, a *Cheap and Popular Edition, without Illustrations, uniform with the Miscellanies, in crown 8vo, 6s.*

PENDENNIS.

Illustrated by the Author. Two vols. 8vo, cloth, 26s.

** Also, a *Cheap and Popular Edition, without Illustrations, uniform with the Miscellanies, in crown 8vo, 7s.*

HISTORY OF SAMUEL TITMARSH.

Illustrated by the Author. One vol. small 8vo, cloth, 4s.

A COLLECTED EDITION OF

MR. THACKERAY'S EARLY WRITINGS.

Complete in Four Vols., crown 8vo, price 6s. each, uniform with the Cheap Editions of "Vanity Fair" and "Pendennis."

MISCELLANIES IN PROSE AND VERSE.

The Contents of each Volume of the "Miscellanies" are also published in separate Parts, at various prices, as follows:—

VOL. I.	s.	d.	VOL. III.	s.	d.
BALLADS	1	6	MEMOIRS OF BARRY LYNDON .	3	0
THE SNOB PAPERS . . .	2	0	A LEGEND OF THE RHINE:—		
THE TREMENDOUS ADVENTURES			REBECCA AND ROWENA .	1	6
OF MAJOR GAHAGAN . .	1	0	A LITTLE DINNER AT TIM-		
THE FATAL BOOTS:—COX'S DIARY	1	0	MINS'S:—THE BEDFORD ROW		
			CONSPIRACY . . .	1	0
VOL. II.			VOL. IV.		
THE YELLOWPLUSH MEMOIRS:—			THE FITZBOODLE PAPERS:—MEN'S		
JEAMES'S DIARY . .	2	0	WIVES	2	6
SKETCHES AND TRAVELS IN LON-			A SHABBY GENTEEL STORY .	1	6
DON	2	0	THE HISTORY OF SAMUEL TIT-		
NOVELS BY EMINENT HANDS:—			MARSH AND THE GREAT		
CHARACTER SKETCHES .	1	6	HOGGARTY DIAMOND . .	1	6

WORKS OF DOUGLAS JERROLD.

In Eight Volumes, crown 8vo, price 4s. each,

THE COLLECTED EDITION

OF THE

WRITINGS OF DOUGLAS JERROLD.

VOL. 1.—ST. GILES AND ST. JAMES.

VOL. 2.—MEN OF CHARACTER:
CONTENTS :—Job Pippins : the Man who "couldn't help it"—Jack Runnymede: the Man of "many thanks"—Adam Buff: the Man "without a Shirt"—Matthew Clear : the Man "who saw his way"—John Applejohn : the Man who "meant well"—Barnaby Palms: the Man "who felt his way"—Christopher Snob: the Man who was "born to be hanged"—Creso Quattrino: the Man "who died rich."

VOL. 3.—MRS. CAUDLE'S CURTAIN LECTURES.—THE STORY OF A FEATHER. — THE SICK GIANT AND THE DOCTOR DWARF.

VOL. 4.—CAKES AND ALE.
CONTENTS :—The Lesson of Life—Perditus Mutton, who bought a Caul—The Mayor of Hole-cum-Corner—The Romance of a Key-hole—Mr. Peppercorn "at home"—The Preacher Parrot—The Lives of Smith, Brown, Jones, and Robinson—Shakespeare at "Bankside"—The Wine Cellar, a "Morality"

—Kind Cousin Tom—The Manager's Pig—The Tapestry Weaver of Beauvais—The Genteel Pigeons—Shakespeare in China—The Order of Poverty—A Gossip at Reculvers—The Old Man at the Gate—The Epitaph of Sir Hugh Evans.

VOL. 5.—PUNCH'S LETTERS TO HIS SON, AND COMPLETE LETTER WRITER — SKETCHES OF THE ENGLISH.

VOL. 6.—A MAN MADE OF MONEY.

VOL. 7.—COMEDIES :
CONTENTS :—Bubbles of the Day—Time Works Wonders—The Catspaw—The Prisoner of War—Retired from Business—St. Cupid ; or Dorothy's Fortune.

*** *These are also sold separately, price 1s. each.*

VOL. 8.—COMEDIES AND DRAMAS :
CONTENTS:—The Rent Day—Nell Gwynne—The Housekeeper—The Wedding Gown—The School-Fellows—Doves in a Cage—The Painter of Ghent—Black-eyed Susan.

THE FOLLOWING ARE PUBLISHED SEPARATELY:—

	s.	d.		s.	d.
THE CAUDLE LECTURES . .	1	0	THE LESSON OF LIFE—THE LIVES OF		
THE STORY OF A FEATHER .	2	0	BROWN, JONES, AND ROBINSON .	1	6
PUNCH'S LETTERS TO HIS SON .	1	6	SKETCHES OF THE ENGLISH . .	1	6

PUNCH'S HISTORY OF THE LAST TWENTY YEARS.

RE-ISSUE OF "PUNCH."

From its Commencement in 1841 to the end of 1860.

In Volumes, 5s. boards, uncut, monthly; and in double Vols., 10s. 6d. cloth gilt,
every other month.

In arranging this re-issue, two modes of publication have been adopted. One in MONTHLY Volumes, each containing the numbers for a half-year, price 5s. in boards, with the edges uncut, so as to enable the purchasers to rebind them according to their fancy.

The other, in volumes published every ALTERNATE MONTH, and containing the Numbers for a year, so that each year will form a distinct volume. The price of these volumes is 10s. 6d., handsomely bound in cloth, gilt edges. To each Volume is prefixed an explanatory introduction.

The following Volumes are already published :—

In boards, price 5s. each, Vols. 1 to 25 ; in cloth, gilt edges :—

	s.	d.		s.	d.
Vol. 1 (for 1841) . . .	6	0	Vols. 12 and 13 (1847) . .	10	6
Vols. 2 and 3 (1842) . . .	10	6	Vols. 14 and 15 (1848) . .	10	6
Vols. 4 and 5 (1843) . .	10	6	Vols. 16 and 17 (1849) . .	10	6
Vols. 6 and 7 (1844) . . .	10	6	Vols. 18 and 19 (1850) . .	10	6
Vols. 8 and 9 (1845) . .	10	6	Vols. 20 and 21 (1851) . .	10	6
Vols. 10 and 11 (1846) . . .	10	6	Vols. 22 and 23 (1852) . .	10	6

Vols. 24 and 25 (1853) 10s. 6d.

** Any Volume or Double Volume may always be had separately.

FROM THE TIMES.

"The complete re-issue of *Punch*, a publication which has come out consecutively week by week for upwards of twenty years, is in its way one of the Curiosities of Literature. . . . . . Suppose a future Macaulay at the close of this century looking up materials for the history of the present portion of it, the *Times* and the statutes at large will supply him with most of them ; but it is simply impossible that he can dispense with *Punch*."

FROM THE EXAMINER.

"As a current comment on our social history, the volumes of *Punch* will have in their way as real, if not as grave, an interest to future students, as the tomes of any serious historical compiler. The pencil sketches show the English year by year in their habits as they lived, and chronicle incidentally every shift and turn of outward fashion. Thus in a pleasant and handy volume one can recover the whole body of English gossip for a bygone year. To the shelves, then, of all household libraries not yet possessed of their enlivening store of wit and wisdom, we recommend the volumes of *Punch* in this their complete re-issue. They are rich in wholesome comic thought, and they are, we believe, the best repertory of comic sketches within the whole range of English and foreign literature."

ONCE A WEEK,

AN ILLUSTRATED MISCELLANY

OF

Literature, Art, Science, and Popular Information,

Is published EVERY SATURDAY, price 3*d.* ; in Monthly Parts, price 1*s.*; and in
Half-yearly Volumes, price 7*s.* 6*d.*

*** *The Seventh Volume was published on the 31st December.*

Amongst the numerous Contributors to "ONCE A WEEK" are the following :—

ALFRED TENNYSON.	HARRIET MARTINEAU.	THEODORE MARTIN.
BRIDGES ADAMS.	MISS CARPENTER.	CAPT. SHERARD OSBORN.
TOM TAYLOR.	G. W. DASENT.	MISS BESSIE PARKES.
SHIRLEY BROOKS.	JOHN ELLIOTT.	JOHN PLUMMER.
DR. WYNTER.	EDWARD JESSE.	COL. ALEXANDER.
SIR JOHN BOWRING.	CHARLES KNIGHT.	GEORGE GROVE.
ROBERT BELL.	MAJOR COOKSON.	MRS. ELLIS.
MISS ISABELLA BLAGDEN.	CHARLES READE.	A. A. KNOX.
GEORGE BORROW.	PERCIVAL LEIGH.	SAMUEL LOVER.
THE AUTHOR OF " JOHN	GEORGE MEREDITH.	T. A. TROLLOPE.
HALIFAX, GENTLEMAN."	MRS. CROW.	MARK LEMON.
MRS. HENRY WOOD.	DUTTON COOKE.	PETER CUNNINGHAM.

And the following eminent Artists are amongst its constant Illustrators :—

J. E. MILLAIS.	H. K. BROWNE.	F. WALKER.
G. DU MAURIER.	F. J. SKILL.	HARRISON WEIR.
CHARLES KEENE.	P. SKELTON.	M. J. LAWLESS.
JOHN LEECH.	JOHN TENNIEL.	J. ROLFE.

ELEANOR'S VICTORY

By the Author of "LADY AUDLEY'S SECRET," "AURORA FLOYD," &c., is now
in course of publication.

THE HAMPDENS

By HARRIET MARTINEAU, is also in course of publication, Illustrated by
J. E. MILLAIS ; and

A NOVEL

By Mr. TOM TAYLOR is in a forward state of preparation.

SPORTING WORKS.

WITH COLOURED ENGRAVINGS, AND NUMEROUS WOODCUTS,

By JOHN LEECH.

One Vol., 8vo, price 14s.,

MR. SPONGE'S SPORTING TOUR. By the Author of "Handley Cross," &c. With Coloured Engravings, &c. By JOHN LEECH.

8vo, price 18s.,

HANDLEY CROSS; OR, MR. JORROCKS'S HUNT. With Coloured Engravings, &c. By JOHN LEECH.

8vo, price 14s.,

ASK MAMMA; OR, THE RICHEST COMMONER IN ENG-LAND. By the Author of "Sponge's Tour," "Handley Cross," &c. Illustrated with Thirteen Coloured Engravings, and numerous Woodcuts, by JOHN LEECH.

One Vol., 8vo, price 14s. cloth,

PLAIN OR RINGLETS? By the Author of "Handley Cross," &c. With Coloured Engravings, &c., by JOHN LEECH.

WORKS PUBLISHED AT THE PUNCH OFFICE.

PUNCH'S POCKET-BOOK FOR 1863. With a Coloured Illustration by JOHN LEECH, and numerous Woodcuts by JOHN LEECH and JOHN TENNIEL.

PUNCH'S ALMANACK FOR 1863. Illustrated by JOHN LEECH and CHARLES KEENE.

Price 2s. 6d. in stiff boards, gilt edges,

PUNCH'S 10 ALMANACKS. 1842 to 1851.

Price 2s. 6d.,

PUNCH'S 10 ALMANACKS. Second Series. 1852 to 1861.

Bound in cloth, price 5s. 6d.,

PUNCH'S 20 ALMANACKS. 1842 to 1861.

"It was a happy notion to reproduce a volume of these Almanacks for the last twenty years, in which we can trace their manifest improvement up to Christmas, 1860."—*The Times.*

ILLUSTRATED WORKS.

In Three handsome Folio Volumes, price 12s. each,

PICTURES OF LIFE AND CHARACTER. From the Collection of Mr. Punch. By JOHN LEECH.

Price 5s. plain ; 7s. 6d. coloured,

YOUNG TROUBLESOME; OR, MASTER JACKY'S HOLIDAYS. By JOHN LEECH.

A handsome 4to. volume, cloth extra, price 22s.,

THE FOREIGN TOUR OF MESSRS. BROWN, JONES, AND ROBINSON. What they saw and did in Belgium, Germany, Switzerland, and Italy. By RICHARD DOYLE.

Elegantly bound in half morocco, price 15s.,

MANNERS AND CUSTOMS OF THE ENGLISH. By RICHARD DOYLE. With Extracts by PERCIVAL LEIGH from "PIPS' DIARY."

Handsomely bound in Two Vols., price 21s.,

THE COMIC HISTORY OF ENGLAND. By GILBERT A. A'BECKETT. With Coloured Engravings and Woodcuts. By JOHN LEECH.

Handsomely bound in cloth, price 11s.,

THE COMIC HISTORY OF ROME. By GILBERT A. A'BECKETT. With Coloured Engravings and Woodcuts. By JOHN LEECH.

With a Coloured Frontispiece and Numerous Illustrations on Wood by JOHN LEECH, price 10s. 6d.,

A LITTLE TOUR IN IRELAND. Being a visit to Dublin, Galway, Connemara, Athlone, Limerick, Killarney, Glengariff, Cork, &c. &c. &c. By An OXONIAN.

Price 10s. 6d. ; or, separately, 1s. each,

MR. BRIGGS AND HIS DOINGS (FISHING). A Series of Twelve Coloured Plates. Enlarged from Mr. JOHN LEECH's original Drawings from "Punch."

BOTANICAL WORKS.

In One Volume, 8vo, cloth, price 36s., with upwards of 500 Illustrations,

THE VEGETABLE KINGDOM ; or, THE STRUCTURE, CLASSI-FICATION, AND USES OF PLANTS. By DR. LINDLEY. Illustrated upon the Natural System.

In One Volume, 8vo, cloth, with numerous Illustrations, price 12s.,

THE ELEMENTS OF BOTANY, Structural and Physiological. With a Glossary of Technical Terms. By DR. LINDLEY.

** The Glossary may be had separately, price 5s.

In One Volume, 8vo, cloth, price 7s. 6d.,

MEDICAL AND ŒCONOMICAL BOTANY. By DR. LINDLEY.

In One Volume, 8vo, half-bound, with 400 Illustrations, price 5s. 6d.,

SCHOOL BOTANY ; or, THE RUDIMENTS OF BOTANICAL SCIENCE. By DR. LINDLEY.

Second Edition, price 1s.,

DESCRIPTIVE BOTANY ; or, THE ART OF DESCRIBING PLANTS CORRECTLY, in Scientific Language, for Self-Instruction and the Use of Schools. By DR. LINDLEY.

Crown 8vo, price 16s. cloth extra,

PAXTON'S BOTANICAL DICTIONARY ; Comprising the Names, History, and Culture of all Plants known in Britain, together with a full Explanation of Technical Terms.

WORKS ON GARDENING.

The Sixth Edition, cloth gilt, price 7s.,

THE LADIES' COMPANION TO THE FLOWER GARDEN. Being an Alphabetical Arrangement of all the Ornamental Plants grown in Gardens and Shrubberies. With full directions for their Culture. By MRS. LOUDON.

Price 5s. in cloth,

PRACTICAL HINTS ON PLANTING ORNAMENTAL TREES. With particular reference to Coniferæ. In which all the Hardy Species are popularly described. By Messrs. STANDISH and NOBLE.

In One Volume, 8vo, illustrated with numerous Plans, Sections, and Sketches of Gardens and General Objects,

HOW TO LAY OUT A GARDEN. Intended as a General Guide in Choosing, Forming, or Improving an Estate (from a Quarter of an Acre to a Hundred Acres in extent). By EDWARD KEMP. [*New Edition in the Press.*

Price 2s. in cloth,

THE HANDBOOK OF GARDENING. By EDWARD KEMP. For the use of persons who possess a small Garden.

In foolscap 8vo, price 1s.,

HANDBOOK TO THE PICTURES IN THE INTERNATIONAL EXHIBITION. By Tom Taylor, M.A.

In square 16mo, price 7s., gilt edges,

JAPANESE FRAGMENTS. By Captain Sherard Osborn, R.N., C.B.

*** This Work is illustrated with Fac-similes of Drawings purchased by the Author in the City of Yedo. Six of them have been reduced by the new patent process of the Electro Block Company, and are coloured after the originals. The Wood Engravings, twenty-two in number, are accurately traced from the Japanese drawings.

"Sherard Osborn's 'Japanese Fragments,' with facsimiles of illustrations by artists of Yedo, is a real novelty ; in fact it has come upon the artist world as a surprise to find there are artists in Japan who can draw with the vigour of Gilray and the delicacy and humour of Richard Doyle."—*The Times.*

" Those who have not yet had the advantage of encountering the literary productions of Captain Osborn have an additional reason for familiarising themselves with one of the best works of the season."—*Morning Post.*

Price 2s. 6d., fcap. 8vo, with Eight Illustrations by Captain May,

THE CAREER, LAST VOYAGE, AND DISCOVERY OF THE FATE OF SIR JOHN FRANKLIN. By Captain Sherard Osborn, R.N., C.B.

In Two Volumes, fcap. 8vo, price 12s.,

SELECTIONS FROM THE PLAYS OF SHAKESPEARE. As arranged for representation at the Princess's Theatre, and especially adapted for Schools, Private Families, and Young People. By Charles Kean, F.S.A.

MACBETH.	KING LEAR.
KING HENRY VIII.	THE MERCHANT OF VENICE.
THE WINTER'S TALE.	KING JOHN.
MIDSUMMER NIGHT'S DREAM.	MUCH ADO ABOUT NOTHING.
KING RICHARD II.	HAMLET.
THE TEMPEST.	KING HENRY IV.

Either Play may be had separately, price 1s.

In One Vol., post 8vo, with Map, price 10s. 6d.,

THE PRINCE OF WALES IN CANADA AND THE UNITED STATES. By N. A. Woods, Esq., the *Times* Special Correspondent.

" It is a most admirable example of the productions of a class of writers whose labours have afforded so much pleasure and profit to their fellow-countrymen."—*Morning Post.*

" As the Prince of Wales's journey has become a political fact of great importance, coming so closely before the recent agitation in the States; and as Mr. Woods has made his work very nearly exhaustive of the subject, we doubt not that it will now and hereafter become a work for historical reference."—*Court Journal.*

" This may be considered as the only authentic historical record of the visit of the Prince of Wales to the United States of North America. It will most assuredly be read with pleasure by all parties.'—*Observer.*

Demy 8vo, with Map, price 16s.,

A DESCRIPTIVE DICTIONARY OF THE INDIAN ISLANDS, &c. By JOHN CRAWFURD, F.R.S.

"It will take its place at once among standard works."—*Athenæum.*

In Three Vols , post 8vo, price 1l. 11s. 6d.,

EVAN HARRINGTON. A Novel. By GEORGE MEREDITH.

"Evan Harrington is a surprisingly good novel ; for we are almost incredulous of our own admiration until the story has fairly carried us away with it, and then we own that there can be no doubt about its power to interest us."—*Saturday Review.*

"Mr. George Meredith is a writer of uncommon ability. Evan Harrington is as clever as any of his former works, and without some of their faults. . . . Evan Harrington has no imitative trick about it, conscious or unconscious—it is a good story on a subject not yet hackneyed."—*Spectator.*

"The pith of the plot has been evolved with such consummate art, that the result will greatly raise Mr. Meredith's reputation as a writer of fiction."—*Oriental Budget.*

New Edition, fcap. 8vo, price 2s.,

THE COMIC BLACKSTONE. By G. A. A'BECKETT, Author of the "Comic History of England," &c. With an Illustration by GEORGE CRUIKSHANK.

Fcap. 8vo, cloth, price 2s.,

THE QUIZZIOLOGY OF THE BRITISH DRAMA. By G. A. A'BECKETT, Author of the "Comic History of England," &c. With Illustrations by G. CRUIKSHANK.

12mo. cloth, price 2s. 6d.,

SCRIPTURAL CHURCH TEACHING. By Rev. H. MOULE.

Fcap. 8vo, price 2s. 6d.,

BARRACK SERMONS. By Rev. H. MOULE.

Cloth, price 5s.,

A SHORT INQUIRY INTO THE HISTORY OF AGRICULTURE, in Ancient, Mediæval, and Modern Times. By CHANDOS WREN HOSKYNS.

Price 1s.,

WHAT SHALL WE HAVE FOR DINNER? Satisfactorily answered by numerous Bills of Fare for from Two to Eighteen Persons. By LADY CLUTTERBUCK.

Price 2s. each,

HANDBOOKS OF COOKERY;—THE TOILETTE;—GARDENING.

SECOND EDITION OF THE SILVER CORD.

In 3 Vols., post 8vo, price 31s. 6d.,

THE SILVER CORD. By SHIRLEY BROOKS, Author of "The Gordian Knot," "Aspen Court," &c., &c.

" If to create excitement from the first chapter to the last be the great object in writing a novel, Mr. Shirley Brooks has achieved a most remarkable success,—for a more exciting story than ' The Silver Cord,' was, perhaps, never written."—*Examiner.*

" A very curious and powerful story."—*Athenæum.*

" There is a wealth of materials in it that is quite surprising. Almost every chapter has its own striking situation allotted to it, and we are constantly kept on the alert watching for something even more startling than all that has gone before."—*Saturday Review.*

" It is not too much to say that in ' The Silver Cord ' Mr. Brooks has produced, under the humble style and title of 'a story,' one of the most consistent and highly-elaborated novels which have issued from the press for many years."—*Morning Post.*

ROYAL EDUCATION COMMISSION.

Price 2s. 6d. boards,

POPULAR EDUCATION IN ENGLAND. Being an Abstract of the Report of the Royal Commissioners on Education. With an Intro- duction and Summary Tables. By HERBERT S. SKEATS.

"Mr. H. S. Skeats' 'Abstract of the Report of the Royal Commissioners' is at once comprehensive, concise, and clear. All the really important points either as to matters of fact or of suggestion are compressed into the compass of one small volume. Yet the arrangement is so good that there is no consequent confusion or obscurity; while the outline of what has been done, is doing, or is proposed to be done for the formation of a sound and wide-spread education among the people, is simple, brief, and intelligible, without being bald and uninteresting from its brevity. It is a useful work well done."—*Economist.*

In One large Volume, crown 8vo, price 9s.,

HEALTH, HUSBANDRY, AND HANDICRAFT. By HARRIET MARTINEAU.

"The work throughout is practical in its character, abounds with good and useful advice, and is the result of the inquiries of a thoughtful, intelligent, and close observer."—*Observer.*

" Full of suggestiveness and sound practical knowledge. Altogether the work is one of vast importance, and we earnestly recommend it to the notice of our readers."—*Press.*

" A series of articles on sanitary matters; some capital papers on domestic and field husbandry (the practical working of a two-acre farm being among the things de- scribed); and a series of fresh and original studies of industrial processes. We can hardly picture to ourselves the sort of reader who would not be in some great or small way pleased and instructed by Miss Martineau's 'Health, Husbandry, and Handicraft.'"—*Examiner.*

In foolscap 8vo., with numerous illustrations, price 1s.,

SEA FISH : AND HOW TO CATCH THEM, By W. B. LORD, Royal Artillery.

" It would be difficult to over-estimate the use and importance of this little book, which, as a teacher, shows how to procure and fabricate the hooks and lines required, the form and nature of the bait used, and the manner or art of successfully using the tackle, when duly prepared. Numerous woodcuts illustrate the form of the float, sink, hook, and bait, the art of knotting the line, and all requisites to be understood capable of demonstration by drawing or diagram."—*Era.*

NEW WORK, BY THE AUTHOR OF "EAST LYNNE," &c.

In Three Vols., post 8vo, price 1l. 11s. 6d.,

VERNER'S PRIDE.

By MRS. HENRY WOOD,

Author of "East Lynne," "The Channings," &c.

"'Verner's Pride' is a first-rate novel,"—*Sun.*

MR. RUSSELL'S AMERICAN DIARY.

In Two Vols., post 8vo, price 21s.,

MY DIARY NORTH AND SOUTH:

OR, PERSONAL EXPERIENCES OF THE CIVIL WAR IN AMERICA.

By W. H. RUSSELL, Esq., LL.D.

"Distinct as to materials, and in many places different as to tone from his Letters, Mr. Russell's 'Diary' is the best of the many sketches of American society published since the rupture of the Union."—*Athenæum.*

UNDER HER MAJESTY'S ESPECIAL PATRONAGE.

In One Vol., large 4to, printed in the highest style of art, and embellished with Photographs, Coloured Borders, numerous Wood Engravings, &c., &c.

THE ROYAL HORTICULTURAL SOCIETY IN 1862.

[In the Press.

LANDSCAPE GARDENING.

ILLUSTRATED BY NUMEROUS PLANS, SECTIONS, AND SKETCHES OF GARDENS, &c.

In One Vol., demy 8vo, a New Edition, much enlarged and improved, of

HOW TO LAY OUT A GARDEN.

By EDWARD KEMP, OF BIRKENHEAD.

INTENDED AS A GUIDE IN CHOOSING, FORMING, OR IMPROVING AN ESTATE
(From a Quarter of an Acre to a Hundred Acres in Extent).

[In the Press.

RUSSIA IN THE TIME OF PETER THE GREAT.

In Two Vols., post 8vo, price 21s.,

THE DIARY OF AN AUSTRIAN SECRETARY OF LEGATION

AT THE COURT OF MOSCOW IN THE REIGN OF CZAR PETER THE GREAT.

TOGETHER WITH A NARRATIVE OF THE DANGEROUS REBELLION OF THE STRELITZ, ETC.

TRANSLATED BY COUNT MACDONNEL. *[Early in March.*

BRADBURY AND EVANS, 11, BOUVERIE STREET, E.C.

www.ingramcontent.com/pod-product-compliance
Lightning Source LLC
Chambersburg PA
CBHW060525030726
47498CB00004B/1077